Stillborn Armadillos

By Nick Russell

Nick Russell
1400 Colorado Street C-16
Boulder City, NV 89005
E-mail Editor@gypsyjournal.net

Also By Nick Russell

Fiction

Big Lake Mystery Series
Big Lake
Big Lake Lynching
Crazy Days In Big Lake
Big Lake Blizzard
Big Lake Scandal
Big Lake Burning
Big Lake Honeymoon
Big Lake Reckoning
Big Lake Brewpub
Big Lake Abduction

Dog's Run Series
Dog's Run
Return To Dog's Run

John Lee Quarrels Series
Stillborn Armadillos

Standalone Mystery Novels
Black Friday

Nonfiction

Highway History and Back Road Mystery
Highway History and Back Road Mystery II
Meandering Down The Highway; A Year On The Road With Fulltime RVers
The Frugal RVer
Work Your Way Across The USA; You Can Travel And Earn A Living Too!
The Gun Shop Manual
Overlooked Florida
Overlooked Arizona

Keep up with Nick Russell's latest books at
www.NickRussellBooks.com

Chapter 1

John Lee hated working the construction zone. Sitting in one spot with his roof lights flashing to warn traffic was boring duty, and it didn't help that the most the feeble air conditioner in the old Caprice could do was to put out a weak flow of air that was only a few degrees cooler than it would have been standing in the shade. With the fan going full blast he was still sweating in the hot, muggy afternoon.

But he had to admit the overtime would come in handy. And from where he sat, Rita Sue Baker did look good standing beside the road in those short shorts. He just wished she would stay there and not come over to talk so much.

Every time Rita Sue rotated her sign around from Stop to Slow and started waving the traffic through the construction site, as soon as the cars started moving she came back to John Lee's patrol car and leaned in the window to talk to him. This offered him a very nice view down her loose fitting blouse, but it also brought him too close to the proximity of her rancid mouth. John Lee wasn't sure if it was because of the rotten teeth, the odor of last night's alcohol, or the cigarettes she smoked one after another. Maybe it was a combination of all three, but whatever it was, it was enough to gag a maggot. He found himself leaning further and further away as Rita Sue talked about some country singer she just adored, told him how lonely she got sometimes at night, what with her boyfriend Randy halfway through serving 90 days on his latest DUI conviction, and how she couldn't decide if she wanted to get a tattoo of a unicorn or a dolphin on her right boob. The loose blouse had made it possible for him to know that a tattoo of Mickey Mouse already adorned the left one.

"What do you think, John Lee?"

"John Lee?"

She reached in the window and poked him on the shoulder. "You in there, John Lee?"

"Oh, sorry, I was thinking about something."

Rita Sue smiled her jagged smile, which was not a pretty sight, and brushed her damp, lank hair from her face as she said, "I just bet you were. Ya know, we shut down here at six, in case you'd like to do more than just think about it."

He was trying to figure out some relatively polite way to tell her that of all the things he had ever thought about, going home with her was six feet below the bottom of the list. But before he could answer, Roy Ballard's shouts caught his attention.

"John Lee, you better get over here."

He started to open the car's door and Rita Sue stepped back just enough for him to get out, but not far enough that he didn't have to brush his body against hers in the process. She made it a point to press herself against him as he did. That close to her, he realized that her oral hygiene wasn't the woman's only shortcoming.

"So whadda you say? Six o'clock?"

Before he could answer, Roy rescued him with a sharp whistle and waved. John Lee left Rita Sue at the police car and walked to where Roy and two other men stood staring at something in the red dirt that the grader had uncovered.

"What's up?"

"Looks like we found us a dead guy," Roy told him.

John Lee looked down into the trench and realized that there might be worse things than Rita Sue to see on this hot Florida afternoon.

***

"So tell me again, where did you find these bones?"

"The road grader turned them up out on Turpentine Highway. Roy Ballard thinks it might be an old Indian from a hundred years ago."

Peter Dawson, the irascible retired doctor who served as Somerton County's coroner, used a brush to clean dirt from the skull and asked, "When did Roy Ballard go to medical school?"

"He didn't, Doc."

"That's right, he didn't. Roy might know all kinds'a stuff about running heavy equipment and overseeing construction projects, but he don't know diddly squat about much else. He's not a doctor, and he's not an archaeologist, either. These bones are too new to belong to an Indian"How do you know tha"How the hell do I know that? Maybe because I spent 50 years patching people together and have seen every kind of body there is, alive and dead. Do you suppose that might have something to do with it?"

"Yeah," John Lee said. "I imagine so."

"I'll tell you two other things," Doc Dawson said. "Besides not being an old Indian, this fellow here didn't die of natural causes."

"What do you mean?"

Doc held up the skull and said, "Look what I found under all the dirt."

He pointed to a round hole in the rear of the skull.

"Is that what I think it is?"

"How the hell do I know what you're thinking? But if you're thinking it's a bullet hole, then you're right."

"Someone shot this guy in the back of the head?"

"Well, unless he had really long arms it would be kinda hard for him to reach around to do that himself."

"Okay, you said two things. What's the other thing?"

"Do you see this here? That there is the femur, it's the longest and largest bone in the human body."

Doc laid another bone beside it and said, "This is the other femur. Now you tell me, what's wrong with this picture, John Lee?"

The deputy stared at the bones and shook his head. "I don't know. I didn't go to medical school, either."

"You don't have to have gone to medical school to see that one of these is almost four inches shorter than the other," Doc said.

"So then what does that mean?"

"It means one of two things. Either this fellow really leaned to one side when he was walking down the road, or else Roy Ballard found himself more than one dead person out there."

Chapter 2

"Well damn, John Lee, you went and opened a can of worms this time around didn't ya? It's always somethin' with you, ain't it?"

Flag Newton scowled at him like John Lee himself had shot whoever the poor souls were that Roy Ballard had discovered. A big man with a shaved head and a walrus mustache, Somerton County's Chief Deputy found most things in life aggravating. Especially if they required him to leave his air-conditioned office at the courthouse and venture out into the world.

"What can I say, Fig? It was a slow afternoon."

Flag shot him a dirty look. He didn't like it when people referred to him by his nickname, and he particularly didn't like it when John Lee did it. Of course, there wasn't much about John Lee that he did like.

"I think we should call in the State Crime Lab. This is more than we normally deal with."

"We don't need to be callin' in nobody from Tallahassee," Flag said. "There ain't nothin' they can do that we can't do ourselves."

John Lee wanted to argue with him, to tell him that they had never had something like this before, what with the discovery of two dead bodies at once, but before he could, Bob Patterson, down in the trench, upped the ante.

"Son of a bitch, this one makes three," Bob said, laying his shovel aside and holding up another skull.

John Lee squatted down and took it from him and brushed away the dirt clinging to the bone.

"That one shot, too?"

"Yep. Same place, back of the head."

"Damn! What have you got us into, John Lee? A goddamn serial killer or somethin'?"

"It's something, Fig, but I don't know what."

"Could it be an old unmarked graveyard?"

Flag turned to the red haired deputy standing with them, a chunky young man with peach fuzz on his upper lip who had not yet outgrown his teenage acne, and said, "Jesus H Christ on a crutch, that's what it is, Red! What we got here is a special cemetery just for people who got themselves shot in the back of the head. Now why'n the hell didn't I think of that before?"

Greg Carson's face colored. "I guess that was kind of a dumb question, huh?"

"Ya think? Damn, boy. If all you're gonna do is stand here and take up space, why don't you get down there and give Patterson a break."

The young deputy nodded and crawled down into the trench that had slowly been enlarged as they excavated the crime scene.

"Give him a break, Fig. The kid's trying."

Flag turned his head and spat tobacco juice at Carson's patrol car, hitting the hubcap dead center with a splat. He looked back at John Lee and wiped his mouth with the back of his hand. "Why you gotta take on the losers and misfits all the time, John Lee?"

Shrugging his shoulders, John Lee replied, "Maybe because when I came on I was one of the losers and misfits?"

"*Was*? Shit, son. What makes you think you still ain't? Just because you married my niece don't mean squat to me. And I'll tell you what. When D.W. finds out you're bangin' both his daughters you might wish your bones was down there in that ditch, too."

As if on cue, a siren bleeped and they turned to see a white Chevrolet Tahoe pull up. Sheriff D.W. Swindle climbed out and lumbered up to them. In spite of the early hour it was already hot, and dark stains were visible in the armpits of the khaki uniform shirt which was stretched tight across his large belly. He pulled a blue bandanna from his back pocket and mopped his face.

"Morning, D.W. Hot enough for you?"

"Hottern' a two dollar pistol. Damned inconsiderate of you to uncover this mess this time a year."

John Lee was tempted to tell him that it wasn't like he set out to find three murder victims the previous day, but the less he talked to his father-in-law, the better.

The D.W. stood for Daniel Webster because his mother had wanted him to be a man of words. Unfortunately, most of the words he uttered were hard to understand due to the chaw of tobacco in his mouth. And those you could understand were likely to have been profane except for the fact that D.W. had toned them down after he got religion at a camp revival meeting following his heart attack the year before.

The religion had not lasted long once he was back on his feet, but when he was at his most vulnerable he had made the man upstairs a promise that he would never swear or smoke cigars again. D.W. didn't think it was wise to renege on a promise to God, but he also figured the big guy was willing to compromise. So Mail Pouch chewing tobacco had replaced the stogies, and he had invented his own method of cursing. When he was offended he would tell somebody to "kiss my rabbit hash" or call them a son of a Suzuki (D.W. hated imported cars and trucks. He believed real men drove Fords, Chevys, and Dodges). When he was really upset he had gone so far as to call someone a "salad eating Frenchman." (D.W. also hated salad and the French.)

"They just found a third skull."

"Well that's just perfect now, ain't it? This one shot, too?"

"Just like the first two. Same place."

D.W. shook his head and looked sourly at the trench. "Why does this kind of thing have to happen to me?"

"Wasn't exactly like it happened to you," Flag said. "It ain't your bones layin' down there."

D.W. ignored his wife's brother. The two men had never gotten along, and probably never would. It rankled Flag to have to take orders from his brother-in-law, a man whom he felt was not at all qualified for the office he held. An office that Flag himself coveted. More than once he had thought about running against D.W. in the next election, but he really didn't need the family drama that it would create. As for D.W., he resented the fact that his wife's hard drinking, heavy smoking brother seemed to have a heart as reliable as an old Detroit diesel engine no matter how badly he abused his body, while D.W. was eating low fat yogurt and dry toast for breakfast. Life just wasn't fair.

An ancient Volkswagen Beetle that had been red at one time but was now a faded orange stopped behind D.W.'s unit and a young woman with curly auburn hair that hung to her shoulders got out and joined them. John Lee and Flag nodded at her, and D.W. tipped his straw cowboy hat and said, "Good morning, Dixie. When you gonna get rid of that slug bug and buy yourself a real car?"

She laughed and said, "Never. It's a classic."

"If you say so."

"How you doin' this fine morning?"

"I'll do better when I get this done and get back to the office. It feels like a sauna out here."

"Well then, let's get to it."

D.W. crawled down into the trench with some difficulty, and said to John Lee, "Hand me that there skull, son."

John Lee gave him the latest skull they had found and D.W. picked up a shovel and turned to face the camera, a grim look on his face. The young woman raised her camera and took several photographs, including one where the sheriff placed the skull back down in the dirt and bent over beside it. To anyone reading that week's *Somerton County News*, the front page picture would look like the sheriff himself had uncovered the grisly crime scene.

"D.W. does know how to work the press," John Lee said.

"That's about the only work that fat bastard ever does," Flag said as he glowered at the scene of his boss taking credit for the discovery.

With her photographs taken, the reporter turned to John Lee to ask him for details, her camera not recording the scene as two deputies had to help their boss back out of the trench. Flag shook his head in disgust and walked away.

"What can you tell me, John Lee?"

"Not a lot yet," the deputy said, and recited the bare facts of the case. How the grader operator had uncovered the first skeleton the afternoon before and how they had collected the bones that he had taken them to Doc Dawson, who after a brief examination had reported that he believed that the person had been shot in the back of the head, and then revealed that the bones indicated there was more than one victim.

"What did you do then?"

"We had already sealed off the scene and posted a deputy here overnight to keep it from being disturbed. This morning we started searching the location more, and so far have uncovered two more skulls and other assorted bones."

The reporter started to ask him something else, but by then D.W. was back, huffing and puffing with the exertion and the heat. "Did you get your pictures, Dixie?"

"Yes, sir."

"Then there's no need for us to stand out here in this heat. Why don't you meet me back at my office and I can give you a full statement there."

"Sheriff, I was just asking John Lee..."

"Now honey, John Lee ain't the spokesman for the Sheriff's Department. I am. So let's you and me go someplace where we won't melt and I'll give you all the details."

She started to protest, but he walked her back to her car and held the door open while she got in.

"Well, at least chivalry isn't dead," John Lee said to nobody in particular.

Once Dixie had made a U-turn and headed back toward town, D.W. got in his Tahoe and started it, then leaned out the window and said, "Call me on my cell phone and fill me in while I'm driving back down so I have the details to tell that gal."

And with that, the sheriff made his own U-turn and tromped on the accelerator, spewing dirt and gravel behind him as he went.

Chapter 3

It took most of the day for the deputies, working in teams, to clear the crime scene. Once the major bones had been found they used wooden framed wire mesh screens to find smaller bones and any other evidence that might turn up. John Lee was taking a break and drinking from a bottle of Gatorade under the shade of a live oak tree when he heard Greg Carson calling his name.

He drained the last of his drink and walked back to the trench, throwing the empty bottle in the back of somebody's pickup along the way.

"What've you got?"

"Some kind of medal or something."

He handed John Lee a flat round disk that looked to be made of copper. The deputy rubbed his thumb across it, but the dirt clung stubbornly to whatever it was. John Lee took a plastic evidence bag from his pocket and dropped the disc inside, then sealed it and wrote the date on it with a black marker.

As he was turning away, Barry Portman said, "Hang on, I got something else."

He picked something out of his screen and held it in the palm of his hand, and said, "It's a bullet."

Barry handed it to John Lee. Looking at the old lead slug, which was slightly deformed at one end, John Lee felt a shudder to think that at one time this had punched its way through a person's skull and plowed through their brain, ending their life.

"Looks to be about a .32 to me," he said.

Barry nodded in agreement.

The sun was getting low in the sky, but it was just as hot.

"Let's give it another hour or so," John Lee said. "Then we'll call it a day."

"Who's got guard duty here tonight?"

"Obie, and he's none too thrilled about it."

"Well shit fire, John Lee, when's the last time Obie was happy about anything? That old boy'd complain if you hung him with a new rope."

"That ain't no lie, Barry," John Lee agreed.

Obediah 'Obie' Long was a sandbagger and chronic complainer who always did just enough to get by, and never a lick more.

"Compared to this, sitting in a car all night doing nothing sounds pretty good to me," Greg said.

John Lee had to give the young deputy a lot of credit. He may look soft on the outside, but the redhead had a lot of heart and had worked hard all day, only coming out of the trench for short breaks when John Lee or the other deputies insisted he do so. Of course, that didn't mean anybody was going to cut him any slack.

"You gonna start bitchin', too? We gonna have to start callin' you Obie Junior?"

"No, sir. I wasn't complaining, just observing."

Barry laughed and slapped the young man on the back and said, "I was kind of hopin' you was, tell you the truth. The way you been workin' your ass off down here today, you was makin' us old guys look bad."

Greg blushed at the compliment, though it was hard to tell because his face was so sunburned. He scooped up another shovelful of dirt and was just starting to pour it into the screen when the soil erupted in front of his face, showering him with red dirt, and the sharp crack of a rifle split the air.

"Everybody down," John Lee shouted, crouching next to his patrol car. He pulled his pistol and scanned the area just as another shot shattered the window of the car's door. Moving in a crouch, John Lee sought cover behind the front fender of the vehicle, where the engine block and tires would provide some protection.

"Everybody okay?"

"Does it count if I shit my pants?"

"Where's it coming from?" Barry asked, a second before a third shot hit the door of the police car. John Lee popped his head up quickly but saw nothing before pulling it back. He looked again and saw something bright, and a second later the rifle fired again, this time the bullet hitting the rear tire of his car.

Jerking his head down, John Lee shouted, "He's over there across the road." He moved to the front of the car and poked his arm around the fender and fired four rounds in a hurry. He knew there was little chance of hitting his target, but at least he wanted the shooter to know he didn't take kindly to being shot at.

There were no more shots fired at them but the deputies weren't taking any chances. John Lee was the only one armed, the others having locked their weapons in the trunks of their cars while they were working in the trench.

He opened his car from the passenger side, staying as low as he could, and pulled the shotgun from the mount in front of the dashboard. Sliding back out, he called, "Here, Barry," and threw the nylon stocked Remington to where the other three deputies were making themselves as small as possible in the trench. Then he reached inside for the radio's microphone and called the dispatcher.

"This is County 16, shots fired on Turpentine Road at the construction site!"

"Say again, 16?"

"I said shots fired. Somebody's shooting at us from the woods on the other side of the road."

"10-4. Attention all units, shots fired at the construction site on Turpentine Road. Unit 16 reports that the shooter is across the road. Approach with caution."

A moment later Flag's voice came over the radio. "Anybody hit, John Lee?"

"Negative, just my car."

"Do you have eyes on the suspect? Any description?"

"No, I fired back a couple of times but I don't think I hit anything."

"You boys hunker down. Help's on the way."

***

"Well this just pisses me off to no end," Flag said an hour later.

"I'm not too thrilled about it either," John Lee told him.

The road was lined with police cars, their red and blue lights flashing in the dark. Four Somerton County units and two State Patrol cars had responded when the shooting call went out. After John Lee had fired back at the sniper there had been no return shots, and whoever it had been was long gone by the time reinforcements arrived. Searching with flashlights, they had not found a blood trail to indicate that John Lee had managed to hit anybody. But they did find four spent brass .308 rifle cases.

"Sumbitch was serious," Calvin McDonald said. "Damn .308

would knock an elk down."

"Well there ain't no elk around here."

"I can tell you one thing," Obie said. "There ain't no way in hell I'm gonna stay out here all night long like a sittin' duck! No sir, I ain't gettin' myself shot for what they pay me."

"How much would we have to pay you to get shot?" John Lee asked. "Because I'd be willing to pitch in a few bucks. How 'bout the rest you guys?"

"That ain't funny, John Lee! You should know more'n anybody, with that maniac tryin' to kill you."

"I don't think he was trying to kill anybody."

"What the hell you talkin' about? If he wasn't tryin' to kill anybody why was he shootin' at you guys?"

"I don't know," John Lee admitted. "But I'm pretty sure that flash I saw at one point, just before he fired his last shot, was a reflection from a rifle scope. If he wanted to hit us, it wouldn't have been all that hard."

"Maybe he's just a bad shot."

"I don't think so, Fig."

"Why the hell not?"

"Because the second and third shots hit the middle of my car. But when I poked my head over the top of my front fender, his next shot, the last one, hit the rear tire."

"Then what the hell do you think he was doin', shootin' at you guys that way?"

"I don't know. Trying to send us a message maybe?"

"Well, whatever the message was, I'd appreciate it if he'd just send an email the next time around," Barry said.

Chapter 4

By the time they had ended their search for the mysterious sniper and had rounded up a second deputy to stay with Obie at the construction site overnight, and he had changed the tire on his car, it was after 10 o'clock when John Lee finally pulled into his driveway.

Magic, his 100 pound German Shepherd, came bounding into the car's headlights and trotted alongside as John Lee drove up in front of the house.

"How you doing, boy? Did you take good care the place while I was gone?"

Magic barked and wagged his tail.

"Good boy," John Lee said, slapping his chest in invitation. The big dog responded by jumping up and putting his paws on his master's chest, rocking the deputy back half a step. He rubbed the dog's head with both hands, pulling on his ears, and leaned down so Magic could lick his nose.

"Are you hungry? Yeah? Me too. Let's go get something to eat."

He walked up the three steps to the deck and unlocked the door, the dog going in ahead of him. Unbuckling his gun belt as he went into his bedroom, he hung it on the hook on the wall, then sat on the bed and pulled his boots off.

Magic stood in the bedroom doorway looking at him expectantly.

"What, you think you're gonna starve to death?"

The dog whined and John Lee laughed.

"Damn, you nag me as much as any woman I've ever known."

The dog whined again and it seemed like he wrinkled his brows, if a dog was capable of that.

"Okay," John Lee said with a sigh, "you win."

He went into the kitchen and opened a can of Alpo and put it in the dog's bowl. Magic started forward and John Lee looked at him and held up a finger. "Don't be in such a damn hurry."

He used the can to scoop out dry Purina and added it to the bowl.

"There you go. Are you happy now?"

Magic waved his tail and barked.

"Okay, you eat that and I'm gonna take a shower. I smell like something dead you'd find to roll in if you got half a chance."

He went back into the bedroom, stripped off his clothes, and stepped into the shower. The hot water felt good as it pounded down on his sore back and he lathered up and watched what must have been two or three pounds of dirt and grime stream off of his body and down the drain. Staying in the water until it turned cold, he finally turned it off and reached outside for the towel hanging on the glass door and dried himself off. Then he brushed his teeth and shaved, wondering why he was brushing when he was planning on eating, but it felt like he could still taste the dust of the road in his mouth.

When he was finally finished John Lee went back into the bedroom and stopped when he saw the naked woman stretched out on his bed.

"Surprise."

He looked at Magic, who was laying in the doorway, and said, "You're one hell of a watchdog, ain't you boy?"

"Now John Lee, don't you be blaming Magic for not doing his job. I mean, after all, I am family, right?"

"I've had a very long day, Beth Ann."

"Well then you climb right into this bed where you belong, mister."

"The only thing I've had to eat today was a burrito from Alvin's Stop and Go."

The woman stretched sensuously and crooked her finger at him. "The Bible says man does not live by bread alone."

"The Bible says a lot of things, and I'm pretty sure it frowns on what you have in mind."

"You just come to bed, John Lee. I promise, we don't have to do nothin' but just hold each other and sleep."

"Uh huh. You sure about that?"

"Why, cross my heart and hope to die!" She drew a cross on her naked breast as if to emphasize the promise.

"I really wanted something to eat."

"You're going to wind up getting fat like Daddy and Uncle Flag if you spend all your time eaten'. Now you come to bed. I promise all we'll do is sleep."

John Lee sighed and crawled onto the bed. Fifty minutes later, as he was finally drifting off to sleep with the woman's head on his chest, he thought to himself that Beth Ann had lied. Again.

***

Magic's barking woke him up. Early morning sunlight was peeking through the bedroom window blinds and John Lee looked at the bedside clock. 7:30. Magic barked again, and then he heard somebody knocking on his door.

"Shit."

Beth Ann moaned something in her sleep and rolled over. He stood up, pulled on boxer shorts and a pair of jeans and went to the door, peeking out the window next to it on the way.

"Shit! Shit! Shit!"

More knocking, this time louder.

"John Lee, you in there?"

He opened the door and D.W. said, "What'd you do, forget to charge your cell phone? I tried to call you three times."

John Lee remembered that his phone was still in the pocket of his dirty uniform shirt, which was on the bedroom floor where he had dropped it when he took it off the night before.

"Ummm... I guess I must have."

"How come Beth Ann's car is here?"

Before he could think of something to say, the woman came out of the bedroom wearing one of his undershirts and padded barefoot into the kitchen, where she turned the Mr. Coffee on.

The sheriff looked at her, then at John Lee, and then at his daughter again.

"Beth Ann?"

"Oh, hi Daddy. What are you doing up and about so early?"

John Lee closed his eyes and groaned, and stepped inside so the sheriff could come in.

"What in God's green earth is going on here?"

"Well, see, it's like this ..."

"Were you two fornicating?"

There was a time when D.W. would have used another word for what they had been up to, but he was still trying to follow that promise he had made to God.

"Come on, Daddy. Don't make a big thing of it, okay?"

"Don't make a big thing of it! You're here almost naked with your sister's husband, and I'm not supposed to make a big thing of it?"

"Daddy, Emily moved out eight months ago so she could find

herself."

"That ain't neither here nor there, girl!"

He turned to John Lee and said, "I thought you were better than that!"

"Now don't you be blaming John Lee," Beth Ann said. "I'm a grown woman, Daddy, and I make my own decisions. I'm the one that started it, not him."

"I don't care who started it," D.W. shouted, pointing a finger at his son-in-law "You oughta' be hung!"

"Oh he is, Daddy. Trust me! That's why I'm here."

"That's enough of your sass, young lady. You get some clothes on and you do it right now."

She gave him a fake pout but walked back into the bedroom with her cup of coffee.

"I'd beat your brains out if you had any!"

"Look, D.W., I don't... what I mean to say is... oh hell, just shoot me and get it over with!"

"I really should. Lord knows I want to."

Beth Ann poked her head out the bedroom door and said, "Ain't nobody shootin' nobody! Now look here, Daddy, I started this. John Lee never came on to me. I'm the one who made the first move, and the second, and the third, too! If Emily was home takin' care of business, this wouldn't of been happening."

"This ain't about your big sister!"

"Sure it is, Daddy. I grew up getting her hand-me-downs. Her clothes, her stereo, even her car when you bought her a new one for graduatin' from college. What makes this any different?"

John Lee wasn't sure he appreciated being a hand-me-down, but he knew a lot worse things could be happening to him at the moment, and he thought there was a good chance that they still would. But before the situation could get worse, D.W.'s cell phone rang. He pulled it from his pocket, pushed the button and curtly asked, "What?"

He listened for a moment, then said, "Yeah, I found him. He'll be there in just a bit."

He ended the call and looked at John Lee and said, "The State Crime Lab has a crew on the way out to that construction site. They should be gettin' there within the next half hour so. Do you suppose you could get your sorry ass dressed and out there to meet them?"

"Yeah, I'm on it."

The sheriff shook his head and said, "This ain't over, John Lee. Not by a long shot."

He turned and stormed out the door and across the deck down to his Tahoe. Opening the door, he turned back to look at John Lee one more time and shook his head, then crawled inside and drove away.

"Well, that was awkward," Beth Ann said. She was sitting on his bed, still wearing just his T-shirt.

"Awkward? I'm lucky he didn't shoot me!"

"I don't know why you two are making such a big thing about this. It's just sex."

"Yeah, well maybe your daddy's kind of old fashioned that way."

He took the jeans off, pulled a fresh uniform from the closet and began to get dressed. "Do you have to leave in such a hurry?"

"Yes, Beth Ann, I have to leave. You heard him say the State Crime Lab was on the way out there to where we found those skeletons."

"Those dead people ain't gonna come back to life, so what's the hurry?"

He shook his head and continued dressing. "You just don't get it, do you? We can't keep this up, Beth Ann."

"Well I don't know about that. Tired as you was last night, you didn't seem to have any problem keeping it up."

"You know what I mean."

She reached out and groped him as he was trying to buckle his pants and said, "You know what I mean, too."

"Stop it, okay? Just stop it? This thing with us, it's just..."

She put her face close to his, until their noses were touching, and said, "It's just sex, John Lee. I ain't planning to fall in love with you, and I know you're still in love with Emily, though I sure don't know why, with all she's put you through. But it's just sex. I'm enjoying it, and I sure didn't hear you complainin' last night. So what's the big problem?"

He started to argue with her but realized it was pointless, and he didn't have the time anyway. "I've got to go. Can you give Magic something to eat before you leave?"

"Leave? I was gonna stay here."

"No, you're not. I never know when Emily's going to come back for something, and I really don't need any more drama in my life, okay?"

"Yeah, I know what she comes back here for. Same reason I'm here. The sooner you understand that, the sooner you'll get her outta your head so you can move on, John Lee."

His stomach was growling as he buckled on his gun belt, and he realized he still hadn't eaten. He filled his oversized stainless steel coffee mug, poured in sugar and powdered creamer, and stirred it. Opening the refrigerator he found three hot dogs left in a pack and took them with him to eat cold along the way.

"You shouldn't eat them 'til they're cooked," Beth Ann said, as he started out the door. "You could get worms or somethin'."

John Lee just shook his head again and got into his car. He figured that dying from whatever might be in the hot dogs was still a better option than having D.W. shoot him.

Chapter 5

There were two sheriff's department cars and a white van from the state crime lab at the construction site when he arrived.

"Sorry I'm late," John Lee said, introducing himself to the three crime scene technicians.

"Looks like we're the ones that are late," said the team leader, a woman named Jayne Emerson, who looked to be in her early 40s, with short gray hair and an aggravated expression on her face. "I don't know why your boss even had us come down if he was going to let you people dig the place up anyhow. You probably destroyed any evidence there was to find."

"I'm sorry," John Lee said. "We're not exactly used to finding something like this around here."

"Exactly," the woman said. "But we are. That's our job. We'd all be a lot better off if you'd stick to writing speeding tickets and let us handle this kind of thing in the future, okay?"

"Yes ma'am," John Lee said, chastised.

She had started to turn away, but jerked her head back to him and hissed, "What did you just call me?"

"Ahhh... ma'am?"

"Let's get something straight cowboy. I am not a ma'am, or a little lady, or a girly, or whatever term of endearment comes to your tiny little redneck mind. You can refer to me by my name. Jayne. Jayne with a Y. There's only five letters in it. Even you should be able to remember that, don't you think?"

And John Lee had only thought his day was getting off to a bad start when D.W. showed up at his door! He didn't say anything because he didn't trust himself to speak. Instead he just nodded and walked to where Barry and Greg were standing drinking coffee next to one of their cars.

"Morning, John Lee. I see you met Jayne with a Y."

"Ain't she a little ray of sunshine?"

"She came outta of that van screaming at us before it even came to a complete stop," Barry told him. "Yellin' 'bout how we had completely contaminated the crime scene and they had driven all the way out here for nothin'.."

"We tried telling her we took pictures and measurements and everything, but she wasn't having none of it," Greg said.

"Don't sweat it guys. She can take it up with D.W. if she wants to."

Another member of the crime scene team approached them.

"Is this the car that got shot up yesterday?"

"Yeah," John Lee said, "and before you start, I had to drive it home because we don't have enough vehicles to spare that we could let it sit here all night waiting for you guys."

The man waved his hand to cut off any explanations. "Don't worry, I understand. Jayne's having a bad day today. Sorry about that."

"Does she ever have a good day?"

The man, maybe 50, with thinning hair, thick glasses and a pug nose, put his hand on his chin as if in deep thought for a moment, and then said, "There was a Wednesday, or maybe it was a Thursday, back in 2003, when she was only a bitch and not a total raving maniac. But it was just that one day."

"You see, guys? The next time you've got Flag riding your ass, just remember it could be worse," John Lee told the other deputies.

"Were you able to recover any of the bullets fired into your vehicle?"

"The one that went through the glass here in the door went out the other side and I have no idea where it ended up," John Lee told him. "The one that went through the door went through the inside door panel on the other side but didn't come out, so I guess it's in there somewhere. And when I changed the tire I could hear the third one rolling around inside when I took it off. Tire's still the trunk."

It only took the tech, whose name was Albert Symansky, a few minutes to dissemble the door panel and recover the deformed copper jacketed bullet he found inside. He used a battery powered Sawzall to cut the tire apart and recover the bullet from inside of it. He bagged each of them in separate evidence bags, then walked across the road with John Lee and spent some time looking for where the shooter may have been positioned.

John Lee told him about his theory that whoever had been shooting at them had not been aiming to kill, and the technician nodded his head in agreement.

"At that distance with a rifle like that, especially with a scope on it, if he had wanted you dead I think you would be. You're a lucky man, Deputy."

Just then Greg shouted his name from across the road. "John Lee, dispatch is on the radio. D.W. wants to see you in his office, ASAP."

John Lee sighed as he walked back to his car. Albert Symansky might think he was a lucky man, but he had a feeling his luck was about to run out.

***

"What am I gonna do with you, John Lee? I'm just speechless."

John Lee didn't say anything, but he was tempted to write the date on the calendar. His father-in-law was much more a politician than a lawman, and he seemed to have a ready made speech for anything and everything that came along. Especially if it was one he could deliver before a group of voters to remind them of what a good job he was doing. And to D.W., a group consisted of anything more than just one person, as long as they were registered to vote.

The sheriff had never really anticipated a career in law enforcement. Actually, growing up he had not given much thought to what he was going to do when he became an adult. Yes, his grandfather, Big Jim Swindle, had worn the sheriff's badge for a decade before an out of work ne'er-do-well named Buster Palmer had gotten liquored up and started beating his wife. When a neighbor called in to report the disturbance, the sheriff went out to their shack on Cass Road to put an end to it. He never got the chance because as he was getting out of his Plymouth squad car Palmer had come around the corner of the house and blown most of his head off with a single shot 12 gauge Stevens shotgun. He then went back in the house, murdered his wife, and killed himself.

Big Jim's son, James Swindle, better known as Junior, had taken up where his father had left off and served as Somerton County's sheriff for over 25 years before he pitched over dead on his 60th birthday. The way the story had been presented to the public, the sheriff had been answering a prowler call when his heart gave out. But it was no secret around the courthouse that he had actually been celebrating the occasion in bed with a 30 year old barmaid named Brenda Davidson when the Grim Reaper came to call.

At the time, D.W. was a young deputy with only a couple of years on the job, but he had already decided that life sitting behind the sheriff's desk was a lot better than life in a squad car, and was more than ready and willing when the county appointed him to fill his late father's shoes. He found that he enjoyed the popularity and being in the spotlight, and while he was more than happy to delegate field duties to Flag Newton and his deputies, he made it a point to get his picture in the paper often enough to convince the public he was on the job. That and kissing a lot of babies, and as many influential asses, assured that he had not lost an election since.

"I just don't understand what this world is comin' to," D.W. was saying. "First Emily runs off to Orlando without a word and we don't see hide nor hair of her for over a month, and then she shows back up in town with that woman she's sharing an apartment with and says she's a bisexual. I don't want to think of my little girl having sex, let alone paying for it!"

John Lee was tempted to explain what a bisexual was, but thought better of it. Sometimes the less D.W. knew, the better off everyone was.

"And now this thing with you and Beth Ann. That just turns my stomach! Now you tell me just how the hell that started."

John Lee wanted to tell him that his daughter had been truthful when she said it was she who had done the pursuing, but he was a grown man and he wasn't going to make any excuses for his own shortcomings. It wasn't like Beth Ann had held a gun to his head.

"D.W., I don't know what to tell you. It just happened."

"No! Thunderstorms happen! Night happens and day happens. Those are just natural forces. But this thing, you and Beth Ann, that's not natural. I've got half a mind to tell you to turn in your badge right now. But with all this stuff with those skeletons goin' on and people shootin' at your car, I got enough on my plate as it is without tryin' to explain to the county supervisors why I fired you. And what the hell were you thinkin' anyhow, not callin' in the state crime lab when you found the first one? That gal that's in charge out there, that Jayne something or other, she called here and tore me a new one because we waited until last night and they had to hear it on the news."

"Wait a minute, why didn't *I* call in the crime lab?"

"Ain't that what I asked ya?"

"Why didn't *I* call in the crime lab?"

"Why you repeatin' yourself, John Lee? Do you think I've gone deaf or somethin'?"

"Son of a bitch!"

"Hey now, you watch your language! Just cause we's kinfolk don't mean you can be talkin' to me that way."

"I didn't mean you, D.W., I meant Fig."

"Fig? What's he got to do with this?"

"After we found the first one I told him we should call in the crime lab and he said no,"

"Well that ain't what he told me. He said he told you to call them and thought you had."

"That's bullshit!"

John Lee turned on his heel and stormed out of the sheriff's office.

"Where you goin'? I'm not done talkin' to you yet."

"You'll have to do that later," the deputy said over his shoulder, "I've got a snake to deal with."

Chapter 6

Flag Newton had been expecting John Lee and frowned when the deputy walked into his office without knocking.

"I hear you got your nuts in a wringer with D.W. I told you it was gonna happen sooner or later."

"You backstabbing bastard. You must have bought some of those penis enlargement pills off the internet, because you're a bigger dick today than you were yesterday."

"You can't talk to me that way!"

"I'll talk to you any damn way I want. Where do you get off telling D.W. that I was the one that didn't call in the state crime lab? I told you yesterday we needed to get them out here and you're the one that said no!"

"I think you misunderstood me. Probably too busy thinkin' 'bout gettin' into Beth Ann's pants and not concentratin' on your job."

"That's bullshit and you know it!"

"What I do know is ya' need to watch your mouth, boy. Who do you think you're talkin' to, anyway?"

"I know exactly who I'm talking to," John Lee said. "You threw me under the bus with D.W. to cover your own ass."

Flag had learned long ago playing high school football that the best defense was a good offense. "I don't see where you filed a report on that shooting yet."

"Really? That's how you're gonna try to change the subject?"

"Regulations say anytime an officer fires his weapon he needs to file an immediate report."

"Yeah, well I kind of had other things going on last night."

"I know that, and the way I hear it, D.W. knows it, too. How's that workin' out for you?"

"How do you know what I was doing last night?"

"There ain't much goes on in this county that I don't know about. And don't you forget that."

"D.W. hasn't been to my house in over a year. It's kind of strange that he showed up this morning, isn't it?"

Flag grinned at him. "I don't know what you're talkin' 'bout, but I'dnot a given a hundred dollar bill to have been a fly on the wall out there."

"You miserable..."

"Watch your mouth! And don't try to change the subject. I want a full report on that shooting on my desk in the next hour, do you understand me, Deputy? And what the hell are you doin' with that unauthorized pistol, anyway? Where's your Glock?"

"There's nothing wrong with this gun," John Lee said.

"It's not authorized. Now hand it over."

"Forget it, you're not getting your hands on my Browning."

"Deputy, I gave you a direct order. You hand me that unauthorized firearm right now, or you hand me your badge."

John Lee knew that Fig had wanted his vintage Browning Hi Power for years, and he had no intention of letting the Chief Deputy get his hands on it because he knew if he did, he would never see it again. So he ignored Fig's outstretched hand.

"The only person who can fire me is the sheriff, and he and I just had that conversation. It's not gonna happen today. And as far as unauthorized weapons, that big .44 magnum you're wearing on your hip isn't exactly authorized, either."

"We're talkin' about you, Deputy, not me. Now which is it going to be, your badge or your weapon?"

"The only thing you're getting out of me is your damn report on the shooting," John Lee said. "If you want anything else, you trot your fat ass out from around that desk and try taking them."

Flag was so angry he was trembling, which only made him more so. John Lee had walked around flaunting the rules for way too long just because he was married to D.W.'s daughter. He needed to be taken down a notch or two. And that was damn sure going to happen, he'd see to that. But this wasn't the time or the place, and he knew that, too.

"Get that damn report on my desk within the hour. And don't think this is over with, John Lee. You and me, we're gonna tangle one of these days. And when we do, I'll show you what for."

"Yeah, well you better pack yourself a lunch, because it's going to be an all day job."

He walked out of the office, and Flag shouted at his back, "One hour. I want that report in one hour!"

***

The bullpen was a large room across the hall from the dispatch center, furnished with six gunmetal gray desks along one wall, each with a cheap office chair and a desktop computer that the deputies used to file their reports and other paperwork, a bank of the same gunmetal gray lockers on the opposite wall, and three long tables with folding chairs in between. John Lee was there writing the report on the shooting that Flag had demanded.

"So I hear you got caught with your finger in the cookie jar. Or should I say nookie jar?"

John Lee looked up and asked, "Are there no secrets in this place, Maddy?"

She sat down across from him at the table and said, "Hell no. Rumors go through here faster than water through a sieve. You know that."

Madison "Maddy" Westfall had been three years behind John Lee in high school, but even then she had been hard not to notice, with her big gray eyes, long ash blonde hair, and legs to match. Her brother Dan had been John Lee's best friend when they were growing up, and he was always telling John Lee that she had a crush on him. But when you're that age, the span is too great to attempt to breach.

When Dan had drowned while swimming in the Suwannee River at seventeen, it had broken his parents' hearts. As so often happens when a child dies, their marriage had not survived the strain. They had divorced and Richard Westfall had moved away. Over time he had taken to drink, and it was only a few years after his son's death that he had driven his car off the road and into a lake somewhere down around Ocala.

Her mother had remarried twice after that, but neither relationship had worked out. She became more and more withdrawn, seldom leaving her bedroom, and never stepping outside the house. Madison had been forced to become the adult in the family while she was still just a girl. She was the one that paid the bills from the monthly Social Security check and an annuity from her father's life insurance policy, she was the one who did the grocery shopping, and she was responsible for the cooking, cleaning, and other household duties. She had handled it all with a maturity far beyond her years, and still managed to graduate at the top of her high school class.

Maddy was only the second female deputy in Somerton County history, the first being the busty and lusty brunette named Carmen Maxwell that Sheriff Junior Swindle had hired and made his personal protégé. Whispers around the courthouse had been that Carmen served in a position directly under the sheriff. Her tenure had ended soon after Junior's death, when she was found in a compromising position in the back seat of her patrol car one night with the pastor of the Third Baptist Church. D.W. had heard the rumors about his father and Carmen and was only too glad to have an excuse to send her packing.

"I could hear you and Fig going at it all the way down the hall," Maddy said. "You know he's going to find any excuse he can to make life hard for you."

"Girl, my life started being hard the day I was born and it hasn't got much easier since then. So if that dickhead wants to try to give me any grief, he's welcome to it."

"Seriously, John Lee, you watch yourself around him. We all know what a backstabbing prick he is. Nobody wants to see you get caught in the middle of the power struggle between him and D.W."

"I appreciate that, but I'll be okay."

She reached across the table and put her hand on his. "Well, like I said, watch your back, okay?"

Her hand felt warm on his, and if his personal life had not already been so complicated, he might have enjoyed it.

"Don't worry about me, it'll take a better man than Fig to take me down."

Sheila Sharp, the daytime dispatcher, poked her head in the bullpen, then stopped when she saw what she thought were the two deputies holding hands.

"Oh, excuse me."

Maddy pulled her hand away and John Lee asked, "What's up, Sheila?"

"Mama Nell has called three times now for you. She said she's tried your cell phone over and over and there's no answer. She heard about the shooting last night and wants to know you're okay."

"Damn, I forgot to charge my phone last night," John Lee said.

"Well, I'm sure you had other things on your mind," Maddy said with a smirk.

"Okay, let me take this report up to Fig, then I'll head over there."

"Here, let me take it up to him," Maddy said. "If you two butt heads again today *I* may have to be writing up a report on a shooting incident."

"You don't have to do that. I'm not afraid of him."

"I know you're not, John Lee, but it's no big thing. Go see Mama Nell and put her mind at ease."

"Okay, if she calls back. tell her I'm on my way," John Lee told Sheila.

The dispatcher left the room and Maddy leaned over and said, "knowing that busybody, by the end of the day everybody in the courthouse is going to think we're doing the nasty."

"Just what I need, more rumors," John Lee said, standing up.

"You know, as long as we're gonna be blamed for it anyway..."

He looked at her, not knowing how to respond, and Maddy laughed at him. "Geez, John Lee, you are so easy! Relax, you and me doing it would be like incest or something."

He breathed a sigh of relief and headed out the door, ignoring Maddy when she called after him, "Of course, they tell me that *is* a proud old Southern tradition!"

Chapter 7

John Lee had never really known his father. Herb Quarrels had been a sailor from Ohio that his mother had met while on spring break in Pensacola. The two had partied for three days and then he had returned to his job at the Naval Air Station there and Lisa Marie came back to Somerton County with a cheap promise ring on her finger and no idea that a new life was growing inside of her. When she missed her period she had called him in tears, and to his credit he had borrowed a friend's car and driven the 300 miles to her home to do the right thing.

Unfortunately, the two 18 year olds may have been mature enough to make a baby, but they weren't ready for the responsibility or commitment that marriage demanded. They moved into base housing at the Naval Air Station, and less than two years later when Herb shipped out for sea duty, Lisa Marie came home with her baby in tow. Six months later, when Herb came back to reclaim his wife and child, Lisa Marie was no longer interested in married life. With her parents, a freethinking couple who had placed few restrictions on her, more than willing to help care for little John Lee, she couldn't see herself returning to the drudgery of being a full-time mother and wife.

Herb hadn't been all that disappointed, and the divorce was amicable. He had only visited a time or two after that, though he faithfully sent a monthly check to help support his son. More often than not, Lisa Marie was not around to cash the check. The world was full of adventures and she was always off seeking another one. She had gone to cosmetology school in Tallahassee, then worked as a waitress in a Key West bar for a while, then signed on a cruise ship, where she served drinks to passengers as they explored the ports of the Caribbean. From there she had moved to New York City for a brief stint, thinking she would get a modeling gig, but that hadn't worked out. Then, because it sounded like fun, she had taken a course in driving eighteen wheelers at a school in Allegan, Michigan. And so it had gone, all through John Lee's childhood. His father had only been a name on an envelope that came once a month, and his mother would occasionally breeze into town for a visit, promising him that she was there to stay, though he never believed her because he knew all too soon she would get some other idea and be off on her her next adventure, the one that she was sure would make her life complete.

Not that he had ever felt neglected or unloved. His grandparents had given him a good home, even though it was not a traditional one by any means. His grandmother never wanted him to call her that, or by any other name except Mama Nell. Though she had been drawing Social Security for a few years, she was the youngest spirit John Lee had ever known.

There was no question that Nell loved her husband Stanley, and their marriage had always been a good one. But everybody, including Stanley, knew he was her second choice. In the summer of 1961, Elvis Presley came to Inverness, Florida to make the movie *Follow That Dream,* and the moment 14 year old Nell had seen him riding in the back of his white stretch Cadillac limousine, she had given her heart to the singer, who was almost twice her age. And when he had smiled that crooked smile of his and pointed his finger at her when she screamed, "I love you, Elvis," she knew he felt the same way.

He had gone on to even greater fame while Nell had stayed a small town Florida girl, and though she had been heartbroken when he married Priscilla six years later, she would always love him. If she couldn't have Elvis, at least she could feel like she had a piece of him when she named her daughter after his.

Stanley seemed to accept the fact that he would always play second fiddle to the man he referred to as Elvis the Pelvis, and he really couldn't complain about the fact that their home seemed to be a shrine to the man, because whenever he was feeling amorous, all he had to do was put on a CD of *Love Me Tender* or *Are You Lonesome Tonight?* and Nell would be putty in his hands.

Stanley was a tall, thin man with a weathered face that came from his years of working as a lineman for Florida Power & Light Company, and a gray ponytail that hung down his back. He had been a young man working for a public utility in Pennsylvania when he had been sent south after a hurricane to help restore power in Florida. And while it was hot hanging off the side of a pole 40 feet in the air, he quickly decided he'd rather do that than spend another winter freezing his rear end off in Harrisburg. Stanley was a hard worker, and when FPL had offered him a job, he had been quick to accept.

Of course, Somerton County wasn't the Florida of the tourist brochures, with the white sand beaches and young women running around in skimpy bikinis. Located in the northern part of the state, just inland from the Big Bend where northwest Florida curved into the Panhandle, rural Somerton County was far less affluent and more what Old Florida was like long before the neon tourist traps and theme parks further south appeared in the landscape. This was piney woods country, with lots of swamps, bayous, and marshland. Good ol' boy and girl rednecks, along with northern retirees looking for a more peaceful and cheaper way to live out their lives shared the county with alligators, a few black bears, and even an occasional rare panther. The small town of Somerton was the biggest community in its namesake county, and that suited Stanley just fine. Sure, it was hot and humid in the summertime, but the rest of the year was fine, and you didn't have to shovel sunshine.

When John Lee's patrol car pulled into the driveway Stanley was in the greenhouse puttering with his plants. An inveterate tinkerer, now that he was retired Stanley spent his days building things. Everything from the greenhouse, which was constructed with PVC pipe and plastic sheeting, to a windmill that he had built and tapped into the solar system he had constructed to add wind power. Stanley had given FPL 35 years of his life, and while he had enjoyed his work and the utility had treated him right, now that he was retired he didn't want to give them any more money than he had to. More than half of his and Mama Nell's electric power needs were provided by the sun and the wind.

Besides building things, Stanley was also a gardener. And he believed that the fact that he grew marijuana along with tomatoes, beans, and sprouts was nobody's business but his own. After all, it was all about having a self-sustaining lifestyle, right?

"Hey there, John Lee. Good to see you ain't got no holes shot in you. Mama Nell's been worried."

"I'm sorry, I should have called, Paw Paw."

John Lee started to go into the greenhouse, then turned away and stepped back outside, shaking his head.

"Paw Paw, you can't be growing pot."

"It's not what you think, John Lee. It's for my glaucoma."

"You don't have glaucoma, Paw Paw. I was with you when you had your eye exam at the WalMart over there in Perry, and the eye doctor said you still had 20/20 vision."

"I know. That shit works good, don't it?"

Before John Lee could reply, the door of the house burst open and Mama Nell came screeching across the yard with her arms outstretched. "You're alive!" She wrapped her arms around him and pulled him close. "I was so worried when I heard about that shootin'."

"Yeah Mama Nell, I'm fine."

She let go of him and then swatted him on the ass. Hard.

"Ouch!"

"What were you thinkin', not answerin' my calls or lettin' me know you were okay?"

"I'm sorry, I've been kind of busy. And I forgot to charge my phone and the battery went dead. Ouch!"

She had swatted him again.

"Mama Nell, I'm 31 years old. I don't need you spanking my rear end all the time."

"Those was love taps. You know how worried I've been? I was just now inside prayin' to Elvis that he was lookin' down on you and was gonna keep you safe."

"Mama Nell, you can't be prayin' to Elvis. He ain't God. Ouch!"

"You watch what you say about the King!"

John Lee wanted to protest, but he was tired of getting spanked, so he let it go.

"Now, you just tell me what the hell happened out there yesterday. What have you got yourself mixed up in that people are shootin' at you?"

"I don't know," John Lee admitted. "It's pretty weird. We found these three skeletons and then the next thing we knew someone was shooting at us from across the road."

"You don't think it was hunters?"

He shook his head. "Nothing's in season this time of year, Paw Paw."

"Maybe target shooters?"

"No, they usually go over there by Loggerhead Pond where they can use that big earth dike as a backstop. Whoever this was, he knew exactly what he was shooting at. And while it scared the bejesus out of us, whoever was doing the shooting wasn't trying to hit us. At that range, with a scoped rifle, he could have, easy enough."

"I really worry about you doin' that job," Mama Nell said.

"I'm fine," he reassured her. These things happen."

"Maybe you should become a singer, just like Elvis. People loved Elvis, they didn't shoot him."

"I don't know about that. Somebody shot John Lennon. Ouch!"

"Don't you be comparin' that limey to Mr. Elvis Presley! Now, I ain't takin' nothin' away from the Beatles, but everybody knows Elvis was a real superstar. And he didn't need three other people up there on stage with him to make him look good. No sir, not Elvis!"

"If you keep hitting me, I'm going to leave, Mama Nell. Ouch!"

"That was the last one, and that was for sassin' me. Now give me a hug. I been so worried 'bout you!"

Chapter 8

He really needed to get back out to the crime scene and check up on things, and he still needed to drop his patrol car off at the shop to get those windows replaced and a new spare tire, but Mama Nell wasn't hearing any of that until John Lee had lunch. And while he much preferred a good bacon cheeseburger over the sprouts and lentils that his vegetarian grandparents served, he was too hungry to argue. Not that it would have done him much good, anyway. When Mama Nell set her mind to something, it was going to happen.

Finally, with his stomach full and Mama Nell assured that he was going to continue to stay alive for at least a while longer, John Lee was able to make his exit. He dropped his car off at the garage, picked up another unit, and drove back to the crime scene. The white crime lab van was gone and Deputy Ray Ray Watkins was sitting in the old Caprice that was too worn out and tired to be used for anything else except parking it alongside the highway to remind people there was a speed limit.

"Where did everybody go, Ray Ray?"

"Ov.. ov... over with."

"What's over with?"

"The cri... cri... crime scene pe... pe... people got... got done and left."

Raymond Watkins had been cursed with a terrible stutter all of his life, and on his first day of school when the teacher told each student to stand up and introduce themselves, when it came to his turn he had managed to say "Ray... Ray...Watkins." From that day forward everybody in Somerton County referred to him as Ray Ray. Some people still teased him about his speech impediment, and wondered how he could do the job of a deputy. More than once Flag had said it was probably better than him being a paratrooper, since he would never live long enough to count to three and pull his ripcord.

"Did they find anything else?"

"Only... only thi... thing they found was a piece of bar...bar... barbed wire."

"Barbed wire?"

The deputy nodded his head and held his hands about seven inches apart and said, "The...the... this big."

"Okay, so we're done here?"

Ray Ray nodded and said, "Wor... work crew com... coming back out in a li... little while to get back at it."

"Work crew? Roy Ballard and his guys?"

Ray Ray nodded again. John Lee knew there had been enough delays on the road project already and that the construction people needed to get back at it, but he would have liked a little more time to investigate the site further. He knew things didn't always work out the way one wanted in Somerton County, where there were not a lot of resources and sometimes they had to make do to get the job done.

"Okay, then I'm gonna head back into town. I don't think you need to worry about anybody coming back and shooting at you at this point, do you?"

"It's... it's okay, John Lee. I can... I can... I can duck faster than I can talk."

John Lee laughed and slapped him on the shoulder and got into his car and drove back to town. There were television news vans from Tallahassee and Jacksonville parked in front of the courthouse and D.W. was in his glory as he preened for the cameras and told them how no matter how long ago those poor folks had been murdered, he was going to get to the bottom of it. "There is no statute of limitations on murder in the great state of Florida, and here in Somerton County we have a long memory and we're committed to making things right," D.W. was saying. "Make no doubt about it, we are going to follow through with this and see justice done!"

John Lee watched from the sidelines for another moment or two as D.W. started fielding questions from the reporters, then went inside. The Sheriff's Department was housed in the back of the courthouse, and he nodded at a couple of folks he knew as he went back to the dispatch office. Sheila Sharp looked up from her radio console and asked, "Did you go see Mama Nell?"

"Yes, ma'am, I did. She feels better knowing that I don't have any more holes in me than the ones I was born with."

"Well, bless her heart. That sweet lady loves you, John Lee. You know that."

"Yes, ma'am, I do. Anything going on here?"

Sheila shook her head. "You saw the circus out front. D.W. is in his glory, and Fig is upstairs pouting because he wanted to be the one talking to the press and D.W. shot him down."

"Two things you never want to get between with D.W. are a pork chop or a television camera," John Lee said.

"No, sir," Sheila said, shaking her head. "He's still not eating much meat. A lot of fish and chicken, but that's about it."

"I wish he'd get himself a steak or a rack of baby back ribs. At the rate he's going, he's gonna live forever."

Sheila laughed and said, "That might not be all bad. Think about it, John Lee, if D.W. was to keel over, Fig would be sheriff. I don't think any of us want that."

"You do have a point."

"Is there anything going on that I can take care of?"

Sheila shook her head. "Maddy is out on road patrol. She called when she stopped a speeder about an hour ago and cleared from that. Otherwise, nothing."

"Did you hear anything about the crime lab folks?"

"Just that Jayne with a Y is a real bitch."

"Yeah, I've had the pleasure of meeting her," John Lee said.

"Barry said they went over the scene quite a bit, and one of the guys that was with her said we did a pretty good job. They took copies of the pictures you guys took and everything and then came here and collected all those bones, then they headed back to Tallahassee. I've got to tell ya' John Lee, I was glad to see those bones gone from here!" She shuddered, as if for emphasis.

"Hell, Sheila, dead people can't hurt you none. It's the living ones I worry about."

"Even so, I'm just glad they're gone."

With nothing else to do, John Lee drove back out to the construction site again, but when he saw Rita Sue, he made it a point to park as far away from where she stood with her sign as he could. He walked into the edge of the trees where they thought the shooter had been and located the spot where the three brass cartridge cases had been found, which they had marked with a small red ribbon stuck into the ground on a wire.

They had been over that ground several times already, both the night of the shooting and that morning, but he wanted to see it for himself one more time. John Lee was not much of an outdoorsman, and he certainly couldn't follow a trail like an experienced hunter might, but he had a good knowledge of local landscape. He knew that there was a fire road about a quarter of a mile further back and they had suspected that was probably where the shooter had parked his car. But a lot of lovers came back there to neck at night, and during the daytime four wheelers and ATVs frequented the area, so there had been a hodgepodge of tire tracks and no discerning evidence of which might belong to the sniper.

If the person *had* even parked there and hiked to his shooting spot. There were trails all through the thick scrub, and who was to say how he had come and gone? For all John Lee knew, he might be back again, he might have the rifle scope's crosshairs centered on his back at that very moment. In spite of himself he felt a shudder much like the one that Sheila had exhibited back at the courthouse. But he told himself that was nonsense. Why would the shooter come back again? What did he have to gain? Then again, why had he been there in the first place?

John Lee poked around for another half hour or so, though he knew it was fruitless. Finally giving up, he walked back through the woods to the road. Rita Sue saw him and yelled, then whistled and waved her arm. As much as he didn't want to, he walked over to where she stood with her sign, holding back two pickups and some kind of foreign car.

"Now what you doin' goin' off in those woods all by yourself, John Lee?"

"I was just looking around."

"We've got a short day, what with everythin' be'in closed down 'cause of those bones and stuff. We never did get together last night..."

She left the invitation hanging there and John Lee figured the best way to handle it was to just get it over with.

"Look, Rita Sue, I don't think that's really a good idea."

"Oh, trust me, I've got some real good ideas for things you and me could be doin'."

"I don't think so."

"Why not?"

"Well, you're in a relationship, for one thing. And I'm married."

"Now John Lee, I wasn't expectin' us to set up housekeeping together or nothin' like that. I'm just talking about a little bit of fun."

"Yeah, but like I said, I'm married."

"I know about your marriage," Rita Sue said. "And I know that wife of yours is livin' with another woman. And I know they ain't just roommates, if you get my drift."

"Be that as it may, as long as I'm married..."

"I'm not gonna say a thing. I mean, I might do some moanin' and screamin', but that's about it."

"Yeah, well, it's not going to happen. Besides, you've got a boyfriend, don't you?"

"Randy? Shoot, he don't care what I do. He's passed me around to both his brothers and a couple of his friends. Besides, he's still locked up. A girl has needs, you know."

"And I'm a cop. I'm not sure the sheriff would take kindly to me sleeping with someone's girlfriend while the man's in jail."

Her handheld radio crackled with a message and Rita Sue said, "10-4" and rotated her sign around then waved the traffic through.

"You're makin' this way too complicated, John Lee. I'll tell you what, you come back in an hour and a half when I'm off and we'll take us a little ride down one of these fire breaks and all you gotta do is sit back and enjoy. I'll make you feel real good."

He felt his skin crawl, and since he knew that nothing he said was going to get the message through to her, he just said, "I'll have to pass" and walked away.

"Well screw you, John Lee Quarrels! You ain't got no idea what you're missin! You think you're the only man in Somerton County? I can have anybody I want. I was just tryin' to be nice to you!"

He ignored her and got in his car and drove away.

Chapter 9

Magic greeted him when he pulled in the driveway and John Lee spent a few minutes playing with the dog before they went inside. He hung up his gun belt, then filled Magic's bowl with food, refreshed the water in the bowl next to it, then got a Dr. Pepper out of the refrigerator before he plopped down on the couch. He picked the remote control up from the end table and turned on the television. A pretty Latina reporter was on the screen, with the Somerton County Courthouse in the background.

"After talking to Sheriff D.W. Swindle, this reporter tried to contact the State Crime Lab in Tallahassee, but nobody there could give us any further information on the case. So all we know at this point is what the sheriff shared with us, that a road construction crew discovered some skeletal remains yesterday afternoon, and further investigation by the sheriff's office revealed that there was not one, but three victims, and all appeared to have been murdered. Sheriff Swindle said that while his deputies were at the crime scene, an unknown sniper fired three rounds at them before disappearing into the forest. Fortunately, nobody was injured, but the suspect remains at large. We will have more details as they become available. This is Marta Gonzales reporting for Channel 27 News."

The screen switched to a story about a tractor-trailer accident on Interstate 10 and John Lee got up and retrieved his pistol from its holster. There had been too much going on and he had not had the time to clean it after firing it at the unknown shooter. He put newspaper down on the kitchen table, removed the magazine and the round from the chamber, then field stripped the Browning and spent the next fifteen minutes cleaning it.

John Lee loved the old pistol that had probably been manufactured sometime in the early 1970s, and the minute he had spotted it on a table at a gun show in Lake City two years previously, he had bought it. Made in Belgium, the Browning Hi Power had been the standard military and police weapon for generations of European agencies. And even though there were newer, fancier, and lighter handguns on the market, he was comfortable with the 9mm pistol and its thirteen round magazine, and the two backup magazines he carried in a pouch on his gun belt give him plenty of firepower. There was nothing at all wrong with the standard issue Glock Model 17s that the other deputies carried, and John Lee himself carried a smaller Glock Model 27 in .40 as his off duty weapon. But authorized or not, he chose to carry the Browning when in uniform.

He reassembled the pistol, pushed the magazine home and chambered a round, then put the safety on and removed the magazine and added another round for the one he had moved to the chamber. That done, he put the dirty newspapers and his cleaning kit away and returned the Browning to its holster.

He noticed his uniform from the day before still lying on the floor on the other side of the unmade bed and thought that the least Beth Ann could have done was to make the bed and put the uniform in the clothes hamper before she left. He went through the pockets, taking his cell phone out and plugging it in to charge, and retrieving a small pocket notebook and pen from one of the shirt pockets. Checking the pants pockets to make sure they were empty, he felt something and reached in and retrieved the evidence bag with the metal disk that they had found at the crime scene the day before.

"Well that's just going to make Jayne with a Y real happy when I call and tell her I forgot about this," he said to himself. "She'll probably say I'm withholding evidence or something."

Magic barked and he heard the sound of a car coming up the driveway. He glanced at his watch, seeing that it was after 7 PM. "Now who the hell is coming around bothering me?"

He walked out to the deck and saw the red Toyota pickup truck. Magic barked excitedly and bounded off the deck to greet the woman who climbed out.

"How you doing, sweetie?"

She bent over and played with the dog for a moment or two, then looked up and said, "Aren't you going to say hi, John Lee?"

"Hello, Emily."

She pulled a small canvas bag from the truck and came up on the deck, where she dropped it and wrapped her arms around his neck and kissed him. Every time she came home like this John Lee told himself that he was not going to give in. He had told himself, and her, over and over that he wasn't a toy that she could take down from the shelf and play with and then put back up when she was done with him. And he meant it every time. It wasn't going to happen again. He was a man and he had some self-respect. There was nothing she could say or do that was going to change his resolve. And then she stuck her tongue in his mouth and ground her crotch into his and everything changed.

Later, as they layed in bed together, John Lee asked, "Does she know where you are?"

"She has a name. It's Sarah."

"Whatever. Does she know you're here?"

"Are you going to start being ugly, John Lee? Can't you just enjoy what we have and let it go at that?"

"What do we have, Emily? Huh, what?"

"We have this."

"Yeah, we have this. Every week or so you show up here, unannounced. You screw my brains out, and when I fall asleep I don't know if you're gonna be here in the morning or not. And if you are, you're always gone by the time I get home from work."

"Do we have to have this conversation every time I come here?"

"Yes, damn it, we do. I can't go on like this forever, Emily. I love you, but I want a full time wife, not somebody who's going to show up when she wants and then take off to go live with her girlfriend the rest of the time. How do you think that makes me feel?"

She moved her hand under the sheet to his crotch and said, "I know how this makes you feel."

He pushed her hand away irritably and said, "Stop it. I'm serious."

She sighed and sat up. "Okay, if you must know, Sarah had to go up to Valdosta. Her daddy's in the hospital with a bad prostate and they're doing surgery tomorrow morning. And *no*, she doesn't know where I'm at. It's none of her business. She doesn't own me, and neither do you, John Lee."

"Is that what you think it is? That I'm trying to own you? Christ, Emily, we're married! I'm not trying to own you. You're my wife and I want you here with me. Is that too much to ask?"

"How many times do we have to have this conversation? I told you, I felt... stifled here. All my life I've had to do what was expected of me. My daddy expected me to be the perfect young lady like a small town sheriff's daughter should be. Then I went away to school and I realized there's a whole big world out there, John Lee. A whole big world, and

I wanted to experience it all. But what did I do? I came back here and I married you!"

"I thought you married me because you loved me."

"I did, and I do. I really do. I just need some more time, okay?"

"How much more time, Emily? A day, a week, a month, ten years? How much time?"

"I don't know. Look, we have tonight. Just enjoy it, okay? Don't make it more complicated than it is."

"It's not enough, Emily."

She pulled the sheet away and moved down his body. He wanted to resist, damn how he wanted to resist. But he didn't. He never had been able to.

Chapter 10

"So you got laid, and then you got a BJ, and when you woke up she was gone. Most guys would think that's the perfect relationship," Maddy said, scooping up a spoonful of cheese grits from her plate.

"I guess I'm not most guys."

"All guys are the same," she said, washing down the grits with a swallow of coffee.

"I don't know, maybe you're right."

"Of course I'm right. I'm always right. Haven't you learned that yet?"

"You can be a real bitch sometimes. Do you know that?"

She laughed and said, "I know. Isn't it great?"

She filled her spoon with grits again and then stopped with it halfway to her mouth and asked, "Look, John Lee, what's the big deal? I mean, was it bad sex?"

"No. I wish it was, it might be harder to resist."

She laughed again and shook her head. "Resist? Seriously? There's no way you're ever going to be able to resist Emily. I mean hell, she's drop dead gorgeous, she's got a great rack, and an ass to die for. Why would any man want to resist that? If I was a little bit more like that Sarah she's mixed up with, I damn sure wouldn't try to resist anything she wanted to do to me."

"You better watch it," John Lee cautioned her. "There's already enough guys around this town that think you're a dyke because you won't put out for them."

"You know the difference between a slut and a dyke, John Lee?"

"No, but I figure you're about to tell me."

"A slut will go home with any guy in the bar. A dyke will go home with any guy in the bar except you."

He laughed in spite of himself.

She reached across the table and stabbed a sausage patty from his plate and set it on top of her grits. Maddy had an amazing appetite and John Lee was always amazed at how much food she could put away. But she never seemed to gain an ounce of weight.

"So, what do you think?"

"What do I think about what?"

"Are you one of the guys that think I'm a dyke, too, John Lee?"

"I never gave it much thought, to be honest."

"Bullshit."

"What?"

"I said bullshit. Are you gonna sit right there and look me in the face and say you've never thought about what it might be like?"

"What, you with another woman? That's more a fantasy than a thought, isn't it?"

"Bite me. You know what I'm talking about."

He felt uncomfortable with the direction the conversation was going and tried to change the subject, wondering aloud if his patrol car had been repaired yet.

"Uh uh," Maddy said with an evil grin on her face. "You're not getting off that easy. Have you?"

"Are you kidding me?"

"I'm just asking a question, that's all. Have you?"

"Have I what?"

She leaned across the table and looked him in the eye and asked, "Have you ever thought about what it would be like, you and me together?"

He started to look away and she put a finger on his jaw and turned him back toward her.

"Have you?"

"Jesus Christ, Maddy! Where's this coming from?"

"Have you?"

He tried to avert his eyes, but felt hers boring into him. Finally he looked back at her and said, "Yeah, I guess I have, a time or two. That's only natural, isn't it. You're a beautiful woman and I've known you forever. So sure, I'm not going to lie and say it's never crossed my mind."

She sat back and smiled and asked, "There, was that so hard?"

"I'd sure hate to be a perp being interrogated by you."

She didn't reply, just scooped the last of the grits from her plate and ate them.

"Well, how about you?"

"How about me, what?"

"You know what I mean."

"I'm a cop, not a clairvoyant, John Lee. I have no idea what you're talking about."

"You're really going to make me ask, aren't you?"

She batted her eyelashes at him innocently and grinned. "Ask me what?"

"Have you ever thought about you and me being together?"

"We are together, right here, having breakfast."

"Jesus, it's like pulling teeth with you. Have you ever thought about you and me... you know, sexually?"

"Oh, God no," Maddy said. "I told you yesterday, you're like a brother to me. Gross!"

John Lee sat back in his chair, confused and not knowing how to respond. He felt like he had just made an ass out of himself, crossed a line he never should have. But she was the one who had broached the subject.

Before he could think too much, Maddy stood up and said, "I've got to get on patrol. Fig's got me working the west end of the county today."

"Yeah, okay," John Lee said. He couldn't wait to be away from her so he could try to figure out what the hell was going on. He had known Maddy forever. She was one of his best friends and he sure had not meant to ruin that. But she *had* been the one that had brought it up in the first place.

She left some money on the table on top of her bill, and as she walked past him she leaned over and whispered in his ear, "Remember what I told you yesterday about proud old Southern traditions."

He heard her chuckling all the way out the door. Martha Darden, who was somewhere between 40 and 60 and had been a waitress at Bernie's Café for as long as he could remember, came by with a glass carafe of coffee and asked, "Do you need a refill, John Lee?"

"No, thank you," he told her. "I need to get out on the road."

***

John Lee liked driving fast. It was one of the best things about his job. How else besides being a NASCAR driver would someone give him a powerful car and pay him to drive it? With Maddy on the west side of the county, he drove in the opposite direction, and once he was out of town he pushed the accelerator all the way to the floor. The car was a Dodge Charger with a 370 horsepower V-8 engine and a stiff suspension that would take the rigors of high-speed pursuit driving. He would have loved to have been assigned the car all the time, it was the fastest and most powerful in the fleet. But Flag guarded it like a precious gem and didn't want anybody behind the wheel. It seemed like he wanted to preserve it as a museum piece instead of a working police vehicle. It was only because John Lee's regular car was still in the shop waiting for the window glass to come in that he had been able to get it.

With roof lights and siren on, he drove out past Wilson's Crossroads, easily hitting 100 miles per hour on the open straightaways, only slowing down when he encountered other traffic. He knew the Charger had more to give him, a lot more, but it would be just his luck to hit a raccoon or something at high speed and flip it. And the way his life was going, he wouldn't be fortunate enough to die, he'd survive and have to face Flag's anger. Even so, the high-speed run had helped relieve some of his frustration and confusion over the conversation with Maddy.

At the county line he pulled to the side of the road and sat for a minute while a slow moving propane truck caught up and passed him, then he made a U-turn and drove back in the direction he had come from, this time keeping it down to about 60. He wished women were as cooperative as cars. He understood automobiles. A car made sense. If he took care of it and treated it right, it would always respond the same way. With women, from his wife to his sister-in-law, and even with Maddy, he never knew what the hell to expect.

Chapter 11

"D.W. wants to see you," Sheila said when he came in.

"Now what?"

"I don't know, he just said that he wanted to talk to you."

"Any news from Tallahassee about those skeletons, yet?"

"Not that I've heard."

He went up the stairs to the second floor, wondering what kind of trouble he was in this time. Had someone seen him driving so fast and called to see what was happening? But if that were the case, Sheila would have taken the call and tipped him off.

He knocked on the sheriff's door and D.W. said, "Come in."

One look told him D.W. was upset about something.

"Have you talked to Flag today?"

"No, I try to avoid him as much as I can. Why, what's he up to?"

D.W. held up a piece of paper and said, "This here is a request for your suspension and the first step to dismissal from the department."

"For what?"

D.W. looked at the paper and said, "Accordin' to him, you are carryin' an unauthorized weapon, you fired said weapon at a suspect and failed to fill out a shooting incident report in a timely manner, and then when he ordered you to surrender the unauthorized weapon to him you refused."

"Are you kidding me? He's really going to try to push that?"

"Got the paperwork right here in front of me."

"Come on, D.W. You know this is bullshit!"

"What can I say? You can look at it for yourself." He handed John Lee the form.

"You do realize how hypocritical this is, right?"

"What do you mean?"

"He's bitching about me carrying an unauthorized weapon, but he's carrying a Smith & Wesson .44 Magnum."

"Yeah, Flag always says if you are gonna dig a hole use a shovel, not a spoon."

"If my Browning, which he's tried to buy from me for over a year and I won't sell to him, is unauthorized, so is his Smith. So he's going to try to hang me for something he's doing himself?"

"Well, besides that, he said you failed to file the shooting incident report in a timely manner."

"Give me a break D.W. It had been a long day and I had other things on my mind."

"Yeah, I know what kind of things you had on your mind. I was at your house yesterday morning, remember?"

"Is that what this is about? You're gonna let him can me for what happened between me and Beth Ann?"

"If I had my way I'd beat your brains out."

"Then do it D.W.! Kick my ass. I deserve it. But this here, this thing with Fig, it's bullshit and you know it."

D.W. leaned forward and rested his elbow on the top of his desk and put his forehead in his hand. "I just don't understand what this world is comin' to, John Lee. Beth Ann tells me that Emily's a part time lesbian or somethin', and you and her are doin'... I don't even want to think about that. When did life get so damn complicated?"

"I don't know, D.W. I don't know what's going on with Emily. I've tried to be patient, hoping she'd get her head together, but I just don't know anymore. And this thing with Beth Ann... just kick my ass and get it over with, okay?"

"I ain't gonna kick your ass, because it wouldn't do any good no how. I know a hard dick ain't got no conscience. Learned that from my own daddy with the crap he was pullin' before he dropped over dead. And I ain't gonna fire you, either. I wish my wife had never talked me into hiring Flag in the first place all those years ago. Worst decision I ever made sittin' here in this office."

"So what about his piece of paper here wanting me suspended and fired?"

"Tell you what, John Lee, why don't you walk down the hall there to Flag's office and tell that son of a Suzuki to wipe his tokus with it. And if he says anythin' else about that pistol you got on your gun belt, you tell him to come see me about it and talk to me with you sittin' here man-to-man. Not sendin' some bullfeather piece of paper like this through channels."

"Will do," John Lee said with a grin.

"Before you go, we need to talk about somethin' else."

A list of all of his possible sins went through John Lee's mind. If he was off the hook on the argument with Fig and nobody had reported his fast run to the county line, and D.W. was not pushing the issue about the relationship between he and Beth Ann, he wasn't sure what was coming next.

"I don't want Flag runnin' the investigation into those skeletons you found."

"Okay. Why not?"

"You know why not. He'd do anything he could do to get his face in front of the press and make himself look important. So I'm puttin' you in charge of the case."

"He's not gonna like that."

"I don't give a donkey's dingdong what Flag Newton likes or don't like. I'm the sheriff, and he needs to remember that!"

"Yes, sir."

"So until further notice, you're off road duty and you only answer calls for assistance when there's nobody else available to handle them."

"Any word from Tallahassee yet?"

"I haven't heard anything," D.W. said. He fished in his desk drawer and pulled out a pink telephone memo slip. "The person you want to talk to over there is named Shania Jones."

"Not Jayne with a Y?"

"No, she's one of the field people. This Shania is in charge of the lab there where they do that stuff. I told her you'd be her contact here at the Sheriff's Department."

"Thanks D.W., I appreciate your faith in me."

"Well, I gotta tell ya' it's a bit strained right now. And I still might take a baseball bat to you one of these days. But of all the people that have pissed me off lately, I trust you more than I do Flag. Now get out of here and go tell him what's what. And tell him if he's got any questions to come see me."

John Lee had expected Fig to hit the roof, and the Chief Deputy didn't disappoint him.

"This is bullshit! Absolute bullshit! It's nepotism, that's what it is, and I won't stand for it! I'll take this to the county commission if I have to."

"So you're going to tell them that your brother-in-law, the sheriff, overruled you in favor of his son-in-law, a deputy?"

"Don't you start any shit with me, you peckerwood."

"Hey, don't kill the messenger. D.W. said if you want to talk about it he's right down the hall."

"And that's exactly where I'm goin' right now," Flag said, coming around his desk and purposely bumping John Lee hard with his elbow as he went by.

As much as he was tempted to punch the man out, Flag was still his superior officer, so John Lee resisted the impulse. Instead he followed him down to D.W.'s office.

"Who the hell do you think you are, overrulin' me like this, D.W.?"

"Accordin' to this here nameplate on my desk, I'm the sheriff. That's who I think I am."

"I won't stand for this. No sir, I won't stand for this for a minute!"

"Well, what are you going to do about it?"

"I'll take it up with the county commission, that's what I'll do."

"Okay, have at it." D.W. pushed his telephone across the desk in Flag's direction.

"Don't think I won't do it, D.W."

"Oh, I don't doubt you'll do it," the sheriff said. "You been lookin' for a way to get in my shorts ever since the day I hired you. So you go ahead and do it. And when you do, I'm goin' to tell them how you tried to force this here deputy to give you his personal weapon after he wouldn't sell it to you. From what I know about the law, that might be considered extortion. Not to mention abuse of your office. And I'm gonna point out to them that you're wearin' an unauthorized weapon, too. The very thing that you're trying to get this man fired for. What was that word you used, John Lee? Hypocrite?"

"And what's this bullshit about puttin' John Lee in charge of the investigation of those bones we found? I'm the Chief Deputy! I should be in charge of decidin' who's gonna do what!"

"It's been over 24 hours and you still hadn't assigned anybody to it, so I figured you were too busy twiddlin' your thumbs or whatever it is you do down the hall there in your office to get around to it. So I took the initiative. That's what I get to do, because I'm the sheriff."

"I should be runnin' that investigation."

"Your job is to be an administrator. Now, if you want to stop being an administrator and go back to being a road deputy, I got no problem with that at all. You two can trade jobs. John Lee, how'd you like to be Chief Deputy? Sit on your ass in an air-conditioned office all day and look important? It can't be that hard. Flag figured out how to do it."

Flag knew that his bluff had been called and he didn't like it. But he also knew that this was a battle he wasn't going to win. Okay, he'd let D.W. and John Lee have this one. But no matter what kind of problems it caused in the family, come next election he was going to run for Sheriff and unseat that fat bastard sitting behind the desk. Without another word he turned and walked out of the sheriff's office and down the hall.

"Why don't you find someplace to go where you're outta' his sight for the rest of the day? I don't want him havin' a stroke here," D.W. said. "At least not 'til he's downstairs. I'd hate to think of one of the paramedics gett'in a rupture tryin' to carry him down the stairs."

John Lee nodded and started out the door, but D.W. called him back once more. "Just to rub some salt in the wound, just keep on drivin' that Charger. Ain't no use lettin' a good car like that sit when it could be out on the road workin'."

Chapter 12

"I'm going to be examining them this afternoon," forensic anthropologist Shania Jones told him on the telephone. "Would you like to come up and watch, or do you just want me to send you a report?"

"I can be there in about two hours," John Lee said.

"Sounds good, I look forward to seeing you."

He called dispatch and told Sheila that he was going to Tallahassee, then fed Magic and made sure his outside water bowl was topped off. It was a little more than 90 miles to the state capital. He followed a two lane road north to Interstate 10, then pointed the Dodge west. There wasn't much traffic and he made good time, arriving at the Crime Lab well within the two hours he had told Shania Jones it would take him.

Shania Jones was a tiny black woman who wore her hair in cornrows and had a beautiful smile and a warm handshake.

"Thank you for inviting me over," John Lee said.

"No, thank *you*. It's always nice when folks have enough interest to actually come and see what we do here. And don't worry, they're just bones so if you're squeamish, you're not in for any unpleasant surprises."

"Actually, I was there when they found the first skull," John Lee told her.

"Well then, shall we?"

She led him into the lab, where they donned gowns, face masks, and paper hats, and pulled on latex gloves. The bones had been laid out on three tables, which were assembled side-by-side.

"We don't have any one complete skeleton," Shania said. "We've tried to put the bones we do have in the right places, based on our observations and past experience. But that's not to say that every bone on Number 1 here shouldn't actually be over there on Number 2 or 3."

"I understand. What do you think happened to the other bones? Everything we found out there is here."

"Oh, it's hard to say. Animals may have carried some off, changes in the earth from temperature variations may have shifted some around.

There are all kinds of possibilities. I'm sure your folks and the team that went out from here found everything there was to find."

"Good, I'd hate to think we missed something. We've never come across a crime scene like this before, so we're kind of out of our league."

"Not to worry, we'll give you all that we have here. So, here are a few things I can tell you to start with. All three of the victims were of African descent."

"How can you tell that?"

She pointed at one of the skulls and said, "The nasal features of the skull, of all three skulls, are the first clue. Notice the shape of the nasal opening on each one?" She went to a glass cabinet on the wall and removed another skull. "This gentleman is a Caucasian of European descent. See the difference in size and shape?"

"I do."

She replaced the specimen in the cabinet and turned back to the table. "I would go so far as to say that these people are all of West African descent. Skulls of people from that region are prognathic. They usually have a protruding mouth/jaw area, and a tendency to have a longer, thinner shape. On the other hand, Caucasian skulls like the one I just showed you tend to be more flat faced, and quite often have occipital buns."

"That's amazing," John Lee said.

"I think so. Now in addition to their race, I feel comfortable in saying that these gentlemen were of a low socioeconomic status. Notice how the teeth are all worn and look like they were poorly cared for? This indicates to me a poor diet along with a lack of any kind of dental care,"

"You just described half the people in Somerton County, black or white," John Lee told her, remembering Rita Sue Baker's smile.

Shania laughed. He found himself really enjoying her company.

"You said gentleman. You can tell their sex?"

"Deputy Quarrels, I don't have to see a penis to know it's a man."

"These days you're never sure either way unless you actually check," John Lee said, then instantly regretted it, hoping he had not stepped over a line. But she put his mind at ease when she laughed loudly.

"There's a lot of truth there. Even in a relatively small city like Tallahassee I've seen some things that just make me shake my head."

John Lee found himself liking her more by the moment.

"Anyway, back to gender. Male skeletons have a narrow deep pelvis and women a wider, shallower pelvis better suited to carry a baby. And you see this notch here in the fan shaped bone of the pelvis? If you stick your thumb in and there is room to wiggle it, it's a female. If it's tight, it's a male. And I know what you're thinking, you sicko, you!"

This time they both laughed.

"I have to admit, you're not at all what I expected," John Lee told her.

"What do you mean? Because I'm black, or a woman, or a scientist?"

"All three," he admitted. "I don't know, I'm just a backwoods boy. I guess I pictured some gray-haired old man with thick glasses and no sense of humor."

"I'm sorry to disappoint."

"Not at all," he assured her. "It's a very pleasant surprise."

"For what it's worth, you're not exactly what I expected, either," Shania said

"How so?"

"A good ol' boy white deputy from the piney woods. I guess maybe a black city girl like me expected a redneck named Bubba with a cheek full of tobacco. But you're not half bad."

"Oh, if you want to meet some of those Bubbas you just described, I know a whole bunch of them," John Lee told her.

She laughed and said, "Thanks, but no thanks. Anyway, back to the subject at hand, the other thing these gentlemen all have in common is that they all did hard physical work. Notice these bony ridges on the wrists? Those are where the muscles are attached and are caused by years of pulling and stretching, lifting, things like that."

John Lee wasn't sure how to broach the subject, but he had to ask. "Do you think these folks could have been slaves?"

"I don't think so. No, I'm sure they're not. The bones aren't that old."

"Do you have any idea when they were killed?"

"Based upon my observations of the condition of the bones you recovered, at least fifty, but less than a hundred years ago."

"Wow. Talk about a cold case. What else can you tell me?"

"Well, at the most, I would say the oldest of these three gentlemen was probably somewhere around 40 to 45 years old when he was killed. The other two were younger."

"How can you tell that?"

"Again, they tell me." She pointed to skeleton Number 1. "Do you see this squiggly line that runs the length of the skull?" She traced her finger along it.

"Yeah, I see it."

"That's called the sagittal suture. Now, let's look at Number 3. Do you notice that it's more tightly closed? When it is completely fused together like that, it's an indication that the person was older than 35 years of age. And this second line, here at the front of the skull? That's the coronal suture, which fully fuses by about age 40. Now let's go look at Numbers 1 and 2. Do you see the difference in their sutures and those compared to Number 3?"

"I do."

"Okay, now I want to show you something else," Shania said. She lifted one of the wrist bones from Number 2 and asked, "Can you see what look like gouges or scrapes right here?"

"Yeah?"

She put the bone down and then walked to Number 3. "Again, we don't have all of the bones, and I couldn't put my hand on the Bible and swear that this particular bone goes with this particular victim. However, this bone here," she said lifting another one, "is also from the right wrist, just like the other one I showed you. And do you see the same scrapes or gouges?"

"Yes, I do."

She went to a table on the wall and came back with a short piece of rusty barbed wire. "This was also found at the crime scene. It's in poor shape and pretty fragile, and I imagine the rest of it rusted away a long time ago. But see this one barb right here?" She held it next to the wrist bone, against the scrapes in the bone."

"You're saying the barb wire did that?"

"I believe so. I think whoever killed these poor guys first tied their hands behind them with barbed wire and that these scrapes on the bone happened when they were struggling to free themselves."

"They had to be fighting damn hard to get loose to do that much damage."

"Wouldn't you be?"

"What I'm going to say now has no basis in fact. It's total conjecture. You need to understand that."

"Okay, understood."

"I don't see those scrapes on the bones of victim Number 1, just the other two. Here's what I think, and again, I'm just making this up as

I go and I could be completely wrong. But here's what I think, for what it's worth. I think they were probably all bound with barbed wire and that whoever murdered these guys shot Number 1 first. The other two, seeing what was coming, were struggling real hard trying to get free. I think that's how they got those scrapes. I think that barbed wire cut right through their skin and went to the bone."

John Lee shuddered, thinking of the terror and misery the men must have suffered before they died. "Damn!"

"Yes, damn indeed," Shania said. "Whoever did this to them was one evil son-of-a-bitch."

Even in a small place like Somerton County, John Lee had been a deputy long enough to know just how cruel people could be. He had seen not only his share of bodies that had been mangled in car wrecks, but also those shot or stabbed or bludgeoned after a night of hard drinking. He had seen victims of domestic abuse too many times. But this, this was something even worse.

"Could it have been the Klan, Ms. Jones?"

"Call me Shania. And yes, that was my first thought."

Black or white, anyone who had been raised in the South knew that the Ku Klux Klan was a true fact of life, and depending on one's politics and view of the world, one either accepted them for what they were and maybe even secretly thought they served a purpose, or else one knew that the racist organization was one of the most shameful examples of humankind in the nation's history. John Lee fell into the latter category, but he knew there were still plenty of bigots and Klansmen out there, even today.

All he could do was look at the skeletons on the three tables in the crime lab and say, once again, "Damn!"

Chapter 13

There wasn't much more that Shania Jones could tell him, but he found himself reluctant to part company with her. By the time they were finished it was after 5 o'clock.

"I really appreciate everything you've been able to tell me," John Lee said. "I never thought spending an afternoon looking at old bones could be so fascinating. Enjoyable, even."

Shania laughed and said, "I've found that sometimes the dead are some of the nicest folks I've ever met. They don't put many demands on you, and they always tell you the truth. That's more than I can say for a lot of people."

"You got that right," John Lee said as they took off their gowns. "Look, please don't take this wrong, but I'm starving. Would it be weird if I asked you if you'd like to get a bite to eat someplace?"

"Well, let me think, a white, how did you say it, 'backwoods boy' deputy sheriff wanting to take a black woman to dinner in the deep South? What could possibly be weird about that?"

"I'm sorry I didn't mean to..."

"Oh, shut up," Shania said, laughing. "I was picking on you. I'm hungry, too. What's it going to be, barbecue or fried chicken?" She saw the look on his face and laughed again. "You really don't get out of the woods much, do you, Deputy Quarrels?"

He laughed with her and said, "Just call me John Lee, okay?"

"John Lee it is. How do you feel about sushi?"

He didn't feel very enthused about sushi at all, so they settled for a Chinese place a few blocks from the lab. Sipping hot tea while they waited for their meals to be prepared, John Lee asked her, "How does a nice girl like you end up spending her days looking at bones?"

"My daddy dropped out of school when he was fourteen to help support his family. After he and Mama got married, he drove a garbage truck. Mama made money on the side fixing ladies' hair. They had seven kids. We never went hungry, and they always made sure we had clothes to wear, but it wasn't like we were *The Jeffersons* or had a lot of money to spend, either. The one thing they impressed on all of their kids was that an education was the key to a good life. All but one of us got a college education. Let's see, one of my brothers is an attorney, another is a schoolteacher, and one is a major in the Army. My older sister runs a community outreach center over in Pensacola, and my younger sister will graduate with a degree in chemistry this year. I started out wanting to go to medical school, but the first time I saw a surgery I passed out. The next time, I lost my cookies. I decided I'd rather work with bones than bodies."

John Lee laughed, then said, "You said all but one of you has a degree."

Her face grew serious, and Shania said, "My brother Jerome was killed in an accident when he was fifteen."

"I'm sorry."

She shrugged her shoulders. "It happens. He was hanging out with a rough crowd, and no matter how much my folks tried to keep him on the straight and narrow, he kept getting himself into trouble. One night Jerome and a couple of his buddies stole a car and the police were chasing them. They wound up crashing into a guardrail doing over 90 miles an hour. Jerome and his buddy Terrance were both killed instantly. Leon, the third boy, the one who was driving, wound up a quadriplegic."

"I'm so sorry," John Lee said.

"Yeah, me, too. But it is what it is, right?"

"I guess."

"Okay, your turn. How did you come to be a deputy sheriff in Somerton County? Do you come from a long line of Southern lawmen?"

"No, though I married into one. My father-in-law is the sheriff over there."

"Oh, I see." There was a subtle change in her body language. "You don't wear a ring."

"My wife and I have been separated for quite a while now."

"I guess it's my turn to say I'm sorry."

"It's complicated," John Lee said.

"Those kind of things usually are."

"It's not like we didn't get along, we very seldom argued about anything. But she always said there was something missing in her life. How did she say it? She felt stifled. So one day when I came home from work she had moved out. Now she's living with another woman."

"Ouch, that must hurt."

He chuckled and said, "I'm not sure what would be worse, being left for another man or for another woman."

"You seem to have a sense of humor about it."

"What was it you said a minute ago? It is what it is."

"Any children?"

"No, closest thing I have to a kid is a big old German Shepherd named Magic. He looks like he would eat you alive, but the most he would do is smother you in kisses."

That wasn't entirely true. Though Magic was as gentle as could be, he was also protection trained, and could easily take down a two hundred pound man if the need arose.

"I like him already."

"Anyway, I never really knew my dad, and my mother is... my mother's a flake. She didn't raise me, she was too busy going off to find herself. She'd pop back into my life now and then for a day or two or a week, and then she was gone again."

"It sounds like your wife and your mother have a lot in common."

"You know, I never thought about it that way," John Lee admitted.

"So who raised you, then?"

"My grandparents. My mother's parents. Paw Paw and Mama Nell."

"Now those sound like good old Southern people."

"You'd be wrong there," John Lee told her. "They don't fit any kind of stereotype you've ever heard of."

"Okay, you piqued my interest. Tell me about them."

The waitress brought their food, and after she left John Lee said, "They're like nobody you've ever met. Mama Nell, I call her that because if I ever called her Grandma she'd wash my mouth out with soap, she's been in love with Elvis Presley since she was little girl. Now, I'm not talking about some teenage crush. I'm talking head over heels in love. She has every record he ever made, not only in vinyl, mind you, but also on 8-track, cassette, and CD. Same with every movie he was ever in. VHS and DVD. Along with dozens of magazine and newspaper stories, and enough souvenirs to fill a WalMart. She makes a pilgrimage to Graceland every year, and if there's an Elvis impersonator playing anywhere from Miami to Biloxi, she's going to be in the front row. Hell, she even named my mother Lisa Marie, just like Elvis did his daughter."

Shania laughed. "And Paw Paw?"

"Let's put it this way. I stopped by their place yesterday and he's growing marijuana in his greenhouse."

Shania laughed so hard she choked on her house fried rice. She held her hand over her mouth and coughed, tears streaming down her cheeks, then took a long drink of water.

"Are you okay?"

"Oh my God, you white folks are funny! Are you serious, Paw Paw is a pothead?"

"I'm serious as a heart attack. Those plants are three or four feet tall!"

"And you're a deputy sheriff!"

"Yeah, we weren't exactly *The Waltons*. More like a cross between *Rosanne* and *Hee Haw*."

"So how does the progeny of a free spirit like your mother who was raised by Mama Nell and Paw Paw end up being a deputy sheriff? Because I still don't get that."

"To be honest, it was just a job, and jobs aren't all that plentiful over in Somerton County. All I've got's a high school education, and I never really wanted to be anything or do anything special. I certainly didn't plan on becoming a cop but it beat driving truck or working construction or anything like that. I just fell into it."

"Was that before or after you married the sheriff's daughter?"

"Before. I knew Emily before I got the job. It's a small town, everybody knows everybody. But we didn't start seeing each other until after I'd been a deputy for a year or so."

"And how does your father-in-law feel about the fact that the marriage is... whatever it is?"

"He doesn't really understand it. He's a small town politician. Don't get me wrong, he's a nice guy, but his world ends at the county line. He and I get along okay for the most part. I don't think he blames me for the separation. He just wants things to go back to the way it used to be."

He didn't tell her about D.W.'s reaction to finding his younger daughter at John Lee's house the other morning. He felt very comfortable with Shania, but that would have been too much information to share.

"And how about you?"

"What do you mean?"

"Do *you* want things to go back to the way they used to be?"

John Lee had to think about that for a moment before he could answer. "To be honest, I don't know. There was a time when I was crushed, when I'd have done anything to get her back. And she has come back a time or two and spent the night, then she just disappears again."

"Do you still love her?"

"I love her, but lately I find myself wondering if I'm still *in love* with her."

That was true. How could he go to bed with Beth Ann if he was still in love with Emily? It was a question he had asked himself more than once.

"Okay, you've given me the third degree. What about you? Is a jealous husband going to be coming through the door any minute now with blood in his eyes?"

Shania laughed and shook her head. "Nope, no need to worry about that."

"No husband?"

She shook her head.

"No boyfriend?"

Again with the headshake, but before he could ask anything else, she added, "And no girlfriend either, just in case you were wondering."

This time they both laughed.

"So how come a beautiful, intelligent, professional woman like you is still single?"

"Why, thank you sir," Shania said with a smile. "I don't know. I was busy with school and getting established in my job. I never had time for a serious relationship. I mean, I've dated a few guys, and there have been a few sleepovers in my life, but not many. I'm not saying I wouldn't want to find the right man someday. But he hasn't come along, and I haven't been out looking. Like I said, it is what it is."

They chatted through their meal, talking about everything from their work to the kinds of music they enjoyed, to their favorite movies and books. Finally, they realized that it was getting late and they were the only people still in the restaurant except for the staff, who occasionally looked at them, wondering how much longer they would be.

Shania wanted to split the bill, but John Lee wouldn't let her. They had walked to the restaurant, and when they got back to the parking lot at the state crime lab, he opened her car door for her and said, "Thank you, I really enjoyed tonight. And thanks again for all the information on the skeletons and all that."

"No problem, John Lee. I enjoyed it, too. You're a nice guy. For a good ol' boy white deputy sheriff, that is."

They laughed and he extended his hand to shake hers. Instead,

Shania, leaned forward and hugged him.

"You drive careful going home, John Lee. And if you ever get back this way again, look me up. Here's my card. My cell number's on the back."

"I'll do that," he said with a big smile. "I'll darned sure do that."

Chapter 14

He took the slower route home, US Highway 19 to Perry, where he picked up US 27 and then turned east on local roads into Somerton County. It had cooled off enough that he could drive with the windows down, and as his headlights cut through the dark he thought about his dinner with Shania. She was one of the most interesting women he had met in a long time. He was glad to have had the opportunity to meet her.

Driving through Somerton he saw Emmitt Planter sitting in his city police car in the parking lot of Dogs-N-Suds and pulled up beside him. Somerton only had four officers on the city police force and they worked closely with the sheriff's department.

"What's up, Emmitt?"

"Nothin' but the cost of livin' and my cholesterol level. How ya' doin', John Lee?"

"Fine as frog's hair."

"That's a nice Charger."

"Thanks. I sure do like it after that old Ford I've been driving the last two years."

"Any news on those bones you fellas found out there on Turpentine Highway?"

"I was just over in Tallahassee at the State Crime Lab. We don't know much more than we did to start with, except that they were black."

"That don't surprise me at all. Lots of niggers got killed around here over the years. Either killin' each other or gettin' out of line and the Klan takin' care of business."

John Lee didn't appreciate the slur but he had learned a long time ago that old prejudices were still alive and well in many people, including some of those who wore a badge. And while the Klan was still around, for the most part, they kept their identities secret. He wouldn't be surprised if more than one person who wore a uniform during the day put on a white hood and sheet at night.

"Yeah well, it's been a long day. I'm gonna head on home. You have a good night, Emmitt."

"You too, John Lee."

He drove away, angry with himself for the fact that he accepted the way people like Emmitt talked. Didn't that make him just as bad? Would he have ignored it the same way if Shania had been with him? Then again, why would she have been with him? That was a can of worms he didn't even want to think about, let alone open.

He was dreading who he might find waiting for him at home. He wasn't looking forward to seeing either Emily or Beth Ann, and he was relieved to have only Magic greet him when he pulled in the driveway.

John Lee felt guilty for being so busy that he had been ignoring the dog lately and spent half an hour in the yard throwing a big rubber Kong toy across the yard so Magic could retrieve it and bring it back to him. Then they would tussle over control until the dog would relinquish it and John Lee would throw it again.

Magic was still going strong, but John Lee was tired and ready to call it a night. They went in the house and he fed Magic, then went into the bedroom to hang up his gun belt and change out of his uniform. As he was going through his pockets he felt the small evidence bag and realized that he had forgotten to show the disk they had found at the crime scene to Shania. He glanced at his watch. It was after 10, but he took a chance and called her cell phone anyway.

"Hello?"

"I hope I didn't call too late. It's John Lee."

"Wow, you don't waste any time, do you?"

"No, it's not like that..."

"It's not? I'm disappointed."

"Really? I mean..."

He heard her laughing over the phone, a sound he had come to enjoy since he first met her earlier that day.

"You white boys are so uptight. What do you need, John Lee?"

"There was something else we found at the crime scene. And I keep forgetting about it."

"Okay, what was it?"

He could tell by the tone of her voice that she was all business again.

"I don't know, exactly. It's a round metal disk, about the size of a fifty cent piece and I think it's brass. It's still got a lot of dirt on it so I can't really tell you much else about it."

"My specialty is bones, but I'd like to see it. Can you take a picture with your phone and send it to me?"

"Yeah, hang on just a minute." He took the disk out of the evidence bag, set it on the kitchen table and took photographs of both sides and sent them to her number.

"It's hard to say," Shania told him after looking at the photos. "Why don't you try to wash some of the dirt off of it and see what you get?"

"Okay."

He went to the kitchen sink and ran some water, doing his best to scrub away the accumulated dirt.

"It's got a hole on top, and then in the center are the letters SL and the number 428 below them on the front. There's nothing on the back side."

"Send me another picture."

He did and waited while she retrieved it.

"I don't know, I've never seen anything like that. At first I thought it might be a token of some kind, but with the hole in it like that, it could be a tag that went on something."

"Like what?"

"I don't know. Anything from an animal trap to a dog tag. Who knows?"

"You said something about a token. What did you mean?"

"There was a time when businesses issued tokens. They called them trade tokens. They were usually good for a discount on something. Like a bar might give them out for a free drink, or a free sandwich if you bought a drink. Almost like they do with coupons today."

"Interesting."

"Believe it or not, cat houses even issued tokens."

"Cat houses? Like brothels?"

"Yes. Do you have any brothels in Somerton County, John Lee?"

"Not that I'm aware of."

"I'm sure if there were, you would know about them."

"What's that supposed to mean?"

"Oh don't get all defensive and start telling me you're one of those guys that never has to pay for it because you get plenty of it offered free. I just meant, you being a cop and everything."

"I wasn't getting defensive, I was just..."

"So do you, John Lee?"

"What do I what? Do I know of any brothels here, or do I get plenty of it offered for free?"

"Your choice, answer whichever one you want."

"No."

"No, what?"

"Your choice, choose whichever question you want."

She laughed again and said, "Oh, I don't think you have to pay for it. I think there's a whole bunch of little gals running around over there in Somerton County that you could have at your beck and call. All you'd have to do is ask."

"If nothing else, you're good for my ego."

She laughed again, and then she said, "My friend, you have no idea how good I am."

He did know how to reply to that, and he heard her laughter over the phone again. "Good night, John Lee. Sweet dreams."

And then the call ended.

***

Cradling the old Remington Mohawk Model 660 bolt action rifle, the sniper hidden in the thick stand of pine trees across the street had watched John Lee playing with the German Shepherd. He was easy to see in the security yard lights. Centering the Bushnell 4X scope's crosshairs on his chest, finger inside the trigger guard, all it would have taken was a light pull on the trigger. It would have been so easy to send a 180 grain bullet tearing through his chest, the soft exposed lead tip and notched copper jacket expanding inside and transferring its energy into a destructive force destroying everything in its path. So very easy.

But what would it accomplish? The damage had already been done, thanks to the road grader, and killing the deputy would only bring more attention to the case. Someone else would just replace him. Shooting at the police car the first time had been a stupid mistake that the sniper now regretted. It would have been better to let it be and see if the whole thing would just blow over. It had been so long ago, what could they have discovered? But there was no use crying over spilt milk. What was done was done.

Who knows? Maybe they would decide that the shots fired at the police car had come from somebody target shooting at a distance. Some careless shooter who didn't even know where his bullets were going. Or maybe a crank. A kid out playing a dangerous game for kicks. The sniper took one last long look through the scope at the deputy. Yes, it would be so easy, but all it would do was complicate things. Still, it was good to know that if it came down to it, taking John Lee Quarrels out would be easy. As easy as shooting fish in a barrel.

Chapter 15

John Lee didn't know his way around the Internet very well but he knew someone who did, and the next morning he called Maddy.

"Are you working today?"

"I go in this afternoon at three. Why?"

"If you're not busy, can I come over for a bit?"

There was hesitation on the line and he wondered if their conversation at breakfast the other day had strained their friendship. He hoped not, but he did know how to approach it.

"You there?"

"Uh... yeah. Come on over."

"Are you sure? If it's not a good time..."

"No, Mama's just having one of her bad days. I tried to get her to come down for breakfast and she wouldn't, and when I took a tray up to her she didn't want to eat."

"I'm sorry. Look, we can do this another time."

"No, really, it's okay. If I spend much more time cooped up in the house with her this way, I might wind up just as depressed as she is."

"All right, I'll see you in a few."

Maddy and her mother lived in a two-story house that her grandfather had built back in the 1940s. It sat on a half acre of land, and the grass needed mowing. Getting out of the Charger, John Lee noted that the place could have used a coat of paint, too.

Maddy met him at the door wearing green shorts and a Jimmy Buffett Margaritaville T-shirt. He followed her inside, and couldn't help noticing how good her legs and rear end looked in the shorts. As if reading his mind, she looked over her shoulder and said, "Caught ya."

John Lee felt his face redden and she chuckled. It seemed like a lot of women were having fun at his expense lately.

"Coffee?"

"Sure. Cream and sugar."

"I know what you like, John Lee." He noticed a little extra wiggle in her walk as she said it, and wondered if it was intentional. Nope. That was another can of worms he needed to leave unopened.

She filled their coffee cups, then asked, "So is this a social call, or business?"

"A little bit of both, maybe."

"Okay."

He took the envelope with the metal disk out of his pocket and showed it to her. "Have you ever seen anything like this before?"

She looked at both sides of it, and shook her head. "No, what is it?"

"I have no idea," John Lee said.

"Where did it come from?"

"We found it out in the trench with those bones."

"Interesting. Did the folks up in Tallahassee have any idea what it might be?"

"I met with a forensic anthropologist named Shania Jones. She could tell me an awful lot about those bones we found, but nothing at all about this."

"Okay, so tell me about the bones."

John Lee shared the things that Shania had told him, and when he was done Maddy shook her head. "Man that's a rough way to go out. Do you think it was the Klan?"

"That was my first thought," John Lee said.

"Can I show this to Mama? Maybe she's seen something like it before."

"Sure."

"Wait here." She took the disk and went upstairs and was gone a couple of minutes. While she was gone, John Lee sat at the table and looked around the kitchen. It seemed like everything had stopped soon after Dan had drowned. The refrigerator, stove, even the electric toaster looked like the same ones his friend's parents had used when they were teenagers. The only new appliance he saw was the electric coffee maker.

"No luck," Maddy said when she returned.

"I was wondering if you could find anything on the Internet about it?"

"It's worth a shot, I guess."

She went to the living room and came back with her Dell laptop computer and opened it on the table. She did a search under dog tags, Somerton County tags, and the letters SL and the numbers 428, all with no success.

"Sorry, John Lee. I tried."

"I appreciate it. I'll show it to Paw Paw and Mama Nell and see what they say. And maybe I'll check in with some of the old folks around the county and see if they have any ideas."

He had a second cup of coffee with her and she asked him about the rumor going around the courthouse about a big blowup between Flag and D.W.

"The way I hear it, Fig went stomping out the door, and when Sheila asked him if he was done for the day, he went off on her and told her that he damn sure wasn't done, he was a long ways from being done, and people around there needed to know that and not forget it."

"Yeah, he was trying to get me suspended and D.W. pulled rank on him. It got pretty ugly."

"And then I heard D.W. put you in charge of the investigation into those bones?"

"Yep, and told me to keep driving the Charger, too."

"Damn, John Lee. Maybe you should've been sleeping with both of his daughters all along!"

"You just had to bring that up, didn't you?"

She laughed at him and said, "Most guys would be bragging about it. I mean what could be hotter than doing two sisters?"

"I don't know. Doing two sisters at the same time?"

Maddy put her hands on both sides of his face and said, "I don't doubt you're good, John Lee, but I don't think even you are that good!"

They laughed and she sat back and asked, "So what are you going to do today?"

"Well, I could mow your grass."

"If that's a euphemism for what I think it is..."

"In your yard," he told her.

"With all the neighbors watching?"

"Get your mind out of the gutter, Maddy. I'm talking about getting a lawnmower and mowing the grass in your yard."

"Yeah, I knew that. No, really, I did."

"I just noticed it's getting pretty long out there."

"I hired Leroy Bolger to do it and he'd come by a couple times a month to mow. But I had to tell him not to do that anymore."

"Why? Couldn't depend on him, or did he do a crappy job?"

"Neither. He started showing up a little too often wanting to talk about other things besides the yard work, if you get my drift."

"What, Leroy's not your type? Looks like he's in pretty good shape from all the work he does. And I hear tell he's only got six or seven more payments due on his pickup and he'll own it free and clear."

"Call me picky," Maddy said, "but I've got a rule that any guy I date has to have more teeth than he does tattoos."

"Girl, you're gonna have to look a lot farther afield than Somerton County unless you plan to be a virgin the rest your life."

"And just what makes you think I'm a virgin, John Lee?"

"I'm just gonna shut up now."

"You should've thought about that a few minutes ago."

"Anyway, do you have a lawnmower?"

"Yeah, there's a riding mower out in the shed next to the garage."

"Has it been started in the last hundred years?"

"Yes, it has. Leroy used it when he cut the grass."

"Let me go check it out," John Lee said.

The shed smelled of dust and old garden mulch. A small collection of rakes, hoes, and shovels leaned together in one corner, looking like nobody had used them since Maddy's father had left. There was a workbench along one wall, hand tools hanging on a pegboard above. Like the rakes and shovels, he was sure they had not been touched in at least a decade.

A tarp covered the mower, an old Toro Wheel Horse, and while it looked like it had seen better days, it started right up. John Lee spent a couple of minutes figuring out the controls, then drove it to the front of the property and mowed the grass on both sides of the driveway all the way to the back of the house. He had the backyard almost done when it ran out of gas.

He had stripped off his shirt and was sweating above his jeans and boots. Maddy came out with a glass of lemonade.

"Damn, John Lee, I may take a picture and put it on a calendar!"

"Flattery will get you anywhere," he told her. "Do you have any gasoline around here?"

"I think there's a can in the shed or the garage, let me check."

She was back in a couple of minutes with a red plastic two gallon can.

"Feels like it's about half full."

"That's enough to do the trick," John Lee told her. He filled the tank and the mower started on the third try. He handed her the empty lemonade glass, gave her a thumbs up, and went to finish the rest of the yard.

Watching him, Maddy had a smile on her face. At six feet tall and 175 pounds, with his dark hair and broad shoulders, there was no denying that John Lee Quarrels was a fine looking man. And as far as she knew, he had all of his teeth and no tattoos.

Chapter 16

John Lee was hot and sweaty by the time he finished mowing the grass, and after he parked the mower back in the shed and pulled his shirt back on, he thanked Maddy for trying to help him find out any information on the disk and drove home to take a shower.

He was just drying off when his cell phone rang. He looked at the screen and the caller ID said it was Shania Jones.

"Hello."

"Are you busy?"

"No, just got out of the shower, to tell you the truth."

"I must have had an impact on you if you are taking cold showers at this time of the day!"

He laughed and said, "Yeah, that's what it is."

"I don't suppose you know how to Skype, do you?"

"How to do what?"

Shania laughed and said, "Never mind. The reason I'm calling is, I showed the pictures of that disc you sent me last night around here, and nobody's ever seen anything like it. The closest thing I got was couple of people who said it might have been a dog tag. But I doubt Somerton County issued any kind of dog tags back when these guys got shot. Do you even require them on dogs now?"

"Yeah, I think they cost a buck or two. But I doubt if half the dogs in the county have one."

"And one of the guys here said he wondered if it was a key fob."

"What do you mean?"

"Sometimes when companies have a lot of vehicles, each one has a designated number, and they use some kind of a tag or something on the keychain so you know which key goes to which one."

"That's interesting, I never thought of that. We use a small square plastic tag for the vehicles here at the Sheriff's Department. It's worth checking out."

"I'd be interested to hear if you find out anything about it," Shania said. "I'll be sending over my formal report sometime this afternoon after I get it written up. It's not going to say any more than what we talked about yesterday, but I'll put a whole bunch of scientific terms on it and dress it up so that it looks like I know what I'm talking about and am earning my pay."

"Sounds good," John Lee told her. Even though they were just talking on the telephone, he felt a little self-conscious doing it while he was standing there naked, especially with her knowing that he had just gotten out of the shower.

"Anyway, keep in touch, okay, John Lee?"

"I'll do that," he told her.

"Oh, and you should look into Skype."

"If you say so."

She laughed and said, "Who knows? It could open up a whole new world for you. Have yourself a nice day, John Lee."

He shaved and put a uniform on, and realized he was humming to himself as he did it. What was that all about? He never hummed.

He called dispatch to check in with Sheila and see if there was anything going on that he needed to know about.

"No, but D.W. just asked if I had heard from you today."

"Okay, transfer me up to him if you would."

"I can't, he went to the Rotary for their monthly luncheon."

"All right, I'll catch him later."

"Before I go, did you hear about your patrol car?"

"My patrol car? No, what about it?"

"Well, it needs a new window in the driver's door."

"No, it needs windows in both doors. When that guy was shooting at us the bullet went through one window and out the other."

"That's not what I mean," Sheila told him.

"Okay, then I have no idea what you're talking about."

"Well, you're gonna love this, John Lee. After his big blow up with D.W. yesterday, Fig went to the garage this morning and saw that they had replaced the windows in your car, but that you were still in the Charger. He hit the roof again, and called D.W. right then and said that you were driving it without his permission. That's when D.W. told him that he had assigned the Charger to you permanently. Buster, there at the garage, he said he heard Fig arguing with D.W. about it, and even though he could only hear one side of the conversation, he said it sounded bad."

"Fig really has had a couple of bad days, hasn't he?"

"Oh, it gets better," Sheila assured him. "Buster said that when he got done with the conversation, Fig threw his phone across the garage and it hit the wall and broke into about a hundred pieces. He said then Fig turned around and put his fist right through the brand new window he had just installed in your old car."

"You're shitting me?"

"That's what Buster said, and it gets even better."

"Really?"

"Yeah, not only did he bust out the window, it sounds like he might have broken a couple of his knuckles. Had to go to the hospital in Perry to get them looked at. And then," she had to pause because she was laughing so hard, "and then when D.W. heard about it, he had Buster write up an incident report and said that the cost of replacing the window was coming out of Fig's paycheck!"

"Damn, that's about the funniest thing I've heard all week," John Lee told her.

He ended the call and laughed all the way out to his Charger.

***

"Nope, I've never seen anything like that," Mama Nell said, turning the disk over in her hand.

"Let me see." Paw Paw took it from her and studied it. "Doesn't look familiar to me, but it looks like the letters and numbers were punched in with individual dies, one at a time. See how they're not exactly straight? The four is a little higher than the other two numbers?" He turned it over and said, "And you can see that it's not flat here in the back. It's dimpled a little bit."

"A die?"

"Yeah. Come on, I'll show you."

He led John Lee through the back door into one of the collection of sheds he had constructed on the property. Inside there was a long tool bench, with various wrenches and screwdrivers hanging from a pegboard above it. Paw Paw opened one of the many drawers under the bench and fished around and pulled out a plastic box.

"Do you remember when I was doing leatherworking?"

John Lee remembered all too well. At one point his grandfather had bought a leather making kit from Tandy and for the next year everybody Paw Paw knew got wallets, belts, leather headbands, and wristbands, all decorated with designs. He opened the box and took out a metal punch and a piece of scrap leather. Placing the leather on the table, he centered the punch on it and hit the end with a hammer.

"See?"

There was a perfect half-moon shaped crescent in the leather.

"You could do the same thing with metal, like that disk of yours if you had some dies or punches with numbers and letters on them."

"Okay, that helps a lot," John Lee told him. "Somebody suggested that maybe this was a tag that went on a key, like for a fleet vehicle?"

"Yeah, that could be. When I worked for FPL we had something similar for all our vehicles. And not just the vehicles, the chainsaws and things like that all had one on them at one time. That was before they started bar coding everything."

"Thanks, Paw Paw, I appreciate it. I need to get back to town to start asking questions."

"Long as you're going back to town, give me a ride."

"Where you headed?"

"Back to town."

Mama Nell had joined them in the shed, and said, "Paw Paw's decided he's goin' to start ridin' a bicycle. I told him at his age he's probably goin' to fall off and break his hip or somethin'."

"I'm not gonna break my hip! Besides, riding a bicycle is healthy for you. I should get one for you, too, and you could ride with me."

"No thank you," Mama Nell said. "We both break our hips who's gonna take care of us?"

"You always look for the worst side of things, woman! Riding a bicycle is good for the environment and good for the health. I don't know why anybody would want to drive a car anyhow."

"Whatever," John Lee interrupted. "If you're going to be riding a bicycle, why do you need a ride into town?"

"So I can ride it back home."

"Well, where is this bicycle, Paw Paw?"

"In the garage."

"Okay, now you've totally confused me."

"We're going to put the bicycle in the trunk of your car and you're going to drive me to town, and then I'm going to ride it home. What's so confusing about that?"

"Well, why don't you just ride it into town and back home again?"

"That wouldn't make any sense. If I was already at home, why would I ride a bicycle into town just to turn around and ride it back home?"

"Because..." John Lee realized this wasn't going to get him anywhere, so he just said, "You better not scratch up my new car putting that bicycle in the trunk."

Chapter 17

D.W. was back from his lunch with the Rotary and John Lee gave him an update on what he had learned in Tallahassee.

"Anything on that slug they found in the dirt with those bones? Or the bullets that got shot into your car?"

"That's a different part of the crime lab," John Lee told him. "Those are the ballistics people and apparently they're swamped. There was a big gang shooting in Pensacola, and half a dozen other incidents that they are working their way through. The fellow I talked to there said he hoped to get back to us in the next two or three days, but he wasn't making any promises."

"Violent times we live in," the sheriff said. "Anything else?"

"Yeah, this." John Lee took the disk out of the evidence bag and handed it to him.

D.W. studied it for a moment and asked, "What am I looking at?"

"I was hoping you could tell me. It's some kind of tag. Someone said it might've been a dog tag, but I don't think we had any kind of dog ordinances back then. And a couple people think it's a key fob, kind of like the plastic tags we use now for Department vehicles."

"That makes sense," D.W. said.

"I thought I'd ask around town, see if anybody remembers seeing anything like this."

"Have at it. But keep in mind, this may not be connected to those bones at all. It could've been dropped or lost at anytime and just be in the same area by coincidence."

"That's true," John Lee said. "But I still think it's worth checking out."

"Sure, but before you do that, I need you to just write me out a quick rundown of everythin' so I can prepare a statement for the press. They're all over this and I don't want to keep them waitin' and give them enough time to get distracted by some other story and forget all about us."

John Lee knew that having the press forget about him would be crushing to his father-in-law. D.W., like any politician, thrived on exposure, and getting face time in front of television cameras was not something a sheriff from a small county like Somerton got very much of. He needed to make hay while the sun was shining. John Lee didn't want to waste much time writing things out for D.W., but he wanted to stay on the man's good side as much as possible. Lord knows he had done enough to test D.W.'s patience lately.

"I'm on it."

As he was going out the door, D.W asked if he had heard about Flag's latest temper tantrum.

"I sure did. I'd have liked to have been there to see that."

D.W. shook his head in disgust. "Man thinks he's fit to be sheriff, and he pulls some dumb stunt like that?" And though there was a frown on his face, John Lee didn't miss the glint of delight in D.W.'s eyes, knowing his nemesis had given him new ammunition to use against him if he ever needed it.

***

"Never seen nothin' like that."

"Sorry, John Lee, nothin' I'm familiar with."

"Ya say it ain't a dog tag? That would a been my guess."

And so it went at Taylor's Hardware Store, Farmer's Supply, Somerton Auto Parts, Overton's Propane, and everywhere else John Lee showed the disk around town. The closest he got was at Gus Martin's Hunting Supply.

"I wouldn't swear to it," Gus said, "but it could be a trapper's tag. Trappers would put a tag with some identifying mark on each one of their traps. That way if the game warden or whoever came across a trap, they'd know who it belonged to."

***

"It very well could be a tag from an old steel leg hold trap," Kevin Stringer, a warden with the Florida Fish and Wildlife Conservation Commission, told him when John Lee sent a picture to his phone. "But there's no way to know for sure, and if it was, no way to know when it was used or who it would have belonged to. We don't have any records dating that far back."

"Well, it was worth a shot," John Lee said.

He was discouraged. He felt like the tag was his best clue to whoever had murdered those three men so long ago, but he wasn't getting anywhere with it. It was late in the day and he had talked to more people than he could remember. His stomach was growling and he was trying to decide between stopping for a bite to eat before he went home, or throwing a TV dinner in the microwave when his cell phone rang and the decision was made for him.

"Where are you?"

"Downtown. What's up?"

"Greg and I are going 10-7 at the Fry Basket," Maddy said. "Want to join us?"

"Sure, I'll be there in five."

It was a short drive to the restaurant, and he pulled in and parked next to Greg's unit. Getting out of the Charger, he could smell the food cooking inside and his stomach growled.

Maddy and Greg were at a table in the corner and as he sat down, the waitress, a pretty young girl with braces on her teeth who was working there for the summer to earn enough money to buy her first car, put a glass of sweet tea in front of him.

"Do y'all know what you want yet?"

She had directed the question at Greg.

"I'll have the shrimp basket," he told her. "And could you bring me a couple extra hushpuppies."

"You got it. How 'bout you, sir?"

"I'll have the same," John Lee told her.

"Catfish for me," Maddy said.

The waitress nodded and headed back to the kitchen to deliver their orders.

"I guess she never heard of ladies first," Maddy said, shaking her head.

John Lee chuckled. "Don't blame her. I'm sure she was blinded by all of Greg's good looks."

Greg blushed. "Yeah right.... ya' think so?"

"Oh, there's no question about it," Maddy teased. "I'm telling you, Greg, if I was a few years younger I'd be all over you."

"Ahh... ahh..."

Maddy and John Lee laughed at his discomfort, although secretly, John Lee was glad that somebody else was Maddy's target for the moment.

"I don't know if it's safe to let you two work the same shift, especially at night," John Lee said.

Maddy laughed out loud, and said, "No worries there, An old lady like me don't hold a candle to that sweet young thing."

"You're not that old," Greg said, and John Lee laughed at the look she gave the young deputy.

The waitress was back with a large cardboard container of hush puppies, which she placed in front of Greg. "Here, I brought you these just so's you don't have to wait for Maggie to get the rest of your dinner fixed."

She hovered over the table until a couple came in and sat down on the other side of the room.

"Wow, somebody's crushin' hard on you, Greg," Maddy said.

John Lee looked at Greg and said, "Just so you know, when shift is over I'm going to come back over and dust that little gal for fingerprints."

"Don't you worry about fingerprints, John Lee. Just have Greg here drop his pants and check his ass cheeks to see if she broke any fingernails off in them."

"You guys stop it," Greg said, protesting, but secretly basking in the good natured attention.

The waitress came back with their orders and made it a point to pat Greg on the shoulder and call him 'honey' when she asked if he needed anything else. John Lee and Maddy exchanged knowing grins when she did not give them the same attention.

As they ate, Maddy asked, "Did you hear about Fig?"

"Yep. D.W. was all over that. Said he's going to dock his pay to cover the cost of the window."

"What an asshole. I mean, D.W. isn't exactly Marshal Matt Dillon, but people keep electing him, so he must be doing something right. Fig makes no secret that he wants D.W.'s job, and then does something that stupid. He's his own worst enemy."

"You got that right, Maddy."

"Any luck with that disk you've been showing around town?"

John Lee shook his head. "I can't count how many people I showed it to and nobody can tell me for sure. Best guess is that it's either a tag for a key for some kind of vehicle or equipment, or else the tag off of a steel trap. But nobody really remembers seeing anything like it."

"This may sound like a stupid question," Greg said, "but did you ask at the Historical Museum?"

"The Historical Mus... holy shit! I never even thought of that, Greg.

Jesus Christ, how fricking dumb am I? That's where I should have started!"

"I never thought of it either," Maddy said. "If D.W. ever gets rid of Fig, he needs to make you Chief Deputy."

Greg was blushing again, this time because of the admiration the experienced deputies were showing him. Meanwhile, John Lee was kicking himself for not thinking of Somerton County's small historical museum, which was tucked away on a side street in an old house that had been around for at least a hundred years. He knew the museum kept sporadic hours, only open a couple of days a week when any of the volunteer docents were available. He had only been in the place once, years ago on a field trip when he was in grade school, and he didn't know what the hours actually were, but he planned to be there first thing in the morning to find out.

Chapter 18

There was a ten year old blue Ford Focus parked in his driveway and John Lee groaned. Magic met him at his cruiser is always, but as soon as John Lee had rubbed his ears a couple of times he ran back to the deck, where Beth Ann was sitting in one of the wooden chairs with her feet propped up on the rail.

"It's 'bout time you got home, I've got to pee."

"There's plenty of trees you could have squatted behind."

She got up and kissed him. She was wearing some kind of strawberry flavored lip gloss.

"Hurry up and unlock the door, John Lee, I'm about to burst!"

He did and she made a beeline for the bathroom, while Magic made one for the kitchen, where he sat next to his bowl and looked back at John Lee expectantly.

"I don't know which of you is a bigger pain in the ass," he told the dog as he fed him. He heard the toilet flush and Beth Ann came out of the bedroom and said, "Wow, talk about relief!"

"What are you doing here, Beth Ann?"

"I just wanted to hang out for a while and... whatever."

"You're gonna keep it up until either your daddy or your sister shoots me, aren't you?"

"Oh, stop be'in such a drama queen, John Lee. Ain't nobody shootin' nobody. You take life way too serious."

"Too serious? Jesus Christ, Beth Ann, your daddy just about walked in and caught us in the act! I expected him to take my head off right there."

"But he didn't, did he? I swear, John Lee, sometimes I think you wake up in the mornin' lookin' for somethin' to worry about."

Beth Ann was 24 years old and just as good looking as her sister, but in a different way. She had been somewhat of a tomboy growing up and still had a casual attitude about everything. Where Emily would have never thought of leaving the house without her makeup just right and her hair brushed to perfection, Beth Ann seldom wore anything but a bit of lip gloss and never took her appearance or herself seriously. Not that she was a slob by any means, she just didn't see the need to waste a bunch of time every morning primping in front of a mirror. Beth Ann accepted herself as she was, and expected the rest of the world to do likewise.

John Lee had always liked her, and enjoyed spending time with her when he and Emily were together, but the thought of them having any kind of relationship other than familial had never entered his mind. Sure, she was a nice looking girl, even sexy, there was no denying that. But she was off limits. Way off limits.

After Emily moved out John Lee had hit a low point and didn't know where his life was going. He considered leaving Somerton, but where would he go? Except for the time he spent away while he was in the Army, it had always been home and he had always expected to live the rest of his life there. The week that Emily returned to Somerton with Sarah and they set up housekeeping, John Lee was sitting on the deck one night working his way through a six pack of Budweiser when Beth Ann showed up with one of her own.

Looking back, he didn't think it was planned, certainly not on his part anyway, but as they drank and talked late into the night, something changed. He had a good buzz on, but he had not been drunk, so that was no excuse for what happened. One minute they were sitting side by side on the porch, and the next Beth Ann was in his lap, her arms around his neck and their tongues doing a dance. Neither of them had said anything as they walked into the house and into his bedroom. There had been no frantic tearing of clothes in a rush to get naked, it just seemed casual and natural. And while Emily had always been reserved in bed, enjoying their love making but always leaving him with the feeling that she was holding back, Beth Ann went about it like she did everything in life, with complete openness and enthusiasm.

Afterward, in the reality of the morning light, John Lee had been full of guilt and was mentally kicking his own ass. He had apologized to Beth Ann and she sat up in bed and asked, "Whatever for?"

"For last night. I didn't plan that and I..."

"Stop it. It's okay. I had a good time."

"Yeah but..."

"But nothin'. Don't make a big thing of it."

"You're my wife's sister, for God's sake!"

"So what?"

"So what? This was a big mistake."

"John Lee, it was just sex. Don't get all bent out of shape over it."

"Can't you see how wrong this is, Beth Ann?"

"If Emily was still here, if she was bein' a proper wife to you, yeah, it'd be wrong. And it wouldn't never have happened. If you was out hound doggin' somewhere and picked me up while she was sittin' here at home, that'd be wrong, too. But it ain't like that, John Lee. She's the one that left. She's the one that's livin' with another woman, and you're the one settin' home alone."

"She's still my wife."

"For how long? You don't know if she's ever comin' home and neither does she. You plannin' to live the rest of your life like one of those celibate Catholic priests or somethin' while she's out gettin' her rocks off with her girlfriend?"

He didn't know how to respond to that, because he didn't know what the future held. Every time he had asked Emily where things were going with them, he always got the same response, that he was smothering her, that he needed to give her room, that she didn't know herself, so how could she answer that?

And so it was that he found himself in this mess. Every once in a while Beth Ann would come over and they'd do the deed. And he had to admit, the sex with her was very good. Maybe the fact that there was a taboo attached to it made it even better. And even though he knew it was wrong, it was something he enjoyed to a great degree.

Then, a few weeks after she had returned to Somerton, Emily walked in one evening as casual as if she had just returned from the grocery store. She had told John Lee that she loved him, that she couldn't picture her life without him, and he thought she was home for good. Those hopes were dashed the next morning when he woke up to hear her crying in the bathroom. He had knocked on the door, asking if she was all right, and Emily had come out and gotten dressed, ignoring him. He kept asking her what was wrong, and she had only said that it had all been a mistake. She wasn't ready for this yet. And then she was gone.

After that, the pattern repeated itself. He might not see her for a week or two and there would be no contact. If he called her, she always told him she was busy and hung up. But then, totally unexpected, she would return and spend the night. The first few times it happened he had been hopeful that life was going to get back to normal, but it never had. He never knew what triggered Emily's need to come back home, or why it never lasted more than a few hours. As time went on, he grew less hopeful. But at the same time, he had never turned her away.

Knowing that the debate with Beth Ann was not going anywhere, and neither was she, John Lee went into the bedroom and hung up his gun belt, then stripped and got into the shower. He wasn't surprised when the door slid open and Beth Ann got in with him, and though he knew he should, he didn't protest. What the hell, sooner or later someone was probably going to shoot him anyway.

Chapter 19

The handwritten sign on the door of the museum said it was open Fridays and Saturdays from 10 AM until 2 PM. It was Thursday.

John Lee cursed, then noticed another small handwritten sign on a 3x5 index card at the bottom of the glass with an emergency number to call. He took out his cell phone and punched in the number and a woman answered on the fourth ring.

"Whatever yer sellin', I don't want it. I don't eat Girl Scout cookies, I know who I'm votin' for, and I've already found Jesus. So if yer one of them solicitors just hang up and stop callin' me."

"No ma'am, I'm not selling anything, I promise. This is Deputy John Lee Quarrels from the Sheriff's Department."

"If that no count grandson of mine got himself arrested again, ya can keep him!"

"No ma'am, it's nothing like that. I'm down here at the Historical Museum and I need to talk to somebody."

Her voice grew concerned. "Is somethin' wrong at the museum? Did somebody break in or somethin'?"

"No ma'am, everything's fine, but I need to talk to somebody. Is there any chance that you could meet me here?"

"Can't ya read the sign on the door, deputy? We're open Friday and Saturday."

"Yes ma'am, I know that."

"And this here is Thursday."

"Yes ma'am, I know that too. But I really need to talk to somebody."

"Ya' ain't got a daddy or a preacher ya can talk to?"

"No ma'am. I mean, yeah, I've got a daddy. But this isn't something I can... look, is there anybody I can talk to?"

"Yer talkin' to me right now, ain't ya?"

John Lee tried to hide his impatience when he said, "Ma'am, this is a police matter and I really need to talk to somebody. Can you please come down here and meet me?"

"I don't even know yer really a deputy. Ya could be one of those serial killers like that there Ted Bundy."

"I promise you, I'm not a serial killer. You could call the Sheriff's Department and the dispatcher will tell you I'm for real."

"Whatever it is ya need, can't it wait 'til tomorrow?"

"No ma'am, it really can't."

There was a sigh and then silence on the line and he wondered if she had hung up on him. "I'm supposed to go to my sister Gracie Ellen's today to help her make potato salad for her husband's family reunion tomorrow. I don't know why, since she don't get along with any of the whole bunch. "

"Hopefully this won't take long," John Lee said. "You'd really be helping me out, ma'am."

There was another audible sigh, and she finally said, "Fine, but you better not be a serial killer!"

"I swear I'm not."

"I'll be there soon as I can. My bunions are acting up so it's going take me a while to get my shoes on."

"That's fine," John Lee said, "I'll be here waiting for you."

It was twenty minutes before an old black Mercury Comet with sagging springs and a piece of clear plastic taped over the opening where the rear passenger window had once been pulled into the driveway. John Lee couldn't help but wonder if Flag Newton was responsible for that one, too. The large woman behind the wheel turned off the ignition and the motor sputtered a time or two before it died. John Lee wondered if it would ever start again.

The woman heaved herself out of the car with great effort and demanded, "You that deputy that called and drug me down here on a Thursday when the museum ain't open?"

He was tempted to tell her that since he was the only deputy there, it was probably a pretty good chance he was the one who had disturbed her day, but instead he just said, "Yes ma'am, and I really appreciate you coming down."

"Well what is it ya want?"

John Lee took the envelope from his pocket and took out the disc. "Have you ever seen something like this before, ma'am?"

She looked at it and shook her head. "What in tarnation is it?"

"That's what I'm trying to find out?"

"You drug me all the way down here when I's supposed to be helpin' Gracie Ellen with her potato salad just to show me that? What the hell is wrong with ya?"

"Please ma'am, this is very important. It has to do with those three skeletons we found the other day."

"Well why you askin' me? I didn't shoot 'em!"

"No, ma'am, I'm sure you didn't. But we found this at the crime scene and we're trying to figure out what the connection is."

"Then why ain't ya talking to Chester?"

"Chester?"

"Yeah, if anybody'd know anythin' 'bout somethin' like that it'd be him, not me."

"Does Chester have a last name, ma'am?"

"Course he's got a last name! Everybody's got a last name. What kind a damn fool question is that, anyway?"

John Lee needed to remind himself that she was an old woman, and a volunteer, and that she had gone out of her way to meet him at the museum. Even if she made it a point to let him know that it was a great sacrifice on her part.

"Ma'am, I really appreciate you coming down here and helping me out, and I know you've got other things to do. If you could just tell me how to get a hold of Chester, that would really help me. And you could go on about your day."

"Damn right I got better things to do!"

"I understand that ma'am, I really do. Now, how can I talk to Chester."

"You can't, he won't be here 'til Saturday."

"Saturday?"

"Ain't that what I just said? I work Fridays and Chester works Saturdays."

"Is there any way I can talk to Chester before then?"

"I don't see how you could, he won't be here 'til Saturday."

"Is there a way that I could call him? Do you know his phone number?"

"No, I don't know his phone number. Why would I know his phone number?"

"Because you work with him at the museum? What if you needed to ask him about something?"

"Then I'd get hold of him when he was here on Saturday."

John Lee took a deep breath, "Ma'am, what if you were in the museum on Friday and a water pipe broke or something like that and you needed to get hold of Chester. What would you do?"

"Why would I call Chester for a broken water pipe? He ain't no plumber."

"I don't know, I just thought there must be some way you can get hold of him if you really had to."

"If I really had to, I'd call him. But Chester don't know nothin' 'bout water pipes. He ain't no plumber."

"Wait a minute. You'd call him? How could you call him if you don't know his phone number?"

"I don't need to know it, it's wrote down in the address book there inside the museum, along with everybody else's numbers."

"I thought you said you didn't have his number."

"No, you asked if I knew his number and I told you I don't, 'cause I don't. You didn't ask me if I knew where his number was wrote down."

John Lee wanted to throttle the woman, but he knew that wouldn't do any good. Instead, he asked, "Could you possibly open up the museum and write his number down for me and give it to me?"

"Deputy how many times I got to tell you? The museum ain't open today. It's open Fridays and Saturdays. And this here is Thursday."

"Right, it's Thursday and you need to go help Gracie Ellen with her potato salad. And I have to figure out who killed those men out there by the highway. And the quicker you get me that number, the quicker you can go do what you have to do and I can go do what I have to do."

"Well ain't you a snotty pants? I'll have ya know that I know Sheriff D.W. Swindle very well and I'm goin' to be talkin' to him about your attitude. Here I come all the way down here on a Thursday, when the museum ain't even open, and I got better things to be doin' and you talk that way to me. Yes, sir, me and D.W. are gonna have us talk!"

"That's fine. ma'am. In the meantime, can you just open the damn door and get me Chester's phone number?"

"There ain't no need for cursin'. After all, I'm doin' you a favor."

"You're right, ma'am and I apologize. Please, would you mind going in and getting me his number?"

"That's more like it, young man. Didn't your mama ever tell ya that ya can catch more flies with honey than with vinegar?"

He was tempted to tell her his mother hadn't taught him much, except to never expect anything just because someone made you a promise. But instead, he just waited while she went inside the museum. She made a point of closing the door in his face and leaving him standing outside.

She came out a moment later with a phone number written in a shaky scrawl and asked, "Are we done now? Gracie Ellen is waitin' on me."

"Yes ma'am, and thank you again for your time."

He started to open her car door for her and she said, "Step back. I don't need you lookin' up my dress when I get in the car."

John Lee was sure that whatever was under her faded print dress was not something he wanted to see. "No problem, ma'am, " he said, backing away. "You have yourself a good day."

She didn't reply, just turned the key in the ignition. The weak battery just barely managed to turn the engine over, and John Lee thought he might have to give her a jump, but then it caught and burst to life in a noisy cloud of blue smoke. She backed out of the driveway and into the street without looking, causing Billy Dickerman to slam on his brakes to keep from broadsiding her. She gave Billy a withering look, like it was his fault that he was driving down the street when she wanted to go someplace, then shifted into gear and drove away.

Chapter 20

A man answered the telephone, and when John Lee asked for Chester, he said that was him. John Lee identified himself and said that he was a deputy investigating the murders of the three men whose skeletons were found recently and that he was at the Historical Museum and wondered if there was a possibility Chester could meet him there.

"Why sure, if you think it'll help you. I'll be right there. Sit tight."

John Lee went back to his car to escape the heat, but before the Charger's air conditioner could cool him down there was a knock on his window. He looked up to see a short, stoop shouldered man with white hair and a goatee.

"You that deputy?"

"Yes, sir."

"I'm Chester Kelly. What can I do for you?"

"I'm sorry," John Lee said, getting out of his car. "I didn't see you drive up."

"Drive up? I only live three houses down. I can walk here quicker'n I could start my pickup and drive here."

"I wish I had known that," John Lee said. "I've spent the last half hour dealing with a lady whose phone number is on the door there as an emergency contact for the museum."

"Hazel? Why'd you call her when I'm almost next door?"

"Hers was the only number there."

Harold walked to the museum door and leaned down to peer at the sign.

"There should be a card there with my number, too." He pulled a key ring from his pocket and sorted through a number of keys until he found the right one and unlocked the door. "Come on in, officer."

He opened the door and bent down to pick up another 3x5 card with his phone number on it and said, "Here it is. Guess I need to put some more tape on it. Come on in, get out of the heat." They were met with hot, stale air. Chester went behind the counter and rummaged around in desk drawers for a moment, then came back with a roll of Scotch tape and re-affixed the sign to the window in the door.

"So you met Hazel?"

"Is that who she is?"

"Yep. Did she bust your balls?"

"Oh, yeah. I don't know why she wouldn't tell me to just walk down to your house and knock on the door."

Chester laughed and shook his head. "That'd be too easy. Hazel's been volunteering here for five or six years now, and I think she drives as many people off as she ever makes feel welcome."

"You might be better off without her," John Lee suggested.

"If I had anybody else that would open up even one day a week, she'd be gone. Most times we don't get enough traffic in here to make it worth keeping the door open, so we have to depend on volunteer help. And she's the last person we had offer to volunteer in as long as I can remember."

"Well anyway, I really appreciate you coming down, Chester."

"No problem. Now what is it I can do for you, son?"

John Lee took the tag from his pocket and showed it to him. "We found this out at the place where those three skeletons turned up. We don't know if it has anything to do with them or not, and we don't know what it is. Some people have said they think it's everything from a dog tag to a key fob, to a tag that went on a steel jaw leg trap. But nobody knows for sure. I know it's a long shot, but I was hoping you might have some insight."

Chester was shaking his head, and John Lee expected him to respond the same way everybody else had, but instead Chester said, "It's not a dog tag or a key fob or any of that stuff people been telling you."

"It's not?"

"Nope. Follow me."

He led John Lee through a series of cluttered rooms, turning on lights as he went. Each room held displays of the county's history, each with its own theme. In one a female mannequin with its right hand missing and a worn-out wig on its head stood in front of a wood burning stove. Another had high school football trophies and other sports memorabilia. It looked like the newest display may have been from the 1950s. A third room seemed to be dedicated to Somerton County veterans. There was a mannequin of a World War I Doughboy, and another wearing a World War II vintage Eisenhower jacket. Everything seemed neglected and forgotten.

In the fourth room they came to, Chester stopped at a glass display case and said, "What you found out there is one of these." He pointed into the case at two identical brass tags, one with the letters SL and the number 236 stamped into it, and the other with SL 103.

John Lee couldn't believe that after running into so many brick walls, he would find two more tags just like the one he had been carrying around on display at the historical museum.

"I'll be damned. What are they, Chester."

"Those are ID tags turpentiners wore,"

"Turpentiners? What are turpentiners?"

"Not *are*, officer, *were*. There haven't been no turpentiners around here since I was knee high to a grasshopper. They're a breed that died out a long time ago."

"Do you know anything about them?"

"About the ID tags, or about the turpentiners?"

"Anything you can tell me will help."

"Oh, I can tell you a lot about those days, if you've got time to listen."

"I've got nothing but time," John Lee assured him.

"Most folks are in too much of a hurry for history lesson," Chester said. "I guess that's why this place don't get much traffic. Folks are too busy playing with computers and texting and all that nonsense to remember the past. Not me, I've been studying it forever. So do you want the *Reader's Digest* condensed version or the full story?"

" I want anything you can tell me. I've already learned more from you in five minutes than I have all week."

The old man smiled with pride and said, "Well then, you're in for a bit of education, officer. Are you from around these parts?"

"Spent my whole life here except for a couple of years when I was gone in the Army."

"And I bet you never heard a word about the turpentine industry in these parts when you was in high school, did you?"

"No sir, I didn't."

"Don't surprise me none. It's one of those things we don't talk about 'round here. One of those dirty little secrets, kinda like slavery and lynching and things like that. Guess that makes sense though, since a lot of the turpentine industry wasn't much more than just another form of slavery. Only difference was, it lasted half way through the 20th century. Pull up a chair, deputy, let me tell you all about it."

Chapter 21

"Do you know where turpentine comes from?"

"I'm sorry, I don't," John Lee admitted.

"Pine trees. Pine trees just like we got all around here. Collecting turpentine dates back to Colonial times. Back then we had wooden ships, and they used pitch, which was rosin made from turpentine gum, to caulk the seams between the timbers on ships' hulls. They also used it on ropes and rigging on sailing ships to preserve them. That's how turpentine products came to be called 'naval stores' and that's what gave birth to the turpentine industry. But turpentine had a lot of other uses, too. People used it to polish furniture and clean floors and windows, and as a solvent for paint. It was also used to heal cuts and insect bites. The whole South was part of the industry, from the Carolinas down to Georgia and here in Florida. Right here in Somerton County the Somerton Lumber Company had half a dozen turpentine camps. It made them rich."

"Somerton, as in the Somerton family?"

"Yes, sir. Ezekiel Somerton first settled this county way back before the Civil War. As I recall, his family was from Alabama and he was kind of the black sheep. I don't know if they drove him off or he left on his own, but he wound up here."

Everybody in the county knew the Somerton family, and though John Lee knew their roots went deep into the past, he had never really thought about how they came to prominence. The Somertons owned several businesses in the county, including Somerton Forest Products Company, one of the biggest employers around. A lot of local people worked for the Somertons, lived on property owned by the Somertons, or did business with them in some form or another. And John Lee had his own unfortunate connection to the family.

"From 1909 until 1923, Florida led the country in production of turpentine gum," Chester said. "It was Florida's second largest industry, and big corporations bought or leased huge tracts of forest land and set up turpentine camps. Things started to slack off a bit with more and more steel ships and when they switched from sail to steam, and then diesel power. But the industry continued way past that. I think the last turpentine camp in the state shut down in about 1952. The last one here in Somerton County closed in 1950."

"I never even heard of them. Where were the camps located?"

"I've got an old map here someplace, I can find it and show you. I know one was just about three miles from where you guys found those skeletons."

"Really? Then they could have come from the camp."

"It's entirely possible," Chester agreed. "Now, you need to understand something about these camps, officer. They wasn't pleasant places to live or work. Before the Civil War they used slaves to work in the woods harvesting turpentine. They'd cut a slash in a tree and when the sap came out they collected it in buckets. Then it was hauled back to camp and run through a still, just like the new moonshine. It was dangerous work and men were killed and maimed by equipment all the time, not to mention getting snake bit or attacked by gators."

"Sounds like a hard life," John Lee said.

"It was, and after the Civil War when they didn't have slave labor no more, they came up with new ways to keep people working. So they hired the negroes who had just been freed, but all they was really doing was making slaves of them all over again. They worked from sunup to sundown Monday through Saturday. The pay was about ten cents an hour, and most of the camps didn't pay with real money. They paid with scrip that could only be used at the camp store. You ever hear the old song about the coal miners and I owe my soul to the company store? It wasn't any different down here in the turpentine camps. If a fella needed to feed his family, or clothe them, or anything else, he had to buy what he needed at the camp store. Besides the camp store, workers lived in little shacks owned by the camp, and they had to pay rent. At the end of the month, he always wound up a little bit more in debt than when he started."

"Then how did he to break the cycle?"

"Most of them never did," Chester said. "The law was on the side of the companies, and if the worker tried to leave without pay'in his debt, the camp captain, who was, like the overseer, could chase them down and bring them back, and whip them or do just about anything he wanted to teach them a lesson. And if one of the workers did somehow manage to get away, any cop could pick him up anywhere and bring him right back."

"And this went on right here, in Somerton County?"

"Not just here. All over the place," Chester told him. "And it wasn't just negroes. The law made it possible to arrest any male age 18 and over who didn't have a visible means of support, and then they had a convict-lease system. The local sheriff could lease out those prisoners to the turpentine camps. It made a lot of good old boy sheriffs rich back in the old days."

Chester stood up and opened the back of the case and took out a short leather riding crop. "That captain I told you about, the overseer who ran the camp? He'd ride around on a horse and use this to whup a worker upside the head or across the back if he didn't think he was performing hard enough. And at the end of that long workday, when they finally drug themselves home from the woods, life in the camps could be just as dangerous. Folks lived in little shacks and shanties almost on top of each other, and there was always fighting and stabbing and stuff like that going on. And the captain and his thugs that helped him keep things in control, a lot of them weren't above taking a woman if they wanted her. Didn't matter if she was black or white, didn't matter if she was married or not."

"And back then the law was part of it?"

"Like I said, a lot of sheriffs and other politicians made a lot of money off the system. That stopped after a fella named Martin Tabert, who was arrested for vagrancy and became part of the convict-lease system, was beaten to death by the overseer at a camp over in Dixie County in 1922. After that the state got so much bad publicity that they put an end to using prisoners that way. But they still had plenty of ways to get workers. The law still said that anyone who accepted anything of value from one of the companies had to work off that debt. And anything of value could be whatever they wanted it to be. Not just something they bought from the camp store or the shack they lived in, it could be as simple as a ride someplace, or getting treated by a doctor when somebody was sick or injured."

"Damn Chester, it really was just like slavery."

"In a lot of ways it was worse. At least back in slavery days the plantation owner owned the slave. He had an investment in him, just like he would a horse or a mule. Now I'm not saying they were nice people, because there was a lot of abuses back then, too. But you're usually not gonna kill a horse or mule just for the sake of killing it. Same way with a slave. But here in the turpentine camps, a worker died or wound up getting killed, so what? There was plenty more where he came from, and it didn't cost you a penny."

"And these workers wore ID tags like these?"

"Yep, that SL stands for Somerton Lumber, and the number was their individual worker number. They were worn around their neck on a string or a leather thong or something like that. That way the overseer and his men knew who was who. When they started their work day the captain noted the number to know they was on the job, and he checked them off at the end of the day. And when they went to the camp store to buy something, they showed that tag. Probably better'n half the people working in the camp stores couldn't read or write much, if any at all. So that was an easy way of record keeping."

"Do you have any way of knowing which workers these tags would've belonged to, Chester?"

The old man shook his head. "Sorry, I don't. And I don't know if the company has any records going back that far, either."

"You said something about the camp captains being able to beat workers if they tried to run away?"

"Not just if they tried to run away. If the boss man felt like they were slacking off, or be'in uppity, or for any reason he wanted to, he could whip them as punishment and to set an example of what happened to people who were shirkin."

"And that was legal?"

"Who was going to complain? And who were they going to complain to?"

Chapter 22

John Lee had never been much of a student when he was in high school. He always did enough to get by, and graduated with a B average, but he was just putting in his time. But over the two hours he spent with Chester, he found himself becoming fascinated with the history of Somerton County. How could he have called this place home for so much of his life, yet know so little about it?

Chester had explained how the turpentine business had enabled the county to survive during the bleak Reconstruction period following the Civil War, and how it had continued to thrive through half of the next century. The Historical Museum had several photographs from the old turpentine camps, faded black and white pictures of men and women who looked tired and worn down by their hard lives. Blacks and whites lived and worked side-by-side, united in their common misery. In one of them, a young white man sat astride a horse, holding a double-barreled shotgun and watching several workers loading a cask onto a horse drawn wagon. A coiled whip hung from his saddle horn. The man looked familiar, although there was no way John Lee could know him, since the picture had been taken so long ago.

"Do you have any idea who this fellow might be?"

Chester studied it and shook his head. "I have no idea. Obviously he's one of the overseers or woods riders. Those were the captains' underlings. Each camp would have three or four of them, depending on size."

John Lee looked at the photograph again. "Sure looks familiar to me for some reason."

"Well, unless you was reincarnated and lived back in those days, I don't see how you'd know him."

"I guess not," John Lee said, then had an idea. "Would you mind if I took up a picture of this with my phone?"

"Help yourself."

While John Lee took a picture of the old photograph, Chester opened up a closet and sorted through several boxes before coming back with an old map, which he opened up on top of the showcase.

"This map dates back to 1939," Chester told him as he carefully unfolded it.

The paper was brittle and the ink was faded, but he was able to point out to John Lee the locations of the six turpentine camps that had been operated by the Somerton Lumber Company. One was north of a line that was identified as Turpentine Road, and though there was no scale on the map, John Lee estimated that Chester's three mile guesstimate was pretty close to where the skeletons had been found. Another camp was a little further west, and the other four were scattered further away around the county.

"Can I take this with me, if I promise to bring it back?"

"I'd really hate to see something happen to it," Chester said. "It's one of the few maps we have of the county back in the old days."

"I understand that," John Lee said. "Listen, we've got a copy machine over at the sheriff's office, can I just take it long enough to make a copy? I promise I'll take really good care of it."

Chester thought about it for a moment and then nodded his head. "Sure, just bring it down to my house when you're done."

John Lee thanked him for his time and promised to be back in just a few minutes. Chester saw him out and locked the museum's door. He shook the deputy's hand and said, "My old lady's got the Alzheimer's and I don't like leaving her alone for too long, so I'm going to head back over to the house."

"You've been a great help to me," John Lee said. "I promise I'll make a copy of the map and get it back to you just as soon as I'm done."

The old man nodded and said, "Whatever was done to those three men out there was a terrible thing. You kinda hate to think things like that happened around here, but they did. I can't help but wonder how many other old bones are buried around this county."

Driving to the courthouse, John Lee wondered the same thing himself.

***

"It's too big to copy all in one piece," Sheila said, "but I can probably make like six copies of different parts of the map and tape them together for you. Will that work, John Lee?"

"Whatever you can do," he told her. "As light as some parts of it are, I'm not even sure how well it will copy."

"I can set the machine to copy it darker than it is," she said.

"Okay, do that if you would. Will that machine blow stuff up, too?"

"Oh yeah, up to four hundred percent."

John Lee showed her the area where the two camps were located closest to where the skeletons had been found and asked if she could give him a blow up of that area."

"You got it," Sheila said. "Give me about fifteen minutes."

While she was doing that John Lee went upstairs to update D.W. on what he had learned.

"Oh yeah, I remember hearin' about the turpentine camps," the sheriff said. "Way I heard it told, it was a good way to get the riffraff off the streets and put them to work."

"Sounds more like slave labor to me," John Lee said.

"Well now, neither you nor me was there, so don't go judgin' things just based on what one person told ya."

"Even riffraff doesn't deserve to be shot in the back of the head like that, D.W."

"I ain't sayin' that, John Lee. Hell, we don't even know if the men those bones belong to came from one of them camps. For all we know it could'a been anything. Bootleggers killin' each other, a family feud, it's hard to say."

"Or the Klan."

"Don't go pokin' sticks at a hornets' nest until you know more than you do now," D.W. warned.

"Wherever this goes D.W., I'm not going to just pretend it never happened."

"Don't expect you to. I'm just sayin' don't be talkin' 'bout things until you know. You know how it is around here, John Lee. There's a lot of good ol' boys 'round these parts that still hang onto the old ways. Just don't go steppin' on toes until we know they're the ones that need steppin' on is all I'm sayin'."

"I understand."

"Okay, get back at it. And keep me posted. I need somethin' to tell those news people."

"Will do," John Lee assured him.

He left the sheriff's office and was headed back downstairs when Chief Deputy Flag Newton accosted him on the wide marble steps. "What's this I hear about you being rude to poor old Miz Darnell?"

"Miz Darnell? I don't know who that is."

"Don't you try to bullshit me, boy! She said you called her and demanded her to come down to the museum and then you got lippy with her. I don't care if you *are* brown nosin' D.W., I won't stand for that!"

"Hazel? Is that who you're talking about?"

"You know damn well who I'm talkin' about! Hazel Darnell. Where do you get off actin' that way?"

"I wasn't rude to her at all," John Lee said. "If anybody was rude, it was her."

"Don't you be makin' excuses, I know what a smart ass you are."

Flag's right hand was swathed in a huge bandage, and he accented his words by thumping John Lee in the chest with it. The deputy was tempted to tell him that if he did it one more time, he was in for another trip to the emergency room, but instead he just said, "Have you ever considered that anal bleaching thing those movie stars are doing out in Hollywood, Fig? Because if an asshole ever needed to lighten up, it's you."

He turned and continued down the stairs, with Flag shouting after him, "There's gonna be a time when you don't have D.W. to protect your ass. And when that day comes, I'm gonna be waitin', John Lee. Oh yeah, I'll be waitin'!"

***

Sheila had done an excellent job on the map, carefully taping six individual sheets together to make a full-size duplicate, and she had also made three separate copies at different magnification levels that zoomed in on the two turpentine camps and the site where the skeletons had been found. She had also been able to increase the contrast so that details showed better than they did on the original.

"That's perfect," John Lee told her. "Let me get this map back to the fellow at the museum. Thank you, Sheila."

"No problem." She leaned forward and rolled her eyes toward the door and said, "You watch yourself with Fig. He's really on the warpath. When old Mrs. Darnell came in here raisin' Cain, I tried to head her off at the pass but he was walking down the stairs and heard it and he was all over it right away."

"Don't fret over it," John Lee said. "He's just pissed off because he can't get his way about my old gun and that Charger, and because he made an ass out of himself and busted his hand in the process."

"I know, but even so, you just watch yourself, okay?"

"I will. I promise."

He left the dispatch office knowing that sooner or later he and Flag were going to have to settle things between them, and he knew when that day came, it wasn't going to be pretty.

Chapter 23

"Here you go," John Lee said, handing Chester the map. "Got it back to you all in one piece, just like I promised."

"Oh, I wasn't too worried about that," the old man said. "Would you like a glass of sweet tea?"

"I don't recall ever turning one down," John Lee replied.

"Well then, come on in."

He led the way into the house, a tidy affair with delicately tatted doilies on the back and arms of each piece of overstuffed furniture. A thin woman with snow white hair that hung halfway down her back was sitting in a rocking chair, her wrinkled, boney hands busy.

"This is Arlene, my wife," Chester said. "Honey, this here is Deputy John Lee Quarrels."

"Pleased to meet you, ma'am."

She didn't look up or acknowledge his presence, her hands busy creating yet another doily.

"Have yourself a seat," Chester said, going into the kitchen. John Lee heard a refrigerator door open and the sound of ice clinking into glasses and then of liquid being poured. Chester returned with a tray holding two large glasses of tea, and a smaller one. He set the tray on the coffee table, handed one of the large glasses to John Lee, then removed a smaller glass from the end table next to his wife and replaced it with the fresh one. John Lee noted that the first glass was still full of tea, the ice long since melted.

"How did you come to know so much about the history of Somerton County, sir?"

"Oh, I've always been fascinated by history. Back in my working years I was over in Jacksonville teaching history at a community college. Arlene here, she's from Somerton, and when we moved back here, I just started doing my research. The museum was closed back then and they were talking about hauling everything off to the dump or selling it or whatever, just to get rid of it. But that would've been a tragedy. I got a group together and we went to the county supervisors and managed to convince them to let us keep it open as long as it didn't cost the county anything."

"I know you're not open all that much, but it still must cost some just to keep the power on," John Lee said. "How can you afford it?"

"Mostly a lot of begging, hat in hand. We charge a couple of bucks admission, and I spend a lot of time sucking up to local businesses, trying to get anything I can out of them. We hang on by the skin of our teeth, and now and then I dip into my own pocket to help make ends meet."

"John Kennedy and Jackie are comin' to town next week," Arlene suddenly said.

"Beg your pardon, ma'am?"

"President John F. Kennedy and his wife Jackie are comin' to town."

"Is that a fact? I hadn't heard about that."

"Yes, siree. He's Catholic, ya' know. But that's okay, I think he's a good man."

"I think so, too," John Lee said. "What's that you're making, ma'am?"

She didn't answer him, lost again in the fog that had taken so much of her mind. Chester looked at her with fondness, as if her comments were as timely as they would've been back in 1962.

He took a sip of the tea, which was delicious and cooled him off well.

"I was thinking," Chester said, "even though it's been a long time since the last turpentine camp closed up, I imagine there's still some old folks around here that remember them. You might ask around, see if anybody remembers any stories about those days."

"I'll do that," John Lee assured him. "Thanks for the tip."

"Of course, you have to remember where you're at, officer. Just because folks remember things don't mean they're going to want to talk about them."

"I understand," John Lee said.

He knew the old man was right. People in Somerton County were not always eager to talk to the police. Sometimes it was because of a natural resentment of authority, sometimes because they themselves or a family member were involved in some kind of nefarious activity, and sometimes because they feared repercussions. And then there were those who just believed in minding their own business. But one never knew, information could come from the most unlikely places.

"Let me ask you something, Chester. Do you think the Klan could have had anything to do with those skeletons we found? They *were* black men."

"You know as well as I do, officer, that's always a possibility. And what did you tell me, that those bones have been out there at least fifty years?"

"That's what they told me at the crime lab up over in Tallahassee."

"There was a lot of bad stuff goin' on back then."

John Lee finished his tea and put the glass back on the tray.

"You've been a big help to me, Chester. I may be back to pick your brain some more, if I can."

"Anytime, officer. You know where to find me."

John Lee stood up and Chester walked him to the door. Before he left, John Lee handed the man a $20 bill and said, "It's not much, but maybe it will help keep things running over there at the museum for another day."

"That's not necessary," Chester said, trying to give the money back, but John Lee shook his head and insisted he keep it.

"Believe me, I probably already wasted that much in gas money just running around town getting nowhere."

As he went out the door Arlene called after him, "Be sure to be on time when President Kennedy and Jackie get here."

"Yes, ma'am, I will," John Lee promised. "You can count on me to be there."

He had just gotten back in the Charger and pulled away from the curb in front of Chester's house when an emergency warning alert came over the radio and then Sheila's excited voice. "All units, shots fired! Officer involved shooting. Homestead Road by the old service station."

John Lee grabbed the microphone off the car's dashboard. "County 16, I'm on my way!"

There was so much radio traffic at once that he did not know if Sheila heard him or not, but he turned on his overhead lights and siren and sped toward the south end of town.

"Who's shot?"

"County 9 on the way."

"Is anybody hit?"

"Is the shooter still on the scene?"

"What does he look like?"

There were so many questions coming at once that the dispatcher could not break through to reply to any of them. Suddenly Flag Newton's voice boomed over the radio. "Everybody shut up! This is County 2, I said shut up! Radio silence, now."

He got his message through and the radio fell silent. "Okay, Sheila what's going on?"

"County 24 reported shots fired," the dispatcher replied. "He's parked at the old gas station. He's not hit and doesn't know who the shooter is. No description."

"24, this is 2," Flag said, "What's your status?"

"Whoever it was shot out my back window," Greg Carson said. "I don't know who it was, I never saw anything. The window just shattered and I heard the shot. Then he fired again and I felt it hit the car."

John Lee whipped into the oncoming lane to avoid hitting a car that pulled out from the curb in front of him, the driver oblivious to his lights and siren. The young woman behind the wheel, talking on her cell phone, glanced up as the police car barely missed her but kept right on talking. Once he was outside of town on Homestead Road it was a straight shot to the old gas station, which had been closed for years now. He floored the accelerator and the Charger shot forward.

The gas station came into view and he could see Greg's car there, but there were no other vehicles and no sign of life. Roaring into the gravel parking lot, John Lee hit the brakes and the Charger began to slide sideways. He was afraid he was going to lose it, but managed to get control and came to a stop sideways behind the other police car. He jumped out, with his pistol in his hand.

"Greg, you okay?"

"Yeah, I'm fine, John Lee."

"Where are you?"

"On the floor of my car."

The other deputy managed to crawl out and ran to crouch beside John Lee.

"You sure you're okay?"

"Yeah, but that's the second time someone shot at me in a week. I'm not liking this at all!"

"Do you know where the shots came from?"

"I think back there behind me. I don't know where for sure."

There were other sirens approaching fast and John Lee got on his radio.

"This is County 16, I'm on the scene. Greg said the shots came from north of the old gas station."

Three cars came into view and one of them pulled off about fifty yards from the gas station where there was a small copse of trees. The deputy got out and pointed a shotgun in that direction, using his car for cover. The other two cars continued on to the gas station. Moments later Flag and a fifth car arrived.

"This is 2. Any sign of movement from those trees?"

"No, sir," somebody replied.

"Okay, John Lee and Carson, I want you guys to head for those trees. Beckett, you circle around and approach from the rear. I'll cover you from here. Move it!"

Chapter 24

John Lee, Greg, and Bob Patterson all piled into the Charger and he drove across the open ground toward the trees, expecting gunshots to ring out at any time. When they were within about 20 yards he turned the Charger sideways and they piled out the driver's side. Still nothing.

"Everybody ready? Okay, let's go."

They moved toward the trees, weapons at the ready. John Lee had holstered his Browning and brought the Charger's shotgun with him. He could feel his heart pounding and a trickle of sweat running down his spine. At any second he expected gunfire to come from the trees.

"Watch for crossfire in case anything happens," Flag cautioned.

With deputies approaching the trees from the north and south, and Flag and another deputy coming in from the east, the only escape route was to the west across an open field and then a marsh. Anybody going that way was sure to be seen.

The tree line was coming closer with every step. John Lee kept his eyes moving, looking for anything out of place. A quick movement, the silhouette of a shooter, anything that might warn them of danger lurking ahead.

"Damn!" He heard a thump and look to the right quickly to where Greg Carson had fallen to the ground. John Lee squatted and kept his shotgun pointed at the tree line. He had not heard a gunshot.

"Are you okay? What happened?"

"I'm okay," a chagrined Greg said as he scrambled back to his feet. "I just tripped over a root and fell."

"You scared me."

"Will y'all stop the damn yakking and concentrate on the situation at hand? Jesus Christ, you act like a couple of girls!"

John Lee ignored Flag and waited until Greg was back on his feet before moving forward. They entered the trees, hyper alert, but there was nothing to be seen. The other deputies met them, and once they knew that there was no armed threat awaiting them they spread out and began a ground search, looking for any evidence of the shooter. But there was nothing. No discarded cigarette butt, no empty shell casings, no footprints. Whoever the phantom shooter was, he was gone and had left no trace.

"Are you sure this is where the shots came from?"

"I don't know for sure, Flag," Greg said. "I was sitting there watching for people blowing the stop sign at the cross road and the next thing I knew the rear window of my unit exploded. And then I heard another round hit my car. I just assumed it came from the tree line because there was no place else where..."

"You assumed? That's what you did, you assumed? Did you even look to see where the shots were comin' from?"

"No sir, I was too busy keeping my head down," Greg said.

"Well, that's just fine, Red. We've got most of the friggin' department out here and you don't even know where the shots came from," Flag shook his head in disgust. "Too busy hidin' yer fat ass to even think about actin' like a real police officer!"

"Back off," John Lee said. "If someone was shooting at me, you can bet your ass I'd be looking for cover, too."

The Chief Deputy turned to him with a snarl on his face. "You shut your god damn mouth, you little prick! I already know you'd be hidin'. Probably up D.W.'s ass. The only bigger pussy around here than him is you! Christ, we got a woman deputy with a real pussy and she's more man than both of you two put together."

"It's way past time for you to shut up," John Lee said.

"Or what? Just what are you goin' do about it?"

"Hey guys, this ain't the time or place," said Andy Stringer, a normally easy-going deputy with a big belly and hands the size of catcher's mitts. "We still got somebody with a gun running around here who likes shooting at cops. How about we concentrate on that and you two can decide who's got the bigger pecker some other time?"

Flag didn't like it, but he turned and walked away, cursing as he went.

Greg stared at the ground, and John Lee patted him on the back. "Don't worry about that asshole, buddy. If I'd have been in your place I'd have probably bailed out of that car on a run and left a trail of shit all the way down to Tampa."

Bob nodded and said, "John Lee's right. Ignore that ignorant jerk. What did he expect you to do, jump out with your handgun and start popping off against a sniper with a rifle? You handled it just right, kid."

The other deputies all nodded or said something in agreement, making Greg feel better. After searching through the trees they moved out on the north side, where Andy said, "Might have something here."

He pointed to tire tracks in the dirt that led out to Homestead Road. "See that?"

Bob squatted down and looked at the wet spot. "Looks like oil."

"Yep, and it's fresh," Andy said. "Somebody was parked here not long ago. And whoever that somebody was, it's a damn good bet it was our shooter."

"Okay, everybody step back," John Lee said. "We need to get photographs of the oil spot and these tracks."

Leaving Andy and another deputy to handle that, John Lee and the others returned to the gas station.

"Bullet came through the back window on the passenger side and out the windshield," said Donny Ray Mayhew. One of the few college graduates on the sheriff's department, Donny Ray was a short, barrel chested man who wore his black hair close cropped, with a mustache and goatee. "No telling where it went from there. I'm just glad there was nobody coming along the crossroad and got hit." He squatted down and looked at the rear of the car and said, "Here's the other one," pointing at a bullet hole in the trunk lid on the right side. "Got your keys, Greg?"

Greg retrieved his keys from the ignition and opened the trunk. Shining a bright flashlight inside, Donny Ray pulled out a folded blanket and opened it to show three round holes where the bullet had passed through. Then he found where it had penetrated into the passenger compartment of the car. Going around to the back door he opened it and they removed the seat. "Bingo!"

There, lodged in the frame of the car's rear seat, was a copper jacketed bullet.

"I'm betting that's going to be from the same .308 rifle that shot at you guys out there on Turpentine Highway the other day." After photographing the bullet's location, Donny Ray removed it and slipped it into a plastic evidence bag.

Flag had been standing at a distance away, talking on his cell phone. With his call ended he came up and said, "A couple of you guys get out there and block the area off and direct traffic. Keep these damn lookie loos moving!"

It seemed like half of Somerton County had a police scanner, and the word was out. A line of cars was slowly moving past, the people inside stopping to gawk at the scene.

Turning back to Donny Ray, Flag said, "Okay, tell me what you've got."

By the time the deputy had finished showing him the damage done to the windshield where the first bullet exited, and the bullet hole in the trunk lid, they heard a siren approaching and D.W. pulled in.

"Who's that with him?"

"Looks like Dixie from the newspaper."

"That figures," Flag said. "Bad enough he lets the damn news people run all over the county, now he's givin' them rides!"

The sheriff and the reporter got out and approached the group, where they were given a briefing.

"Are you okay, Greg?"

"Yes, sir, I'm fine."

D.W. walked around the car, pausing in several places so Dixie could take photographs. When he was sure she had everything she needed, the sheriff put his arm around Greg's shoulder and squeezed.

"Why don't you go ahead and write your report, then take the rest of the day off, Deputy."

"I don't need to do that, sir. I'm okay."

"Now you listen to me, young man. I know you're a brave officer, but anytime someone shoots at you, that takes a toll on a person. So you turn in your report and you go home. That's an order, okay?"

John Lee noticed that while the two men were talking, Dixie was taking photographs. He was sure the picture of the concerned sheriff comforting the young deputy who had been under fire would look good on the front page of the newspaper.

Flag hung around for another half hour, barking orders and berating deputies for what he considered to be poor performance or rookie mistakes. About the time that John Lee was seriously considering seeing if the man's bandaged hand would fit into his big mouth the Chief Deputy got into his car and headed back to town. Bob Patterson watched him drive away and shook his head. "Is he getting worse by the day?"

"I don't know if he could get any worse," John Lee said.

"Guys, this shit is getting serious," Andy Stringer said. "When was the last time someone shot at one of us, before this week?"

"I think it was a couple of years ago," Bob said. "Remember, we raided that meth lab at that trailer park out on Palmetto Road and that tweaker started shooting at us with a shotgun?"

"And now in less than a week it's happened twice. If that don't raise the pucker factor, there's something wrong with you."

"For what it's worth," Donny Ray said, "Just like last time, I don't think whoever was shooting actually wanted to hurt Greg. He took pains to shoot at the far right side of the back window and the right side of the trunk. He could just as easily have shot at the driver's side."

"I take damn little comfort in that," Bob said.

"Neither do I," Greg added.

"So far he's been good or we've been lucky," John Lee said. "But how long is that gonna last? That bullet that went through the trunk and ended up stuck in the back seat? It could have just as easily have ricocheted up and went through the back of the front seat and taken out Greg where he was laying there."

Andy nodded. None of the deputies said anything, but they were all well aware of the fact that whoever the elusive sniper was, they needed to put an end to it before somebody got killed.

Chapter 25

"Damn, I take a day off and convince Mama to let me take her down to Crystal River to see her sister, and I miss all the fun!"

"Trust me, it wasn't much fun," Greg said.

"I'll tell you what," Maddy said, "between this fool running around shooting at us and Fig punching out patrol cars, it's a good time to be in the auto glass business."

The deputies assembled for the hasty meeting that the sheriff had called all laughed loudly, then stopped quickly when Flag and D.W. entered the room.

"Okay y'all, I appreciate those of you who are off duty comin' in, and we'll try to make this quick so you can get out of here," the sheriff said. "We don't have any leads on who's doin' this shootin', but there's no question in my mind that it's the same person. We sent that bullet that we recovered from Carson's car over to the crime lab and they jumped right on it, since this is the second incident in a couple days. The bullets found in John Lee's car and the one from yesterday were all fired by the same rifle. It's a 30 caliber, most likely some kind of huntin' rifle. This is our number one priority right now, findin' out who's doing this. I need y'all to be talkin' to everybody you can, find out if anybody's been sayin' anythin' about it, if anybody's heard any rumors, anythin' at all."

Several deputies nodded, and Andy asked, "D.W., do you think this is tied in with those skeletons they found out there at the construction site on Turpentine Highway?"

"The reporters asked me the same thing this mornin'. The first time it happened, that's what I thought. But after yesterday, I'm not so sure."

"Could it be somebody who's got a hard on for the Sheriff's Department? Or maybe Greg here in particular, since he was at both incidents?"

"That's a good question," D.W. said. "Carson, do you remember arrestin' anybody or givin' someone a ticket that got particularly upset?"

"I've been thinking about that," Greg said. "And the only thing that comes to mind is a fellow by the name of Earl McRae. I pulled him over a couple of weeks ago for wandering over the center line while I was following him. He didn't want to do a field sobriety test and wanted to argue with me about it. I wound up arresting him for DUI. Ray Ray came out to back me up and McRae was making all kind of threats. But it was nothing I haven't heard before."

"I know that old boy, he does have an attitude," said Deputy Paul Schaffer. "I've stopped him two or three times. He always wants to mouth off and give me a ration of shit."

"We need to find out where this guy is," Flag said. "Maddy, have Dispatch run a records check, see if we can get a current address for him."

Maddy was tempted to say something to the effect that there were nineteen deputies and three city officers in the room, and many of them were closer to the door than she was, but she knew that to the Chief Deputy she was always going to be just a woman and never quite measure up, and that nothing would be gained by challenging him about it at that time.

"Okay, anythin' else anybody can think of?"

There were a couple of suggestions. One was a man who had been arrested recently for domestic violence who was known to be aggressive towards the police. The other was a man who had blamed the Sheriff's Department for setting up his son for a drug bust. It was the son's third conviction, which had earned him a long sentence in the state prison. In the first case, they learned that the man in question was back in jail, this time down in Hernando County after an altercation with his estranged wife at her parents' home in Brooksville. The second possibility, the aggrieved father, could account for his time and had alibis for when both shootings took place. That left Earl McRae.

The man lived with his wife and four kids in a rundown place six miles from town. He was known to carry a gun frequently, and all of his neighbors had learned to keep their distance. If somebody complained about one of his teenage sons driving too fast down their gravel road, or of his dogs running loose and killing their chickens, McRae instantly went on the offensive and wanted to fight. There had been more than one case of slashed tires or sugar poured in automobile gas tanks after someone had lodged a complaint with the Sheriff's Department when talking to the man directly had failed. One elderly woman who lived nearby had reported that McRae had come onto her property with a shotgun after she had called and told him one of his sons had smashed her mailbox with a baseball bat. In that case, as in each other one, there

had never been enough evidence to act upon.

"We need to go have a talk with this clown," Flag said. "And we need to do it now!"

***

Four marked cars pulled into the McRae place at once, with two deputies in each vehicle. Two more parked on the road and deputies moved in on foot. Four or five large dogs surrounded the cars, barking and snarling. A girl who looked to be about seven or eight years old was playing in a tire swing, and two shirtless teenage boys were bent over the hood of an old International Scout.

"Call these damn dogs off," Flag ordered.

One of the boys put his fingers in his mouth and whistled and the dogs backed off at a distance.

"What the hell you want?"

"We want to talk to your father," Flag said.

"He ain't here."

"Where is he?"

"How the fuck do I know? It ain't my day to watch him."

"What's your name, boy?"

"Puddin Tane. Ask me again and I'll tell ya' the same."

"You a smart ass, ain't ya'?"

"Better to be a smart ass than a fat dumb ass like you!"

Before Flag could respond, one of the deputies out near the road came on the radio and said, "Heads up, suspect just passed us and is pulling in the driveway."

McRae was driving a rattletrap old Ford pickup that looked like it would blow away in the first strong windstorm, and he jumped out before the vehicle even came to a complete stop.

"What the hell you doin' on my property? Get the hell out of here!"

"We've got some questions for you, Mr. McRae," John Lee said.

"Yeah? Well stick your questions up your ass. This is private property and you ain't got no business here. Now move it!"

Earl McRae was a small, bald, thin man, not much over five feet tall, and he wore bib overalls with no shirt under them. He had a stubbly beard, thin, mean lips and a mouth that had never met toothpaste. But though he might not be large in stature, every ounce of him was full of malice and venom.

"We can do this easy or we can do this hard," Flag said. "Makes no never mind to me."

"I told you to get off my property," McRae shouted, pointing towards the road. "And I ain't goin' tell you again!"

"Just settle down," John Lee said. "There's no need for all this screaming and hollering. All we want to do is ask you a few questions."

"Oh yeah? Let me get my shotgun an' I'll let it do the answerin' for me."

He turned back towards the truck, where a battered old sixteen gauge pump action Mossberg shotgun rode in a rack across the back window.

"Stop right there. Don't you move another step!"

The man ignored John Lee's orders and jerked open the truck's door. Instantly half a dozen deputies pointed their weapons at him.

"Don't do it!"

"Freeze!"

"Put your hand on that shotgun and you're a dead man, McRae!"

He ignored them all and was reaching inside the truck when Flag strode forward quickly and kicked the door with all of his might. The door slammed on the man's arm and he howled in pain. Forgetting all about the shotgun, he charged at the much larger Chief Deputy. Flag, for all his size, had spent many years fighting with drunken rednecks and was quick on his feet. He stepped aside and shoved a leg out, tripping McRae, who sprawled on his face in the dirt. Before the little man could move, three deputies had pounced on him. He put up a hell of a fight, but they managed to get him handcuffed and jerked him to his feet.

"What the hell's the matter with you? For such a little man, you're 'bout the biggest idiot I've ever seen," Flag said.

McRae cursed him and spat at the Chief Deputy."

"You got no right comin' on my property and treatin' me this way!"

"All you had to do was answer a couple of god damn questions, ya idiot."

Before the man could respond, John Lee heard a noise behind him and two deputies shouted warnings. He turned to see one of McRae's sons coming at him with a raised hammer. The boy swung it at his head, but John Lee managed to duck, hearing the air swish past his ear from the narrow miss. He drove his shoulder hard into the young man's chest, knocking him backwards against the International. The teenager still had the hammer, so John Lee grabbed his wrist and twisted, at the same time slamming his elbow into the side of the boy's head. Two more deputies swarmed over him and brought him to the ground, while another put his hand on his holstered pistol and ordered the other son to keep his hands up and not to move.

Just about the time John Lee thought the hostilities had ended, the door of the home flew open and a woman as short and thin as her husband, and just as mean, came out with a baseball bat.

"Y'all get your hands off my husband and boy or I'm gonna knock some son-of-bitch's head off!"

"Drop that bat right now," Bob Patterson ordered. "Do it, I won't tell you again!"

The woman ignored his orders and advanced toward him, the bat raised over her shoulder. John Lee knew that if she swung it she could kill the deputy. He drew his Browning from its holster and pointed at her.

"Stop, lady. Stop or I'll shoot!"

She ignored him, and just as John Lee centered his sights on the side of her head Maddy fired her Taser, sending 50,000 volts through her and sending her to the ground, where she convulsed in spasms, wetting herself.

The dogs were barking and snarling and threatening to attack, but the second son managed to keep them at bay. Meanwhile the girl on the swing had run inside, where she hid with her younger sister in the bathroom.

Finally, with three of the McRae's in handcuffs and lodged in the back of police cars, and a call in to a relative to come and take charge of the remaining children, the deputies searched the property. They found a dozen firearms, from the shotgun in Earl's truck and a small .25 semiautomatic pistol in the pocket of his overalls, to an assortment of .22 rifles and shotguns, and three other handguns. But there were no center fire rifles of the type that were used to shoot at the deputies' cars.

"So was all of this is just a big waste of time?"

"Don't know, John Lee," Flag said. "Let's haul these three back to town and do some talkin' to them. If nothing else, we'll charge 'em with assault on police officers and be'in stupid and ugly."

Chapter 26

It took most of the rest of the day to interrogate the McRaes and do all of the paperwork associated with the raid upon their home. And it all led to nothing.

While they were able to charge all three of them with assaulting police officers and resisting arrest, when they finally were able to get Earl to talk to them, he had an alibi for the day before.

"I spent the whole day at my brother Jerry's house helpin' him put a transmission in his car. You can ask him or his wife or his kids. Hell, ask his neighbors, we was workin' right there in the front yard!"

"Well then, why the hell didn't you just say that instead of actin' like such an asshole and startin' a big fight?"

"Cause it's the principle of the thing! I told y'all to get off my property and you didn't. None of this would'a happened if you'd a just listened to me."

"And none of this would've happened if you would've just acted like a rational human be'in," Flag said.

"I got my rights and I exercised 'em."

"Yeah, well you done exercised yourself into about 90 days in jail is what ya' did. Not to mention that you could've got yourself and your kid and wife all shot."

"You'd a liked that, wouldn't ya'? The law's been after us McRaes forever and we never bothered nobody."

"Yeah, you're just a god damn prince, ain't ya'?"

"Call it what ya' want, I made my point."

"Yeah, ya' sure did. If yer point was that ya' can't fix stupid!"

***

Like she did a couple of times a week, Beth Ann was waiting for him when John Lee got home. He didn't even try to talk to her about it. They grilled steaks on the back deck, and after they ate and washed the dishes they went into the bedroom. There had been no discussion about that, they both knew why she was there and they both accepted it for what it was.

Afterwards, lying together in the dark bedroom with her head in the crook of his arm, Beth Ann said, "You're awfully quiet tonight. What are you thinkin' about?"

"I almost shot a woman today, Beth Ann. My finger was on the trigger and I was just getting ready to pull it when Maddy zapped her with a Taser and put her down."

"That's awful, John Lee."

"Yes, it is. I don't know which is more awful, the fact that it came so close to happening, or the fact that I was ready to do it. I don't remember making a decision that I was going to, a lot of things were happening at once and I was just reacting."

"Well, ain't that what you're trained to do?"

"Yeah, but then what? No amount of training is going to prepare you for what has to happen if you do pull that trigger."

"You didn't think you'd ever have to shoot somebody?"

"I don't know. I mean, I always knew it was a possibility. Twice before I've had to pull my gun on somebody, but both times they backed right down. Not this time, not this crazy lady."

"Well, I'm just glad you didn't have to."

"Me, too."

Beth Ann rolled on top of him. "You just forget about almost shootin' that crazy lady, John Lee. 'Cause you've got a crazy lady right here, wonderin' if you're ready to shoot again."

As it turned out, with just a little bit of effort, he was. Later, with her sleeping beside him, John Lee stared at the ceiling wondering if Doris McRae had any idea how close she had come to being dead, and how people like the McRaes could be so hostile toward authority that they were willing to die to make whatever kind of crazy point Earl thought he had to make.

***

John Lee wasn't the only one who couldn't sleep. After filling out the report on using her Taser, Maddy had returned home and tried to get some rest before going on her shift in the afternoon, but she was too wired to sleep. It had been a quiet night, with only a handful of routine calls. Obie Long was working the shift with her, and she had spent a long 90 minutes parked beside him in the Dollar General parking lot, listening to him complain about everything from his electric bill to the fact that Flag knew he only liked working the day shift, which was why he routinely assigned him to nights. Maddy wanted to remind him that it was a rotating schedule and everybody worked all shifts at some point. She also wanted to say that he should like the night shift, when there usually wasn't much happening and he could spend most of it sleeping, but she didn't want to encourage him.

When she went off duty at midnight she hung around the office for a while, talking to Kathleen Whitman. She and the dispatcher had gone through school together and been casual friends since they were girls. Kathleen had married her husband Steve right after graduation and they had spent ten years moving from one Air Force base to another, from North Dakota to Texas to Germany, and then back home after Steve was injured on duty and had to take a medical discharge.

It was after 2 AM when Maddy left and started home, but she knew sleep wouldn't come easy. She checked on her mother, who was snoring away, thanks to the sleeping pills that she took every night, and then watched half an hour of late-night infomercials.

"Screw this," she finally said. She went out to her car and drove away, with no real plan in mind. But she knew where she would end up. She circled the courthouse square and waved at Emmitt Planter, sitting in his city police car at his usual spot in the parking lot of Dogs-N-Suds. She drove out past the abandoned gas station where the sniper had shot at Greg Carson, and then found herself cruising slowly toward John Lee's house.

Would he be awake? What would he say or do if she showed up at his door in the middle of the night? Was this a bridge she really wanted to cross? And if she did, what would happen afterward? How would it affect them long term? Should she just turn around right there and go back home and forget the whole thing? How many times had she made this same late night drive and backed down at the last minute?

No, not this time! John Lee was her friend, if nothing else. It wasn't like he was going to laugh in her face. It didn't have to mean anything more than just a night, did it? No, this was the night she was going to stop.

She slowed down at his driveway and started to turn in. Her headlights illuminated the Ford Focus and she stopped.

"Shit! God damn it!"

She shifted into reverse and backed out and drove away.

Inside the house, Magic had barked when the car pulled in the driveway. Still awake, John Lee had heard it and got out of bed and walked into the living room. By the time he got there all he could see were a set of red taillights driving away. He watched them for a moment until they were gone, then reached down in the dark and patted the dog's head.

"Good boy. Must have just been somebody turning around."

He went to the kitchen, opened the refrigerator door and took a long drink of milk from the plastic bottle. He put it away, thinking about how Emily had always complained when he did that, and how he had always asked her what the problem was, since it was just the two of them there and it wasn't like they hadn't exchanged plenty of other bodily fluids.

"John Lee? Where are you?"

He walked back into the bedroom.

"You okay?"

"Yeah," he said, getting back into bed and spooning Beth Ann. "I was just getting something to drink."

Chapter 27

"Who is the phantom sniper who has been shooting at Somerton County deputies in the past few days?" the television reporter on the early news asked. There was a picture of Greg's police car with the shattered back window and a close up of the bullet hole in the trunk lid.

"This is the second time in a matter of days that deputies in the normally quiet rural county have come under fire. In both instances, the first on Monday, and again yesterday, somebody with a high powered rifle has taken pot shots at deputies in marked police cars while they were parked. In the first incident, three shots were fired at Somerton County deputies investigating the discovery of three skeletons by a road construction crew on Turpentine Highway. And then yesterday, Deputy Greg Carson was parked at this abandoned gas station a few miles outside of the town of Somerton when two shots were fired at him. One bullet blew out the back window of Deputy Carson's police car and exited through the windshield, and the second penetrated the trunk and was found lodged inside the car. Reinforcements quickly arrived, but they were unable to find the person or persons responsible for these attacks. Fortunately, nobody has been injured to this point, but needless to say, Somerton County deputies are on high alert, as is the rest of the population."

The scene switched to an accident involving a bus and a bicyclist and John Lee's phone rang.

"Did you see that stuff on the news just now?"

"Yeah, I saw it, D.W."

"We need to do somethin' about this, John Lee. If we don't put an end to it real soon it's goin' to look like I'm some kind'a fool."

"Flag's got everybody out asking questions and trying to get any information on it," John Lee assured him.

"I don't trust Flag. He's lovin' every minute of this. You mark my words, he's goin' to use this against me if he decides to run for Sheriff."

John Lee was tempted to say that he was more concerned about people shooting high powered rifles at deputies than he was about his father-in-law's political future, but he didn't. With Beth Ann prancing around wearing just her tiny red panties, it seemed like the wrong thing to do.

"First we got those skeletons, and now this. This is making me look bad, John Lee. Real bad!"

"We're all working on it, D.W.," John Lee said again.

"Any more news on those skeletons?"

"Nothing new."

"Well, keep at it."

"Yesterday you said the shooter was the top priority. What do you want me to focus on, D.W.?"

"Both of them!"

"Okay, one may be tied to the other, but we don't know that."

"Just do somethin'," the sheriff said. "Wrap up either one and it will at least take some of the heat off of me."

John Lee was tempted to say that he couldn't concentrate his efforts on two things at once, but Beth Ann distracted him with a particularly emphatic wiggle of her butt as she walked by. He ended the call with promises to do his best and to keep D.W. posted on his progress. But it would be a while before he started on that, because the sheriff's daughter walked back into sight again, this time with the red panties hanging off of her finger and an inviting smile on her face.

***

"Yeah, I know where this place is," Paw Paw said. "We've got a power line that runs right down through here." He traced a line on the map with his finger.

"Is there anything left back there?"

"Beats me. Years ago when I was up on a pole I could look over in that direction and there was still some stuff laying around. Not much more than trash, but you could tell that something had been there."

"And what about this one," John Lee asked, pointing to the second turpentine camp near where the skeletons had been found.

His grandfather shook his head. "Nope, can't help you there. Want to go look?"

"I was thinking about driving out there to see what I can find."

"That car of yours won't make it back there," Paw Paw said. "We had to use four wheel drive trucks to get in and out. Let's take my Jeep."

"The Department's got a couple of 4x4s, I can get one of those."

"What for? My Jeep's just fine. And if we bang it up, you don't have to explain to Fig Newton how you did it."

John Lee couldn't disagree with that logic, though he dreaded riding in Paw Paw's ancient old gray Jeep Wagoneer. Built sometime in the early 1960s, the vehicle had seen a lot of hard use over the years. There was no air conditioning, the ride was rough, and the seats didn't have much padding left in them. But he had to admit that the old workhorse had never let them down on any of their backcountry adventures.

"When do you want to go?"

"No time like the present. Let me go tell Mama Nell."

"Grab a can of Off while you're in there so the mosquitoes don't eat us alive," John Lee said to the old man's back as he went into the house. While he was waiting he wandered over to the greenhouse and looked inside, shaking his head.

"Those beans are getting big, aren't they?"

"I thought I told you to get rid of those pot plants, Paw Paw."

"What pot plants?"

"The ones in there that I just saw."

Paw Paw climbed into the Jeep and started it, and asked, "You getting in, or what?"

John Lee got into the passenger seat and reached for the seatbelt, then remembered there wasn't one.

"Seriously, Paw Paw, you can't grow marijuana."

"What marijuana?"

"The marijuana that you have in your greenhouse. *That* marijuana!"

Paw Paw grinned at him and said, "Son, I don't know what you think you saw, but you need to get your eyes checked. You're going blind or something."

"Paw Paw..."

"Hey, you know what? Maybe, you should get yourself some cannabis. I've heard it's good for your eyesight!"

"Just drive the damn Jeep, Paw Paw, and try not to run us into a ditch or something, okay?"

The old man laughed out loud and said, "Don't you worry about my eyesight, John Lee. It's 20/20!"

They drove through town with Creedence Clearwater Revival blasting through the stereo, singing about a *Bad Moon Rising* and *Green River*.

"Now that's real music," Paw Paw said as the band segued into

Proud Mary. "I love your Mama Nell, but that Elvis shit gets old."

He coasted through the third or fourth stop sign without touching the brake pedal. "Not that that's all bad, mind you. I got to tell you John Lee, some men want their women to dress up in that frilly see-through stuff because they say it makes the sex really hot. But all I got to do is put on a cape and one of those sequined Elvis costumes she's got, and she'll rock my world until all I can say is, "Thank you. Thank you very much."

"That's way more about your sex life than I need to know," John Lee said, shuddering.

"What? You think just because the hair turns gray the horny goes away? You have no idea, kid! That's about the time a woman comes into her prime."

"Can we talk about something else? Anything in the whole world, Paw Paw? Please?"

Paw Paw blew the stoplight at Third Street and Main, drawing blares of protest from the horns of two drivers who had to slam on their brakes to avoid a collision. He ignored them and turned to John Lee with a wicked grin and asked, "Do you want to know what I'm taking for my erectile dysfunction?"

***

"See, there's another one. Proves my point!"

Paw Paw was referring to a dead armadillo on the shoulder of the road. For as long as John Lee could remember, the old man had always pointed out the dead animals, which were a common sight along Somerton County roads.

"I'm telling you, John Lee. There's never been a live armadillo. They're all stillborn on the side of the road."

John Lee didn't want to get into the same old discussion again, but it beat the hell out of hearing about his grandparents' sex life and how it was flourishing thanks to Elvis and Viagra. Given the alternative, he played along.

"Paw Paw, for them to be born dead alongside the road there had to be a live one to give birth, right?"

"There's another one right there. That's two of them in what, a quarter of a mile?"

"Yeah, so what?"

"So we've seen two dead ones. Have we seen any live ones?"

"No, we haven't."

"Well, there you have it," Paw Paw said, slapping the steering wheel for emphasis. "Stillborn armadillos. I'm telling you, John Lee, I don't know how the scientific community has overlooked this all these years. One of these days I'm gonna write a paper on it and send it up to the Smithsonian, there in Washington, D.C. You just wait and see, I'm gonna do it!"

Before John Lee could reply, Paw Paw made a hard right turn with no warning, throwing him sideways in his seat and then bouncing him off the roof of the Wagoneer.

"Jesus Christ, Paw Paw, are you trying to kill us both?"

"Nope, I'm just driving up this here power line road to take you where you want to go."

They thumped down into a dip and back up again with a tooth rattling jolt.

"You might want to hang on to your gonads," Paw Paw advised. "It's gonna get rough up here in just a little bit."

Chapter 28

Describing the rough track paralleling the power lines as a road was quite a stretch of the imagination, but they took it for some distance before Paw Paw finally stopped the Jeep.

They got out, and he said, "Let me see, I think it's just over there a little bit."

"You think? How can you tell? It all looks the same to me."

The area was a mass of trees and brush and there did not seem to be anything discernible about this particular location from any other they had passed, but Paw Paw set off through the waist high tangle like a homing pigeon.

"Why don't you slow down before you get bit by a rattler or something?"

"Oh, hell, John Lee, if I was worried about things like that I wouldn't have lasted a day with FPL. When people's power goes out, do you think they care about a bunch of critters minding their own business out in the middle of the woods?"

John Lee was in excellent physical condition, but he still had to work to keep up with his grandfather's long strides. Mosquitoes and gnats flew in his face and he had to constantly wave them away. At one point he walked into a massive web from a golden silk spider and cursed as he tried to wipe it off his face, hoping none of the big arachnids were on him.

Eventually Paw Paw stopped and said. "Here we are."

At first John Lee couldn't tell the difference between this and any place else they had walked past, but then Paw Paw pointed to some old boards. "There used to be more, but most of it has probably rotted away or been overgrown. See over there, that straight line? There aren't many straight lines in nature."

They walked to the spot Paw Paw had indicated and he kicked with his foot, uncovering weathered and crumbling concrete.

"This was probably part of a foundation for one of the buildings."

"Could be," John Lee said. "From what I hear, most of the workers lived in wooden shacks. But they may have had something here. I know there was a camp store and things like that."

"Yep," Paw Paw said walking the length of the line, then making a left turn. He followed the foundation around a roughly 10 x 20 foot rectangle.

Once he looked past the trees and brush, John Lee began to see how the camp may have once been laid out. They dug around and found some pieces of heavy rusted metal, numerous flattened rusty cans, lots of broken glass that had come from bottles, and other trash that indicated that at one time people had lived out their lives in this place.

"I'd love to come out here with a metal detector and see what I could find," John Lee said.

"Probably a whole lot more of the same," Paw Paw replied.

John Lee took his GPS from his pocket and found the location he had marked for the construction site where the skeletons had been found.

"2.9 miles overland to where we found the skeletons."

"Make sense that they probably came from here," Paw Paw said. "Now what?"

"I don't know," John Lee admitted, looking around. He took the blow up of the map that Sheila had copied for him. "Do you suppose we could find this other one over here?"

"It would be a crapshoot. I knew where this one was from being up on the power poles and seeing, but otherwise how would we have ever known it was here?"

"Yeah, you're right."

"In this country you could be ten feet from something and not know it," Paw Paw said. "If you want to, we can look around, but I don't know of any roads or trails going off in that direction."

"No use breaking our necks or getting lost back there," John Lee said.

He marked the camp's location on his GPS so he could find it again and they spent another hour prowling around, but all they found was more trash from long ago. John Lee stared at the old turpentine camp and wondered about the people who had lived and worked here. Their lives had been so different than his own, toiling from sunrise to sunset six days a week for little pay, always getting deeper and deeper into debt to the company with no hope of escaping their situation except by fleeing, hoping they could outrun the company's horse mounted posse and their dogs. Some may have made it, but he knew that most didn't. He wondered if the three poor men whose skeletons they had found had been among those who been hunted down and suffered the swift justice of the brutal system.

***

Every law enforcement officer in Somerton County, from the deputies and the small city police force to the state patrolmen who came through were on high alert, aware that at any time bullets could ring out and the sniper could strike again. He did, but this time around, the results were tragic.

Maybe the shooter had aimed to miss, like he had every other time, or maybe he had gotten bolder. Either way, Ray Ray Watkins paid the price.

People are creatures of habit, and one habit that nearly every Somerton County deputy seemed to have was to park at a wide pull off on the shoulder of Cemetery Road, six miles outside of town. From there, the road ran straight as a yardstick for over two miles. It was a favorite place for teenagers to drag race, testing their cars and their skills against one another. Over the years more than one unfortunate youngster had died or been maimed in accidents on that stretch of road, and deputies knew that if they went out there late in the day, there was always a good chance of interrupting a race and writing a ticket or two.

Ray Ray was parked there late Sunday afternoon, waiting for any action that might come along. He never saw the shooter hidden behind a tombstone in the cemetery, he never knew that he was breathing his last when a large fly flew past his face. He didn't know how it had gotten into the car, since he had the windows up and the air conditioning on. But twice now it had buzzed him, and he didn't plan to let it happen a third time. He rolled up the magazine he had been reading, turned sideways in his seat, and leaned over the back of it looking for the irritating thing. That's when the back window exploded in a shower of glass and the bullet plowed into his forehead before exiting in a misty cloud of gore.

There wasn't much traffic on Cemetery Road and nobody thought much of the police car sitting there, since it was a common sight. It was only when a couple from out of town, lost and dangerously low on gas, pulled in to ask the officer where they could find the closest station or convenience store that his body was found, slumped sideways across the front seat of his patrol car.

Chapter 29

County and state police cars, an ambulance, and two vans from the State Crime Lab were parked along the shoulders of the small two lane road. Many deputies had tears in their eyes as they tried to go about the job of processing the crime scene. They had all seen death in its many forms before, and in a small county like Somerton, oftentimes the victims were people they knew. Neighbors, people they had gone to school with, friends from their church, softball league teammates. It was never easy, but they all knew it came with the job.

But Ray Ray Watkins had been one of their own, and that made all the difference in the world. Every one of them had worked alongside him, had shared meals with him during their shift breaks, had depended on him to have their backs, just like they had his. And every deputy knew that it could just as easily be them lying there dead in the front seat of the police car.

Their emotions ranged from disbelief to profound grief to rage, and back again. "Who would want to hurt Ray Ray? Why, he never had an enemy in the world!" "This just can't be happening. I keep thinking it's a nightmare and I'm going to wake up." "We need to find the prick who did this and we need to take him out once and for all!"

Normally someone who never passed up an opportunity to preen for the news cameras, D.W. had ordered deputies to keep the media at a distance and tell them he would issue a statement later, but right now the top priority was investigating the crime scene and taking care of his people.

"From all appearances, I'd bet the shooter was over there in the cemetery," said Ralph Doherty, a state crime scene technician.

Ray Ray's cell phone began to ring again from inside the car, like it had over a dozen times. John Lee looked at D.W., who looked at Doherty. "That's his wife calling."

"Do you want to answer it?"

"No, sir, I don't. But somebody has to. I imagine by now she's goin' crazy."

The sheriff looked at John Lee, who nodded and reached inside the car to retrieve the phone from the dashboard. He pushed the answer button and said, "Hello."

"Oh, thank God, Ray Ray... I heard about a deputy being shot and I kept calling and calling."

"Marcella, it's not Ray Ray, it's John Lee."

"John Lee? Where's Ray Ray?"

"Marcella...."

"I want to talk to Ray Ray. I'm out here on the road and they won't let me in and I just want to talk to him. I just want to know he's okay."

"You stay there, Marcella. I'll be right down."

"No. No, no, no! No, don't you come down here, John Lee! I want Ray Ray. I want my husband."

"Marcella..."

All he heard was a scream and then the call ended.

***

"That poor woman. Two little kids at home and another one in her belly. It ain't right, John Lee. It just ain't right!"

It was after 2 AM and John Lee felt dead inside. It had seemed like he was in a trance as he went through the motions of helping to process the crime scene, filled out endless reports, tried to comfort his fellow deputies, and then drove to the hospital in Perry to check on Marcella Watkins, who had collapsed when he and D.W. had delivered the news that her husband had been murdered.

They were driving back to Somerton County, D.W. behind the wheel of his white Tahoe. John Lee watched the white lines of the highway unfold ahead of them, but all he could see in his mind's eye was Ray Ray's bloody body. That and the look of anguish on his widow's face.

"I'm tellin' you somethin' and I want ya' know I mean it. When we catch this son of a bitch, if he gives you any excuse at all, blow him away. You pass the word out to the rest of the guys, okay?"

"Yeah, I think everybody feels that way right now, D.W., but is that right? We're the police, not judge, jury, and executioner."

"Ain't nobody respects the law more'n I do, You know that. But whoever did this to poor Ray Ray, far as I'm concerned he don't deserve anythin' more than what he did to him. Only difference is, I want him to know it's come'n. And why."

As tired and as emotionally wrung out as he was, John Lee was still surprised at his father-in-law's words. He had always thought of D.W. as more politician than lawman, more concerned with the next election than the case at hand, except for possibly how that case might impact his political future. This was a whole different side to the man, one he had never seen before.

"I know I told you to keep workin' on those skeletons, but put that on the back burner for now, John Lee. There ain't nothin' more important than findin' the bastard that shot Ray Ray."

John Lee agreed with that. The first shooting out at the construction site while they were excavating the crime scene had led him to believe that it was tied into the deaths of the men they found there. But the subsequent attacks showed that whoever was doing them was on a vendetta against the Sheriff's Department for something, and there was little likelihood it had anything to do with whatever had happened to those men so many years ago.

***

Early Monday morning, heavily armed deputies raided the home of Dennis McRae, the older brother of Earl McRae The same brother who had provided his alibi for the day Greg Carson's patrol car had been shot at by the sniper. They brought in Dennis, his wife Georgette, and Earl's son, Lonnie.

"I swear to God, I didn't have anythin' to do with any of the shootings. Good Lord, man, just because my name is McRae don't mean I'm as crazy as my brother!"

"You think it's just a coincidence that Deputy Carson and Deputy Watson arrested your brother for drunk driving, and both of them got shot at? And now one of them is dead? Dead right after we arrested Earl?"

"I don't know nothin' about that," Dennis insisted. "I'll put my hand on the Bible and swear to it, or take a lie detector test, or whatever you want me to do!"

Fig's face was red and he leaned so close into the other man's that spittle sprayed him when he said. "Oh, you're gonna take a lie detector test, all right. And when it shows that yer lyin' to me I'm gonna see that I'm sittin' right there in the front row when they stick a needle in your arm for killin' that deputy!"

"I didn't kill nobody. I swear I didn't. I keep tellin' you, I'm not like

Earl. Not like him at all. I mean we're kin and all that, but he was trouble from the day he was born. You check my record, I've never had so much as a speedin' ticket. I'm a deacon at Grace Lutheran Church. You can ask anybody from there, I was there at the church yesterday afternoon helpin' get ready for Sunday night services. Poor old Sister Standridge, she had an accident when she was leavin' Sunday mornin' services and I was steam cleanin' the carpet."

"An accident? What kind of accident? I don't remember any reports of an accident out by the church yesterday."

"Not a car accident, you know, an *accident.*"

"No, I don't *know*! You start talkin' straight to me, mister, or you're never goin' to see light of day again."

"She crapped herself! Poor old lady's 86 years old and she usually wears those Depends or whatever you call 'em. I guess she ran out or somethin'. I don't know. Anyhow she made a mess when she stood up from the pew and started walkin' out after mornin' services was over. Poor old woman was humiliated. Some of the ladies took her in the bathroom and got her cleaned up, and I told Reverend Leyendecker that I'd rent a steam cleaner and come back and get things cleaned up and ready for evenin' services. You can check with Christopher Rosenfeld, too. He came down and opened up the Ace Hardware for me so I could rent the cleaner. Had to call him at home, since he's closed on Sunday. I went home and changed clothes, then went and picked up the steam cleaner and went back to the church. Some of the other men from the congregation helped out and we figured while we had the machine anyway we'd steam clean the whole carpet. We moved all the pews and worked all afternoon. It took longer than we thought it was goin' to, so we wound up hav'in evenin' services in the Fellowship Hall because the carpet in the church was still too damp to walk on."

Flag looked at Bob Patterson and said, "Make some calls. See if his story checks out."

Bob left the room and Flag turned back to Dennis. "I'm tellin' you right now, McRae, if your story don't hold water, you and me are goin' to have a problem."

Bob was back in twenty minutes and motioned for Flag to join him out in the hallway.

"Man's story checks out, just like he said. Reverend Leyendecker says he's a good man, that Dennis has even come to him to ask him to pray for Earl and his family because of the direction their lives are headed. I don't think he's our man, Flag."

"What about Earl's son? Not the one we arrested, the other one? The one that was staying with the uncle and his wife?"

"His name is David, I know him. I don't think so. Just like the difference between Earl and Dennis is like day and night, it's the same way with the two brothers. Jackson, the one we've got in custody, who came at John Lee with that hammer? He's a psycho just like his dad. But David, he's a... I guess we can't say retarded anymore, but he's real slow. My wife had him in her fifth grade class for two years in a row. She said he was a good kid, never gave her any trouble, but he just wasn't able to grasp even basic stuff. He played Little League for a while when he was younger and half the time he couldn't remember which direction to run when he hit the ball. He stopped coming when his dad showed up one night all liquored up and got into an argument with the umpire and caused a big scene."

"Shit," Flag said. "I was sure Ray Ray's killin' was revenge for us lockin' up those others." He turned and stared at the door of the interview room, then said, "Cut him and his wife and the kid loose."

Watching him walk away, Bob shook his head and said, "Least he could do is apologize to the man in there for us showing up like we did and dragging them in here while they were still half-asleep."

"Have you ever known Flag to apologize for anything?"

"No, John Lee, I haven't."

"Doesn't mean we can't."

Dennis McCrae looked up when they came back into the room, his eyes hopeful. "Did you talk to Reverend Leyendecker? Did he tell you I was at the church all day yesterday?"

"Yes, sir, he did," Bob said sitting down across the table from him. "You're in the clear, Mr. McCrae."

The man, who looked so much like his brother but who was so very different, seemed to sag with relief and tears came to his eyes. "I wish... I wish Earl would get on the straight and narrow. I really do. Him and his wife and Jackson, they're just... they need the Lord's help but they won't take it. David and the two little girls, we try to show them there's another way, but it's hard when that's all they've ever known or seen."

"Listen, Mr. McCrae, I'm sorry we put you and your wife and son through all this. We just..."

Dennis raised his hand to stop John Lee. "No apology necessary, Deputy. I know y'all was just doin' your job. It ain't the first time me and my woman has been looked down on because people just associate the McCrae family name with Earl and the messes he's always gettin' into. We prayed last night. We prayed for the soul of that poor deputy that got killed, and we prayed for his family. And we prayed that the Lord keeps his hand on all of you so somethin' like this don't happen again. And we'll do it again tonight."

John Lee didn't know what else to say to the humble man except, "Thank you, sir. Right now we need all the prayers we can get."

Chapter 30

Representatives from law enforcement agencies across the region came to Somerton for Ray Ray's funeral. Led by highway patrolman on motorcycles, the cortege stretched all the way from the high school gymnasium where the services were held because there were too many people to fit into the church, all the way out to the cemetery. Stores downtown closed for the day and it seemed like almost every citizen in the county was either at the funeral or lining the roads leading to the cemetery, their heads bowed as the hearse passed.

Riding in the car behind the limousine carrying Ray Ray's wife and children and his parents, John Lee had a lump in his throat as he saw so many people turn out to honor the fallen deputy. Sitting beside him in the front seat of his Charger, Maddy patted tears from her eyes with a Kleenex.

"It just doesn't seem real, does it?"

"No, it doesn't," John Lee told her. "I keep feeling like I'm gonna wake up and this was all just a bad dream."

"That could have been you or me, John Lee. It could have been any of us. Why Ray Ray?"

"I don't know. Why does a fellow at one end of a boat catch fish all day and the man at the other end doesn't get a bite? Why does lightning hit one guy on a golf course and miss everybody else? Why does a drunk cross the line and hit a car head on instead of the one that was right in front or right behind it? Fate? Luck of the draw? I don't know Maddy. I really don't."

During the services, deputies and agents of the FDLE were assigned to watch the crowd, and some in covert locations were taking photographs. It was not unknown for perpetrators to show up at the funerals of their victims, even if they didn't know them. There was such a big turnout, in a county where almost everybody knew everybody to some extent, that John Lee wondered what they might find out, if anything. Looking away, across the road to the spot where Ray Ray had been killed, John Lee wondered if the sniper had waited right where they were standing at attention. Had he been right here when he raised his rifle and fired? They had searched the cemetery, going over every inch of ground, but had not found any evidence that would lead them to the shooter.

And then, it was all over. The minister said his final words, off in the distance rifleman fired a 21 gun salute, with tears in his eyes D.W. presented Marcella with the folded flag as his deputies held their hands in salute for their fallen comrade, and then the mournful tones of *Taps* echoed across the cemetery. People lingered for a while, coming to Marcella and Ray Ray's parents to pay their respects, to tell them how much they had loved Ray Ray, and every deputy promised them that they would do whatever it took to see that justice was done and that his killer was punished. Eventually everyone drifted away and the three men who been waiting a discreet distance away came and lowered Ray Ray's coffin into the ground.

***

There was a gathering at the church, with lots of food donated and more good words said about Ray Ray. Eventually John Lee, Maddy, and several of the deputies left and went to John Lee's house, where they sat on the deck, grilled burgers and hotdogs, drank beer, and talked about their friend.

Somebody laughed when they recounted how an excited Ray Ray had once stuttered a response to the dispatcher's call sending him to help a woman in labor who wasn't going to be able to wait for the ambulance. "10... 10... 10... "

"Jesus Christ, Ray Ray, just hurry up and get there before the kid's in kindergarten," another deputy's voice had said over the radio. A voice that sounded very suspiciously like John Lee's.

"Hey, do you remember the time Ray Ray took a call from a neighbor who thought someone had broken into a vacant house, and he caught Gloria Mathur's from the real estate company doing the nasty with some handyman on the couch?"

"I remember that," Maddy said. "When I got there, Ray Ray was just coming out the door and his face was so red. I asked him what was going on and he said, "They... they... they was fornica... fornica... they was fucking, Maddy!"

Someone raised his beer can and said, "To Ray Ray. We love you, brother. When we find the prick who did this to you, he's going to burn in hell!'"

The other deputies raised their bottles and cans and said, "here here" or nodded their heads in agreement. At some point both D.W. and Flag showed up and put in an appearance. Both were subdued and neither stayed long.

Finally, people began drifting off, some to return to their families, others to try to get some rest before going on duty, and eventually only John Lee and Maddy were left.

"I guess I ought to clean this mess up."

"I'll help."

"You don't have to do that."

"I don't mind, John Lee."

It didn't take long, since almost everybody had been throwing their paper plates and cans in the large plastic trashcan at the end of the deck. John Lee put whatever leftovers there were in the refrigerator and fed Magic while Maddy washed the few utensils that had been used.

When they were done, they sat on the deck in the dark, listening to the crickets chirping and the occasional buzz as some flying insect incinerated itself in the violet light of the bug zapper, each lost in their own thoughts. Lightning flashed far off in the distance, too far away for them to hear any thunder.

At some point, Maddy yawned.

"Tired?"

"It's been a long day. I don't know if I'm so much tired as just emotionally drained."

"I know the feeling."

She yawned again and said, "Excuse me."

"Maybe you need to get to bed."

She didn't look at him, but after a long pause she said, "I don't want to sleep alone tonight, John Lee."

When he didn't say anything she turned to him, studying his face in the light from inside the house.

"Well, aren't you gonna say something?"

"I'm not sure what to say, to be honest with you."

"Well say *something*, please. Anything. Because right now I'm sitting here wishing I was anyplace else in the world."

"Why?"

"Why do I wish I was anyplace else in the world, or why don't I want to sleep alone tonight?"

"Maddy, you and me? Is that a good idea? I mean, we're so close, and we're such good friends. I don't want to screw that up by having sex. Don't get me wrong, I'm not saying you're not beautiful and desirable, because you are. I just don't want to lose what we have."

"Did I say anything about sex, John Lee? I just said I don't want to sleep alone."

"I'm sorry, I guess I just took it the wrong way."

"John Lee, you don't think I'm just as worried as you are that we could mess up what we have? Do you think I haven't asked myself that a hundred times? Hell, do you know I was out here the other night? That I was gonna knock on your door and I was going to spend the night with you? Until I saw Beth Ann's car here?"

"I'm sorry, Maddy. I..."

"Sorry for what? Banging your sister-in-law? You don't need to apologize to me for that. I don't have any claim to you. Personally I think it's kind of weird, but what the hell, you're a man and she's a woman, and it's not exactly like Emily's giving you any reason to believe she's ever coming home to stay."

"It's complicated..."

Maddy laughed and snorted, which made him laugh, too.

"Really, ya think?"

They sat in silence a little while longer, then Maddy stood up and took his hand and led him inside. In his bedroom they undressed without either of them saying anything. Her back to him, she unbuttoned her shirt.

"You do know you're facing a mirror, right?"

John Lee couldn't help looking, and while she wasn't putting on a performance, Maddy didn't seem shy at all about being naked in front of him except for just her panties. Her breasts were considerably smaller than either Beth Ann's or Emily's, but he found himself stirring at the sight.

Noticing, Maddy asked, "Are you going to be able to control that thing, or do I need to bring a Taser to bed?"

He pulled a T-shirt from his dresser drawer and offered it to her. Maddy put it on and they crawled into bed. She snuggled up against him and said, "Just hold me, John Lee. There may be another time, I don't know. But right now, I can't go back to that house and lay there in my empty bed and listen to Mama snoring through the wall. I need my friend to hold me. Okay?"

Chapter 31

For ten long days the Florida Department of Law Enforcement and the Somerton County Sheriff's Department carried out an intense, fruitless investigation into the murder of Deputy Raymond Watkins. They looked at every case Ray Ray had been involved in since he was a rookie, from issuing a simple traffic ticket to arresting drivers under the influence of alcohol or drugs, or any other infraction. They came up with nothing.

They delved into his personal life, looking for anything there, but there was nothing to be found. No illicit affairs, no disputes with neighbors, no arguments over something as trivial as a barking dog. As much as they hated to, they even looked at his family life. He and his wife got along wonderfully, she was the girl of his dreams who had always looked past the stuttering to see the man he really was, and he always put her on a pedestal. There was no large life insurance policy to be garnered. He was a devoted father, well loved by everybody who knew him, from his family to his neighbors and coworkers.

In the end, they were not able to find one thing that would offer even a hint of why someone would want the friendly, dependable family man dead.

"Early on there was talk that maybe the shooter was just some kind of crank, out for thrills," Donny Ray Mayhew said, at a meeting to discuss the case and bounce ideas off each other. "Is that what this all comes down to? Somebody shooting at deputies for kicks?"

"People have been killed for less," said Adam Levy, one of the state investigators assigned to the case.

"Well, there hasn't been another shootin' since Ray Ray was killed. So either the shooter accomplished what he set out to do, or else maybe it *was* some kind of a nutcase out gettin' his jollies at our expense. John Lee, you said early on that you didn't think he was tryin' to hit anybody out there at the construction site, and Donny Ray, you said the same thing after Carson's car was shot up," D.W. said.

"This sounds terrible, but I almost wish the bastard would try it again," John Lee said. "Don't get me wrong, I don't want anybody else hurt, but if he's crawled back under whatever rock he came out from, we might never find him."

"Oh, I want to find him, all right," said Rick Pye, a former Marine who had served in Afghanistan.

There were murmurs from other deputies, all of whom were frustrated at the lack of progress on the case, and all of whom wanted to avenge Ray Ray in some way. And while he wanted to see the killer brought to justice, John Lee couldn't help but think that it was probably just as well that the shooter had not resurfaced. Not just for officer safety, but because he would have hated to see one of his fellow deputies step over the line and do something out of frustration and anger that could ruin their career and their life.

The Federal Bureau of Investigation had been brought in, in the hope that the FBI might shine some light on the case, but even that astute law enforcement agency, with all of its resources, drew a blank. It would seem that whoever the sniper was who had been shooting at Somerton County deputies, he had gone deep under cover and was not coming out anytime soon.

FBI agents compared the attacks with sniper incidents and attacks on police officers nationwide, looking for some connection. And while violence between police and citizens seemed to be all over the news lately, there was nothing locally that would indicate the incidents were hate crimes or had any relationship to things happening outside of the area.

"There's been a lot of problems with niggers and white cops all over the country lately," Flag said. "I wonder if some of our local jigaboos have been watchin' too much TV and decided to join in the fun."

"Really, Fig? You're the second highest law enforcement officer in the county, and that's the way you talk?"

"The day I need you correctin' me in public, John Lee, that's the day one of us needs to start considerin' a new career."

"I think you're right. Have you ever thought about the fast food industry, Fig? I bet with enough practice you can learn to ask, 'do you want fries with that?'"

There were snickers from several of the deputies in the room, and Flag started to get up from his chair, but D.W. interrupted.

"That's enough of that kind of talk, Flag. This department and the local African-American community ain't had any problems like that. So let's just drop it and move on, okay?"

Flag didn't like it, but the looks on the faces of the state and federal investigators told him that he had stepped over the line. There was a time when all that politically correct bullshit didn't matter, but he knew that if he was ever going to be sheriff, he was going to have to learn to play the game, no matter how he really felt about things.

"So what else do we know?" Adam Levy asked.

"We've checked with gun shops as far away as Macon, Georgia and east all the way to Mobile," an FBI agent named Angela Waterbury said. "The .308 is a very common rifle round, but it's pretty much for big game. Except for feral hogs, I don't know what people would use it on around here. But that's not to say there aren't a lot of them around. It also has the military designation of 7.62 and was the standard for small arms among NATO countries since the 1950s. Here in this country, it was used in the M-14 rifle and M-60 machine gun. The M-14 was phased out when the M-16 came along, but the Army and other services still use sniper rifles chambered for it."

"Wait a minute," D.W. said. "You're tellin' me this is a sniper round?"

"Among other things, in the military version, the 7.62. But again, it's also used by civilians all over the place for big game hunting. And the casings you found were stamped .308, so they were from civilian ammunition."

"But the ammo's interchangeable, right?"

"To a certain extent," she said. "The 7.62 actually has higher pressure than a lot of the civilian .308 rounds. So over a period of time, it would possibly damage some civilian rifles. What are you getting at, Sheriff? Do you by any chance have any survivalist types running around here?"

"Not that I know of. How about any of you guys?"

"Oh we've got a few lunatics who think the sky's falling and the government will be taking over any day," John Lee said. "But they've all been accounted for and we haven't been able to find out anything that would indicate any of them were involved in this."

"So we're right back where we started," Flag said bitterly.

"I wish I had more to tell you," Special Agent Waterbury said. "Our profilers are trying to work up something on it, but we don't have one thing to go on."

The meeting ended with nothing accomplished except more frustration on everyone's part. John Lee was going out the back door of the Sheriff's Department when Flag accosted him.

"Listen to me, you limp dick. If you ever mouth off to me like that again in front of anybody, I'm gonna break you in two. I'll kick your ass so bad even your Mama won't recognize you."

"I'll tell you what," John Lee said, "Why don't we just settle this right here and right now, Fig? You keep telling me about what you're going to do, but you're beginning to sound just like a used car salesman. Lots of bullshit promises and nothing behind them. I see you've got the bandage off your hand, so why don't we send your ass back to the ER and they can put some new ones on you? Hopefully around your mouth, because I'm getting damn tired of listening to it."

The Chief Deputy's face had gone from red to purple and he was shaking with rage. John Lee, for his part, had an insolent smile on his face. Fearing that they were about to come to blows, Sheila Sharp tried to intervene.

"Umm... Flag, John Lee, y'all both need to calm down. We got citizens walking around here, listenin' to you two."

"Mind your own business, Sheila," Flag said, never taking his eyes off John Lee.

"How 'bout I make it my business?"

Neither man had seen D.W. approach. He pushed himself between them and said, "Flag, I'm on my way to a meetin' of the County Supervisors to bring them up to date on everything that's goin' on with this investigation. I'd hate to have to tell them that I just relieved you from duty for threatenin' a subordinate in public and using racial slurs in a staff meetin'. And I'd sure hate to have to tell my wife about why her brother's out of a job. But I'll do it. Don't think I won't. That way you'll have a lot of time to plan your campaign against me, come next election. And I'll make sure that my own campaign will let folks around here know that you were fired from this department, and why. Now what's it goin' to be?"

Flag was seething, but he knew anything he said would only make matters worse for him. But the time was coming. Oh yeah, the time was coming. And when it did, people were going to know what happened when you crossed Flag Newton. Yeah, people were going to know all right. And these two were going to be the first to know!

Chapter 32

The ringing telephone woke John Lee up and he fumbled for it on the nightstand next to the bed, managing to knock it to the floor in the process. He cursed and rolled over to reach it and pushed the button to answer the call.

"Hello?"

"Good morning, John Lee. It's Shania."

He had been up late the night before and not been able to sleep well. His brain was still foggy. "Who?"

"Shania Jones. Am I that easy to forget?"

"Oh, no. Of course not. I'm sorry, I'm still half asleep."

"I'm sorry, I can call back another time."

"No, this is a good time."

He sat up and looked at the bedside clock. 9:15 AM.

"What's up, Shania?"

"I was just calling to check in with you since I hadn't heard anything from you."

"Yeah, sorry about that. It's been pretty crazy over here."

"I know, it's been all over the news. I didn't want to call too soon because I knew you were busy, but I just wanted to let you know that I'm so sorry for the loss of your friend."

"Thank you."

"So how are you doing? I can't imagine what that must feel like."

"It's kind of like losing a brother. So yeah, I think maybe you can imagine."

There was silence on the other end of the line for a moment, and then she said, "For what it's worth, John Lee, eventually it gets easier to live with. It still hurts, and you never forget, but you learn to put it in a compartment so you can get on with your life. I think if you don't, it would eventually eat you alive."

John Lee thought of Richard and Alice Westfall, and how each had been affected by losing Dan, so long ago. In one way or another, their son's death had indeed eaten both of his parents alive. Maddy, for her part, seemed to have been able to compartmentalize her brother's loss.

Thinking about her, he couldn't help but remember the night they had spent together following Ray Ray's funeral. The next morning both had been subdued, and he didn't know if it was because of what had happened to Ray Ray, or what had not happened between the two of them. Maddy had dressed and bent over to kiss his cheek as he still lay in bed.

"I need to get home and check on Mama."

"All right."

She got to the door of the bedroom and John Lee had called her name. "Maddy? Are we okay?"

Maddy had nodded, and said, "Yeah, John Lee. We're okay."

She had turned away and then stopped and turned back to him. "Thank you."

"For what?"

"For being you. For being my friend every time I've needed you there. For last night, for not wanting more or expecting more, or...."

"I'll always be here for you Maddy. You know that."

"Yeah, I know that."

"Are you there, John Lee?"

Shania's voice on the telephone brought him back to the present.

"Sorry, I guess I drifted off there for a minute."

"Listen, I'll call you back another time."

"No, I'm sorry, Shania. I didn't get much sleep last night. It's been really crazy here."

"I understand. Like I said, I just wanted to check in with you."

"I appreciate that, I really do."

"Have you been making any headway in finding out who killed your friend?"

"Not yet. Between our people and the state investigators, and the FBI, we haven't found out a damned thing. I've got to be honest with you, Shania. I don't know if we ever will."

"That's got to be so frustrating."

"It is."

"Do you think... do you think whoever did it will start up again?"

"I don't know. I hope not. But on the other hand, I almost wish something *would* happen to move things along. I mean, not anyone getting hurt or anything like that, but at least if he resurfaces maybe we'll have a chance of getting him."

"Please be careful, John Lee."

"I will."

"I imagine all of this has put the investigation into those three skeletons on the back burner."

"Yeah, it has. But I don't know. We're not getting anywhere on Ray Ray's murder, and there have been so many people looking at it from every direction that we're almost stumbling over each other. I think maybe I might ask my boss about getting back on that, at least until something develops with Ray Ray's case."

"Well, you stay in touch, John Lee. And if you get back over this way, give me a call, okay?"

"I'll do it," he promised.

He got out of bed, let Magic out, then filled the dog's bowls with food and fresh water before he got in the shower. He felt guilty for not touching base with Shania before then, but he really had been swamped, putting in long hours day after day without taking any time off since Ray Ray had been killed. Maybe he was right, maybe it was time to talk to D.W. about getting back to work on the case of the skeletons they had found out on Turpentine Highway.

***

D.W. didn't like that idea at all. "Those men been dead a long time, John Lee. And whoever killed them has probably been dead almost as long. I doubt you'll find out anything. And meanwhile, we got us a cop killer runnin' loose around here."

"I know that D.W., but it's not like we're getting anywhere on Ray Ray's case."

"Were not just goin' to forget it!"

"Of course not! All I'm saying is that we've got so many people looking at the same things over and over again, and all we do is keep butting our heads against a wall."

"That's how you solve these things, John Lee. You just keep at it and keep at it and keep at it."

"I know that. But so far we're not accomplishing anything. Meanwhile, think about this, D.W. Sooner or later the news folks are going to ask you about those skeletons. And we both know that Fig is always looking for any way he can to make you look bad."

"Fig can kiss my wrinkled white ass for all I care!"

"Yeah, but what if he decides to tell those reporters that you're ignoring the murders of three black men completely and are focusing every resource we have on the death of a white deputy."

"The two ain't the same at all. You know that."

"I know it, and you know it. That's not the point. Those reporters are always looking for a new story or a new angle. All Fig has to do is plant a seed in their minds about how three dead black men are not as important as one dead white man is, here in Somerton County. You know that one of them is going to take that and run with it. And as soon as one does, the rest are gonna jump right on the story, too. The next thing you know, Ray Ray's murder is completely forgotten and they're all trying to crucify you. Calling you just another bigoted white small town southern sheriff."

He could tell that the message hit home when D.W. shoved back his chair and got up and paced back and forth across his office, muttering to himself. After a moment he stopped and said, "You're right, that salad eatin' Frenchman would do somethin' just like that to throw me under the bus. And those reporters? They don't give a tinker's damn 'bout me, I know that. All they're lookin' for is the next story. Damn, why didn't I see this comin'?"

"There's been too much going on to focus on everything, D.W."

"Oh yeah? Well as of right now, you start focusin' on those skeletons. Losin' Ray Ray is a tragedy, and we're goin' to catch the cotton picker that did it and we're gonna put him away forever. But in the meantime, you keep trying to figure out what happened to those three men out there on Turpentine Highway. And try to find somethin' fast, before Fig and those reporters put their heads together and find some way to try to stick it to me!"

Chapter 33

Troy Somerton kept him waiting for over fifteen minutes. John Lee spent the time sitting in a chair leafing through old building industry magazines and listening to Charlotte Thompson answering the telephone and directing calls to different parts of the large complex that included a lumber store, building supplies, warehouses, and a construction yard where utility sheds, wooden decks for mobile homes, and trusses were built. After directing him to a chair and telling him that her boss would be with him as soon as possible, given that he didn't have an appointment, Charlotte had pointedly ignored him.

John Lee knew she was still mad at him because he had arrested her daughter for shoplifting at the Dollar General six months earlier. She considered it somehow his fault that Danielle had $36 worth of makeup and other merchandise shoved inside her backpack when the store's manager stopped the girl on her way out the door. Between claiming that the whole thing was a set up to harass her daughter, and warning John Lee that she would have his badge before it was all over with, not once did she ever acknowledge that maybe, just maybe, her lack of parenting skills and the fact that she spent most of her time holding down a barstool at Bill Gator's Pub might have something to do with it being the fourteen year old's third arrest in just over a year.

Eventually her phone buzzed and she picked up the receiver, listened for a moment, and said, "Yes, sir." She hung up, and without looking at John Lee, said, "He'll see you now."

"John Lee Quarrels! How you doin', man?"

Troy came around his desk, a massive, dark wooden affair that took up almost as much floor space as a '55 Rambler, and gripped his hand hard. Troy was a couple of inches shorter than John Lee, the time he had spent sitting at a desk was beginning to show. His face and neck were thicker, and there was the beginning of a potbelly stretching the front of his light gray polo shirt with the Somerton logo, a stylized red S, embroidered on it.

"I'm good, Troy. How about you?"

"Oh, busy, busy. Have yourself a seat."

He walked back behind his desk and sat down as his face grew serious. "I was so sorry to hear about Ray Ray Watkins. That was a terrible thing. Just terrible."

"Yes, it was."

"How are you holdin' up, John Lee?"

"We're all doing the best we can."

"Do you have any leads yet?"

"Nothing so far. Maybe that reward you announced the other day will help."

In a front page story in the *Somerton County News,* Troy had announced that Somerton Forest Products Company was offering a $50,000 reward for anybody who could provide information leading to the arrest and conviction of the person or persons responsible for the murder of Deputy Raymond Watkins.

"I hope so, I really do. It's a small price to pay to see justice done. Now, what can I do for you today, John Lee?"

"Well, it's about those three skeletons we found out there on Turpentine Highway a while back."

Troy nodded. "Yeah, I read about that in the newspaper. What'd they say, they was fifty years old or somethin' like that?"

"We're not really sure how old they are," John Lee told him. "At least that old, maybe more."

"I don't want to think about things like that happenin' around here," Troy said, shaking his head. "But I guess back in those days... well, you know."

"No I don't know. That's why I'm here, Troy."

"I'm not sure what you mean."

"How do you think those three men wound up dead out there?"

"Lord, man, I don't have any idea! Happened before either one of us were born. My first thought was maybe the Klan."

"That was mine, too."

Troy laughed and said, "Now John Lee, I've been known to drive my Corvette a little too fast on some of the back roads, and I've got the tickets and the insurance rates to prove it. But that's about as unlawful as I get. You really don't think I have anything to do with the Klan, do you?

"No, no, not at all. That wasn't what I was getting at. Troy, do you remember when this company used to be called Somerton Lumber Company?"

Troy laughed again. "Boy, you're really going back in history now. Yeah, way back when my daddy was a boy that's what it was called. That's before we diversified and got into building materials and small construction and all that."

"Do you know when the name changed, by any chance?"

"Not off the top my head. Maybe sometime back in the 60s or 70s, I really couldn't say. Why?"

"Do you know anything about the turpentine business?"

"Turpentine? I know we sell it down in the building supply store. What's this all about, John Lee?"

He took an evidence bag from his pocket and set the brass tag on Troy's desk. "Have you ever seen one of those before?"

The other man picked it up and studied it for a moment, then set it back down. "Can't say as I have."

"Are there any company records anywhere, Troy, from back in the old days?"

"I don't know. What exactly is it you're lookin' for, John Lee?"

"Well, as I understand it, back in the old days this whole region of the country was filled with turpentine camps. They tapped into pine trees and got the sap and distilled it into turpentine. They used a lot of it on the old wooden ships."

"That's interestin', I don't think I ever knew anything about that."

"Yeah, apparently that's how your family's company got started. A fellow over at the Historical Museum was telling me that Somerton Lumber Company had six turpentine camps around the county."

"Really? I'll have to get over there and check that out."

"Yeah, they've got some stuff on display there about it."

"That's just fascinating," Troy said. "I'll have to ask my Daddy about it. Though I guess that was before his time, too."

"How is your grandpa these days, Troy? Is he still doing well?"

"I'll tell you what, John Lee, I wouldn't be a bit surprised if that old man outlasts all of us. He always says that he's going to live forever because Heaven don't want him and the Devil's afraid he'll take over. He has his moments, and he's slowed down a whole lot, but trust me, he can get just as cantankerous as all get out. A week ago he decided it was plantin' time and he went out to one of the barns and started up a tractor and drove that thing right through the back wall and into Mama's flower garden before we even knew what was happenin'!"

They laughed at the story, and then John Lee said, "Anyway, that brass tag there with the numbers on it and those initials, SL? The man at the museum told me that stood for Somerton Lumber, and those numbers on there were a number issued to an employee at one of the turpentine camps. Kind of like an identification tag. I guess each employee had one, and each one had a different number on it."

"Really?" Troy picked the tag up and looked at it again. "Did you get this at the museum?"

"No. They've got a couple of them on display," John Lee said, "but that one you're holding there came from where we found the skeletons of those men that got themselves killed out there. One of them was carrying it with him, or more likely he had around his neck on a string or something that went through that little hole there in the top."

Troy dropped the tag onto his desk like it was hot.

"Sorry, didn't mean to spook you," John Lee said.

"No, just surprised me, I guess. I mean, it's kind of morbid to be holding somethin' in your hand that came out of a grave."

"Yeah, I felt that way at first, too," John Lee said. "Sad fact is, though, that whoever killed those men out there and buried them like they did never marked those graves. I expect their kinfolk always wondered what happened to them."

"Be a terrible thing to live with, never knowing where somebody you loved disappeared to like that," Troy said.

"Anyway, John Lee said, "I was hoping that maybe you had some kind of records somewhere, in an old warehouse or some such, that dated back to those days. That might tell us who it was that had this tag. That way if he still had any family around the county, at least we can tell them and see the man gets a decent burial."

"I don't know, but I'll sure look into it for you, John Lee," Troy promised. And I'll tell you somethin' else. If you think those men worked for the company way back there in the day, I'm goin' to make sure that all three of them have Christian burials. You just tell me whenever y'all are finished with the remains and I'll talk to Edgar Ross over at the mortuary and see that it's taken care of. I mean after all, if they were Somerton people, they're like family, right?"

"That's mighty good of you, Troy. I don't know if we'll ever find out who they are. I think our best shot is if you can find some records somewhere. The way I understand it, there was like a company store or commissary or something where workers could buy stuff they needed, and they kept track of it based on those ID numbers so they could settle accounts at the end of the month. My thought was if you had any records of that kind of stuff, it might help us out."

"I'll sure do what I can, John Lee. How about you check back with me tomorrow afternoon? I'll get a couple people on it and see what we can come up with. Hell, if we could find something like that, it might make an interesting display to have down there in front of the store. Kind of give people an idea of how far we've come."

"I appreciate that," John Lee said, standing up and picking up the tag and returning it to its envelope.

"We need to get out on the water somewhere and go fishing one of these days," Troy said. "Remember when we used to do that, back when we was kids?"

"I do remember," John Lee replied.

"We had a some good times back then, John Lee. I'm sorry we grew apart as we got older. But workin' and life and everythin' gets in the way, I guess."

"Yeah, it does. Hey, thank you for your time Troy. It's really good to see you again. I'll check in with you tomorrow and see if you've come up with anything."

"I'll do my best. Thanks for stopping by. And I'm serious, we need to get together and do somethin' one of these days. Ever since Daddy retired, it seems like I spend half my life sittin' behind this desk and the rest of it in a meetin' someplace. I need to get outta' here and have some fun for a change."

They shook hands again and John Lee left the office, Charlotte ignoring him as he walked by her desk.

Chapter 34

"You ask me, when ya' catch the bastard, ya' oughta' take him out in the swamp and strip him naked and tie his ass to a tree. Then leave him there for the gators and snakes."

"I heard that! Or just shoot him right between the eyes and be done with it."

"Shootin's too good for what he done to Ray Ray."

The three old men wearing feed store caps were seated at the counter at Sparky's Diner, turned sideways on their stools so they could talk to John Lee.

"Any truth to the rumor that it's a drug gang movin' into the county?"

"Not that I know of," John Lee said. "This area's not exactly a hotbed of drug activity, and even if it was, why would they draw attention to themselves by shooting at deputies?"

"Ya' never know what people goin' to do when they get wired up on that stuff."

The waitress set a glass of sweet tea in front of him and asked, "Do ya' know what you want?"

"I'm thinking the steak fingers."

"Make that two," Maddy said as she slid into the booth across from him.

The old men nodded at Maddy politely, then turned back around, but not before giving her admiring looks.

They hadn't talked much since the night after Ray Ray's funeral, and when they had it had been somewhat strained, both of them avoiding the topic. So John Lee had been surprised when she called him and asked if they could meet for lunch.

"What's happening?"

"Not much," she said. "I guess Joe Taylor pulled over a drunk driver last night, some clown who lives someplace down around Gainesville. As it turned out, he had like a dozen warrants out for DUI, failure to appear, and grand larceny. While Joe was putting him in the back of the car, the guy got aggressive and tried to bite him. They had a little tussle, and in the process the guy's dentures fell out on the road. Joe said he was tempted to pick them up and bite him with his own teeth."

They laughed and John Lee said, "I remember back when I was a rookie I arrested somebody for DUI, I can't remember who now, but he started out by telling me that his tax dollars paid my salary. Then he started puking. Puked all over my shoes. Puked so hard his dentures came out. I told him to pick them up and he said he wasn't touching them, I needed to do it because I was a public servant."

"Oh, gross! Don't tell me you did!"

"Sure I did. I put on latex gloves, I picked them up from all that mess and I shoved them right back into his mouth!"

"You could've waited for another time to tell me that besides when we're eating lunch."

"Hey, you brought it up."

The three old timers had finished their lunch and each left a quarter on the counter as a tip and shuffled out the door, tipping their ball caps to Maddy as they went.

"So, I'm kind of surprised you called and wanted to meet."

"I think we need to talk, John Lee."

"It's been my experience that whenever a woman tells me that we need to talk, something bad is about to happen."

"No. No, not at all." She reached across the table to put her hand on his, then took it away as the waitress came back with their orders.

"Will that be all?"

"Looks good," John Lee said.

"I'll check in with ya' in a bit, see if you need refills on your tea."

When she left, Maddy said, "I just wanted to clear the air between us."

"Okay."

"That night... I hope I didn't put you in an uncomfortable situation."

"Maddy, contrary to what guys have probably told you, nobody ever really died of blue balls."

She laughed, a sound he had not heard in a while and had missed. "You always see the good side of everything, don't you, John Lee?"

"I saw a couple good sides of you that night."

Her face turned slightly pink and she said, "Yeah, I guess you did. Such as it was."

"Looked damn fine to me."

"I don't exactly have boobs like Emily. Or Beth Ann."

"You know what they say, Maddy, any more than a mouthful goes to waste."

"You'd have to work pretty hard to get more than a mouthful from me."

"How hard?"

Maddy laughed again, this time so loud that someone at the far end of the counter turned and looked in their direction.

"I could ask you the same question. But judging from the tent I saw in your briefs that night, I think I've already got a pretty good idea."

It was John Lee's turn to blush, which she seemed to take delight in as she smirked at him and sipped her tea.

"Anyway, that thing I said about coming by and seeing Beth Ann's car there? Let's not let that make things weird between us, okay?"

"As opposed to sleeping together and not doing anything?"

"Yeah, as opposed to that, I guess." She reached across the table and took his hand again and squeezed gently. "I was really vulnerable that night, and I had had a few beers, which I don't do very often. I mean, I wasn't out of it or wasted or anything like that. But I appreciate the fact that you didn't want more. And the fact that you were more concerned about our friendship than you were about just getting your dick wet."

"Oh, I wanted, Maddy. I'm not gonna lie to you about that."

The waitress was coming back with a pitcher to refill their tea and he pulled his hand away again. With their glasses topped off and with assurances that they didn't need anything else, she went down the counter, making sure everybody else was okay.

"So we're okay?"

"Yeah, we're okay."

"Good. I've been worried about that."

"Me, too."

They finished their lunches, paid their bill, and left the waitress a good tip. Outside, before she got into her patrol car, Maddy said, "I have to ask.... when I said I drove by your house that night, planning to knock on the door? What would have happened?"

He smiled at her and said, "Let's just say that if you ever do decide to come knocking, I won't leave you standing out there on the deck very long."

"So now I guess I've just got to find a night when you're not otherwise engaged, huh?"

"Oh, don't let that stop you. I've heard that three is a very interesting number."

"Trust me, John Lee. It's been so long that if I ever do work up the courage, you're going to have more than you can handle without needing anybody else there."

She kissed the air between them, got in her car and drove away, leaving him standing there in the parking lot.

Chapter 35

Charlotte Thompson ignored him the same way when he went back the next afternoon, but at least Troy Somerton did not keep him waiting as long. John Lee was only two paragraphs into a story about solar panels in one of the builders' magazines when Troy opened the door to his office and said, "Come on in, John Lee."

As soon as they were seated, Troy said, "I'm sorry, but I haven't come up with much of anything to help you. Apparently there was a tornado came through here back in '64 or '65, somethin' like that. I guess it destroyed several buildings around town, includin' a warehouse where we had all of the company records stored."

John Lee remembered hearing about the big tornado of 1965 when he was growing up. As he recalled, it had killed two or three people as it tore a mile-long swath through Somerton County, taking out everything in its path.

"Well that sucks."

"I did mention it to my Daddy. He said the turpentine camps were gone by the time he was born, but he remembered his father and his granddaddy talkin' about them."

"Really? What did he have to say about them?"

"Oh, no details, just that they were there. I guess it was quite a business at one time. The company had three or four camps spread out around the county."

"Six."

"Six? Six what ?"

"Somerton Lumber operated six turpentine camps at one time."

"Then you know more about it than Daddy can remember. Like I said, he just recalls hearing about them, but no details."

"What about your grandfather, Troy? He's old enough that he'd probably remember."

Troy shook his head. "Oh, I'm sure he'd have all kinds of stuff to tell you about them. Now, whether it was true or not, that'd be the hard part to figure out. Like I said yesterday, he's slowed down a lot, and you don't really know when you're talkin' to him how much is real and how much is garbled. Somebody on the TV was talkin' 'bout the Vietnam War on television the other night and Grandpa started tellin' us about the Tet Offensive or some such, and how they fought for days without end."

"I didn't know he was in Vietnam."

"That's just the point, John Lee. He wasn't. He was born in 1927, he'd have been too old for that. Now, he was in World War II, right at the tail end. But apparently he saw some TV show or movie about that Tet thing and he decided he'd been there. The week before, he was tellin' us all about how he come drivin' along some country road with a lady friend and came on the scene right after Bonnie and Clyde got killed. I think he'd have been about seven years old when that happened."

"So he likes telling tall tales."

"No, sir," Troy said, shaking his head. "Nope, in Grandpa's mind, it really happened just that way. Like I said, he gets things all mixed up in his head. Half the time he calls me by my Daddy's name and I have to keep tellin' him who I am. I know your grandma and grandpa are younger than him, but do they ever do that? Get things confused like that and call somebody by someone else's name?"

John Lee didn't want to think about when Mama Nell might be calling Paw Paw Elvis, and he quickly pushed the mental image that came into his mind away. "No, they're both pretty sharp. Still crazy in their own way, but sharp."

"That's a good thing. Enjoy them while you can. Hey, John Lee, do you remember how when we was kids your Mama Nell dressed you up like Elvis for Halloween every year? How after the second or third year you were so sick of it that as soon as you was away from the house you took that darn costume off and hid it in the bushes and put on some raggedy clothes and rubbed dirt on your face and pretended you were a hobo instead?"

John Lee chuckled at the memory. "Yeah, I do. And I remember that you hid that Elvis costume and I was afraid I was gonna get a butt whoopin' when Mama Nell found out the truth."

"I had you goin' there for a while, didn't I?"

"Oh yeah. I don't think I ever managed to get even with you for that one, Troy. Just where are those roads that you drive that Corvette of yours so fast on?"

They both laughed, and Troy said, "I ain't tellin'. They say payback's a bitch."

"Yes, it is. And this payback's got a lot of years of interest built up."

"Damn, John Lee, we need to get together more often, like I said yesterday. We used to have such good times together. Me and you, and Patrick, and Dan. Real good times!"

At the mention of Dan's name they both grew somber for a moment.

"I sure do miss him."

"I do, too Troy."

"Do you ever hear from Patrick anymore?"

"It's been years. He came back to town for the funeral when his Mama died and I saw him there. Said he was living up in Tennessee someplace, working for the post office."

The intercom on Troy's desk buzzed and he pushed the button, "Yes?"

"Sir, Mr. Swanson from SWB Insulation Concepts is on the telephone. He says he's got those quotes you asked for."

"Thanks, Charlotte, tell him I'll be with him in just a minute."

A button on the telephone on his desk began to blink. "I'm sorry, John Lee, I've really got to take this."

"I understand," John Lee said, standing up.

Troy extended his hand across the desk and they shook.

"If I come up with anything else about those turpentine camps or anything at all that can help you with findin' out who those skeletons belong to, I'll be in touch."

"I appreciate that," John Lee said, going to the door.

Just as he opened it, Troy said, "Don't forget, we need to get together. We'll go fishin' or something, okay?"

"Okay," John Lee replied, but Troy was already on the phone, taking care of business. Charlotte never looked up as he passed her desk.

***

It was 10 o'clock at night and John Lee was watching a rerun of an old sitcom with Bob Newhart running a Vermont country inn on one of the cable channels when his phone rang.

"John Lee, we've got shots fired downtown, officer involved shooting."

"I'm on my way," he said grabbing his gun belt from the hook in the bedroom. "Anybody hurt?"

"Obie called it in. All he said is someone is shooting at him. He's parked at the grade school. He thinks it's the sniper again."

John Lee paused long enough to work the dial on the gun safe in his spare bedroom. If the sniper was still there, he wanted to have more than his pistol or the shotgun from his patrol car, both of which had limited range, to go up against the man's scoped rifle. He opened the heavy steel door, pulled out his Colt AR-15 and a bandolier with six loaded twenty round magazines. Running out to the Charger, he threw the bandolier on the passenger seat, set the rifle on the floor on the passenger side, flipped his lights and siren on, and raced toward the school.

The radio was alive with chatter as other deputies responded and said they were on the way.

"Hurry up, they're shootin' at me again," Obie said, the terror in his voice evident. "I think they've got a machine gun!" Everybody could hear the rapid gunshots going off in the background.

"John Lee, where you at?"

"Three blocks away."

"Come in from the back," Flag ordered. "We'll see if we can catch this bastard between us."

"10-4."

"Listen to me everybody," Flag said, "Don't take any chances. If you see the son of a bitch, shoot him!"

John Lee wondered how many citizens with police scanners were hearing Somerton County's Chief Deputy ordering them to shoot the suspect on sight. Then again, given how upset everyone was over Ray Ray's death, he didn't think there would be any complaints if that's exactly what happened.

A block from the school he turned his lights and siren off, and as he got close to the rear parking lot he turned his headlights off as well. Getting out, he pulled the charging handle on the AR-15 to chamber a round. Every sense on high alert, he scanned the parking lot, looking for any sign of danger hiding in the long shadows.

There was nothing, but then he heard a scuffling noise and he crouched down behind the hood of the Charger, aiming the rifle toward the sound. The sound grew louder and a shape emerged from the darkness, running fast.

"Freeze! Make one move and I'll shoot!"

The suspect skidded to a stop, and a second later another fast moving form crashed into him and both of them went down.

Holding it away from his body so as not to make himself a target, John Lee pointed his tactical flashlight and the rifle at them and said,

"Don't you move! I mean it, don't even fart or you're dead."

"Don't shoot! Please don't shoot!"

John Lee looked over the rifle's sights at them, his finger still on the trigger. Then he saw the faces in the harsh light of his flashlight and said, "Son of a bitch!"

One of the suspects grinned and said, "Hi, John Lee."

Chapter 36

"Are you two completely out of your friggin' minds? Do you know how close you came to gettin' your stupid asses blown away?"

John Lee was pretty sure the two teenage boys were more afraid of the Chief Deputy's rage than they had been of him and his rifle.

"What in the hell were you idiots thinkin' anyway, pullin' a fool stunt like that?"

"It seemed like a good idea at the time," Herbie Matthews said.

"A good idea? Really? Do you think this is funny?"

"No, sir," said Stephen Atterbury, staring at the floor as he shook his head.

"With all that's going on in this town, I'm surprised you're both not dead right now. Do you know what an AR-15 will do to you?"

"Yeah, in videogames."

"Videogames? Son, life isn't a fuckin' videogame! In real life, bullets tear people to pieces and they die. I'll tell both you little peckerheads somethin' right now. You're damn lucky it was John Lee back there behind that school instead of me or somebody else. 'Cause with a call for shots fired at a deputy after what happened to Ray Ray Watkins, most of us would have blown your asses away, com'in at them out of the dark like that, before you ever got close enough to see who it was!"

"We're sorry," Stephen said. "We just thought we was goin' to give Obie a scare. We didn't expect all this to happen."

"What the hell *did* you expect to happen?"

The boy shrugged his shoulders. "I don't know. Just that he'd get all excited, maybe piss his pants or something like that."

There was a knock on the door and the dispatcher poked his head in and said, "Their parents are in the lobby."

"You go talk to them, John Lee. I'm pretty sure if I do, I'll ask them if they'd mind if I just beat both these mutts' heads in."

The boys looked at John Lee in a panic, and he wasn't sure if it was because they were afraid of what their parents might do when they saw them, or what Flag would do to them without any witnesses present.

Dave and Karen Atterbury had been in John Lee's class in high school and were worried that she'd have enough credits to graduate. Not because Karen, a student who was more interested in having fun with her friends than studying, wanted to avoid having to go to summer school, but because she was already three months pregnant and beginning to show. Their son Stephen, born that September, was the first official child born to anyone from their class, though a couple of girls had gone away to "visit relatives" out of state between their junior and senior years.

Herbie's parents, Gene and Lorraine Matthews, were a few years older. All four of them were concerned as to why they had been called to the sheriff's department late at night, so soon after hearing all of the sirens as police cars tore through town.

"What's happening, John Lee? Are our boys all right? Nobody will tell us anything and everyone looks so grim."

"Yeah, they're fine, Karen. But it was close, I'll tell you that."

John Lee had been shaken by how close he had come to pulling the trigger when Herbie had come rushing at him out of the darkness. He was thankful that he had not obeyed Fig's order to shoot on sight.

"What the hell happened?"

"Well, it seems like the boys thought it would be funny to crawl up on the roof of the grade school and light a bunch of firecrackers and throw them on top of Obie Long's patrol car. He thought somebody was shooting at him and he called it in and every cop in the county responded. I came into the back parking lot just as the boys came running out of the darkness and almost shot them."

"Wait a minute," Lorraine Matthews said. "You almost shot my son?"

"Yes, ma'am. Almost," John Lee said.

"Are you out of your god damn mind? Did they have a gun?"

"No, ma'am. But you have to understand it was dark and we were responding to a call of shots fired. And with what happened to Deputy Watkins just..."

"I don't give a flying fuck what happened to Deputy Watkins. You almost shot my son?"

"Like I said, we had reports of shots fired. And all of a sudden they come running at me out of the darkness..."

"I want to talk to your supervisor right now!"

"Calm down, Lorraine. We've known John Lee forever. If he..."

"If he what, Karen? He almost shot our *sons!*"

"But he didn't," Dave Atterbury said. "Let's just be glad about that and find out what the hell's going on before anybody starts throwing blame around."

"Oh, I know who's to blame. That little punk of yours, that's who to blame. Herbie's never been in trouble before."

"Well, neither has Stephen. For all we know..."

"Just shut up, Karen. If you were a better mother maybe you'd know..."

"Don't tell me to shut up!"

"Ladies, let's calm down, okay?"

"Calm down? You almost killed my son and you want me to calm down?"

The slap caught John Lee by surprise, but before he could react Lorraine was on the attack, raining blows upon his face and clawing at his eyes with her fingernails. He threw up his left arm to try to protect himself and tried to push her away with his right. She was screaming and cursing at him and somehow managed to get past his upraised arm and close enough to rake her fingers down his right cheek.

"Stop it! Stop it, Lorraine," Karen was shouting as the woman's husband stood dumbfounded at what he was seeing. Bob Patterson and Dave Atterbury managed to grab her and pull her away before she could do any more damage.

"Settle down," Bob ordered.

Lorraine fought both of them, trying to get free and back at John Lee.

"I said stop it, lady!"

Completely out of control, she only seemed to fight harder, managing to hit Dave in the mouth, splitting his lip, which exploded with a spray of blood.

Bob pulled the pepper spray canister from a pouch on his belt and gave her a blast in the face. Lorraine shrieked and threw her hands to her face. Bob took advantage of the opportunity and wrestled her to the floor, where he handcuffed her hands behind her.

He jerked her to her feet and sat her down in a chair, then turned to John Lee. "Are you okay?"

John Lee wasn't okay. He could taste blood in his mouth and his cheek felt like it had been flayed open. But he nodded his head. "Check on Dave, she got him a pretty good lick."

"I'm okay," Dave said, wiping his mouth with the back of his hand, which came away bloody.

"My eyes are on fire," Lorraine screamed. "Somebody do something!"

"Paramedics are on the way," said the dispatcher.

A moment later the door opened and Sheriff D.W. Swindle strode into the lobby. Seeing the scene before him, with one of his deputies and a civilian bloodied, and a handcuffed woman wailing that her eyes were burning, he stopped in his tracks.

"What in holy hell is goin' on here?"

"It's a long story D.W. You might as well pour yourself a cup of coffee," John Lee said. "Because I think we're going to be here all night."

Chapter 37

It didn't take all night long, but it took most of it. While paramedics flushed Lorraine's eyes to wash away the pepper spray, then attended to Dave Atterbury and John Lee's injuries, Flag gave D.W. a rundown of the night's events, from Obie's first report of shots fired to deputies responding en masse, believing another sniper attack was taking place, and to John Lee apprehending the boys as they attempted to flee. Donnie Ray Mayhew was called in to take statements from the dispatcher and everyone else who had witnessed Lorraine Matthews' attacks on John Lee and Dave Atterbury.

When he had heard it all, D.W. said, "This is 'bout the biggest mess ever." He was already trying to figure out how he was going to put a spin on this to make his department look good. "I'm just glad you didn't shoot those boys, John Lee."

"Believe me! I'm glad, too."

"Maybe you shoulda'," Flag said. "Might give folks 'round here the message that you don't play games with the sheriff's department."

D.W. ignored him, but once again John Lee wondered how the news media and the general public would react to statements like that. His father-in-law might not be the image of the southern lawman in any good sense of the term, but Fig certainly was in every bad sense.

"So what do we do now?"

"What do we do? I'll tell you what we do," Flag said, leaning over to use the antique brass spittoon next to the sheriff's desk. "We lock those two little bastards up for disturbin' the peace and vandalism, and trespassin' on school property, and anythin' else we can think of. And then we lock up that crazy ass woman for attackin' John Lee and that other fella. That's what we do!"

"No."

"What?" Flag turned to John Lee in surprise and asked again, "What did you say?"

"No, I don't want the woman locked up."

"Why the hell not? Have you looked in the mirror and seen your face?"

As a matter of fact, John Lee had, and it wasn't a pretty sight. His bottom lip was split and swollen, and Lorraine Matthews had carved four deep furrows in his cheek with her fingernails. But he stood his ground. "I imagine if I just found out that my son just came that close to getting shot, I'd go a little crazy, too."

"Bullshit. What if she'd a had a gun and started shootin'?"

"But she didn't have a gun, Fig."

"That ain't the point! We can't let people go around attackin' deputies and just forget about it and say it's okay because they're upset about somethin' and fly off the handle."

"Look, this is a big enough mess as it is. Let's not make it any worse. I know both boys. They're just typical kids. Yeah, they pulled a stupid stunt, but when you think about it, it is kind of funny."

"Funny? What in the hell is funny 'bout it?"

"Think about it," John Lee said. "We all know what a slacker Obie is. I'd bet money he was probably sound asleep in his patrol car when those firecrackers went off. It's the most action he's seen in at least ten years. I can just imagine him scared shitless thinking World War III landed right on the roof of his patrol car."

Bob Patterson chuckled, and even D.W. grinned in spite of himself.

"That is funny, John Lee," Bob said. "Obie's always complaining about how rough the job is and how he hates working the swing or night shifts. For the next twenty years he'll be telling the story about the big shootout he was in at the grade school. He'll ride the story so long he'll never have to buy a cup of coffee in this town again."

"How about this? Let's keep the boys in a cell overnight to teach them a lesson. Then we can charge them with disturbing the peace or something," John Lee said. "As for the mother, like I said, if I was in..."

"No!" Flag shouted. "We're not lettin' her walk out of here like nothin' happened! What kind of message does that send to the public? That whenever you get upset you can attack a deputy and it's okay because you're havin' a bad day?"

"All I'm saying is..."

"No, Flag's right," D.W. said. "I think I know where you're comin' from, John Lee. But you got no reason to feel guilty for what happened out there. Or almost happened. If anythin', be glad you had the levelheadedness not to shoot. But that don't change the fact that there ain't no excuse for that woman attacking you like that. I want her charged with assault on a police officer. From what I'm hearin' so far, she's not willin' to take any kind of responsibility for what her boy did."

"That's a felony conviction, D.W."

"Time it gets to court, she'll plead it down to simple assault or somethin' like that and pay a fine and maybe get some community service. It could be worse. It could be a lot worse."

Thinking back to how he had aimed his AR-15 at what he had believed to be the sniper who had killed Ray Ray Watkins and shot at two other police cars, John Lee nodded in agreement. D.W. was right, it could have been a lot worse.

***

Night was fading into day when John Lee pulled into his driveway. Every bone and joint in his body ached, the scratches on his face were throbbing, and he was so tired that it took all he could do to pick up the AR-15 and walk into the house. He didn't even have the energy to stop and pet Magic along the way.

He hung his gun belt on the hook in the bedroom, started to the spare room to put the rifle in his gun safe, then said, "The hell with it." He leaned the rifle in the corner of his bedroom and laid across the bed, still wearing his boots, Levi's, and the dark blue Sheriff's Department T-shirt he had been wearing when the dispatcher called to tell him about shots being fired at the grade school.

Magic whined with concern, unaccustomed to his master acting this way. Then, instead of going to the padded dog bed in a corner of the living room where he usually slept, the big German Shepherd laid down on the floor beside John Lee's bed and guarded him while the exhausted man snored.

***

Two very remorseful boys were lead into D.W.'s office the next afternoon, heads down and shoulders slumped.

"How'd ya'll like your night in jail, boys?"

They shook their heads, and Dave Atterbury said, "Stephen, look at the man and talk."

"We didn't like it very much at all, sir."

"No, sir, we didn't," Herbie Matthews added.

"Do you boys know how close ya' come to gettin' yourselves

killed?"

"We're sorry," Stephen said. "It was pretty dumb, what we did."

"What you boys don't understand is that when you do somethin' like that, it sets off a whole chain reaction," D.W. told them. "What's that they call it, John Lee? A chain of unintended circumstances? See, that's what happened. Y'all thought it'd be funny to throw those firecrackers at Deputy Long, but because you did that, over a dozen deputies who were off duty came a runnin' 'cause they thought somebody was shootin' for real. Now, you boys think about somethin'. Over a dozen deputies drivin' real fast through the community thinkin' someone was shooting at Deputy Long. What if one of them would'a got in an accident and killed somebody or killed themselves drivin' at a high rate of speed like that? How would ya' feel knowin' you were responsible for that?"

"Not very good at all. We never thought about something like that happening," Stephen said.

"Nope, ya' didn't think at all. But that ain't the only thing. What if Deputy Quarrels here would've shot you? Put yourself in his place. He's out there in the dark and he thinks someone's been shootin' at another deputy, and then y'all come runnin' at him like that? I'll tell ya' right now boys, if it had been me you'd both be layin' in the morgue with tags on your toes right now. No question 'bout that. Think about that for a minute. Think about your families and what that'd do to them. Think about Deputy Quarrels. Think about what he'd have to go through know'in he killed two kids because they was bein' stupid."

There were tears in both boys' eyes by now, but D.W. wasn't through with them yet. "You know those unintended consequences I talked about? I want you to look at Deputy Quarrels' face. You see those big deep scratches? You see how his lip is all puffed up like that? Stephen, look at your father. See how he's got a big fat lip, too? Herbie, do you know why your dad's here, but not your mom?"

"No, sir," Herbie mumbled.

"Speak up," his father said to him.

"No, sir. I guess 'cause she's really mad at me."

"No. Your mom is in jail, son."

Herbie looked at the sheriff, his eyes huge. "My mom's in jail?"

"That's right. When she heard that Deputy Quarrels almost shot you two fools, she went off on him. She done that to him. Clawed his face open and hit him in the mouth. Hit Mr. Atterbury here, too, when he tried to pull her off'a him."

"My mom did that?"

"That's right. She's goin' to see the judge in just a little bit. Assault on a police officer is a felony in this state, boy. Your mama could go to prison for ten years."

"No. No, it's all my fault! It was all my idea, I talked Stephen into it. He didn't even want to do it in the first place. Please don't put my mom in prison! I'll do anything. You can lock me up forever, but don't send my mom to prison."

"I'm afraid it ain't that simple," D.W. told the crying boy. "What's done is done. Now it's up to the judge and the court."

"I don't want my mom to go to prison." Herbie was crying so hard he was shaking. His father put an arm around his shoulder to try to comfort him.

D.W. gave the boy a moment to calm down, then said, "I could send you both to reform school for 90 days. That's what they call prison for juveniles here in Florida. Trust me, it ain't no vacation. But here's what I'm goin' to do. I want both of you to apologize to Deputy Long in person when he comes back on duty, since he's off now, recoverin' from the scare you put in him and almost having a heart attack. And I want you both to apologize to Deputy Quarrels here. And I want you both to write me a 500 word essay. No, make that 750 words. About how you realize how dumb what you did was. And then I'm going to want each of you to give me twenty hours of community service. I don't know that's goin' to be yet. Pickin' up trash alongside the highway or washin' patrol cars or somethin'. I guarantee you, it's probably less'n the judge would give ya' and you ain't goin' to wind up with this on your records. If you do that and you keep your noses clean, we're gonna forget all this. But," and with that the sheriff pointed a stern finger at them, "if you so much as jay walk or sass your parents, or anythin' at all, you're gone. Do ya' understand me?"

"Yes, sir," Stephen said. "I'm sorry for what we did, Sheriff, I really am." He turned to John Lee and said, "I'm sorry. Thank you for not shooting us, John Lee."

John Lee shook his hand and said, "That's okay, Stephen. You mind what the sheriff said, and the next time you think you want to do something funny, think about those unintended consequences he told you about."

"I will," Stephen promised.

Herbie was still crying as he apologized, but John Lee believed he was sincere as well.

When the boys left with their fathers and Stephen's mother, D.W. shook his head. "I hope I got through to them."

"Oh, I think you did," John Lee said.

"How's the face?"

"Hurts like hell."

"Yeah, you ain't as pretty as ya' used to be. What time's the mother's arraignment?"

"Three o'clock."

"I wonder if a night in jail did anything to help her attitude?"

"I guess we'll find that out soon, won't we?"

Chapter 38

As it turned out, the time she spent behind bars had only served to increase Lorraine Matthews' rage. When Maddy brought the handcuffed woman into the courtroom she looked at John Lee with unveiled hatred in her eyes.

Seeing his mother, Herbie had rushed forward to throw his arms around her. Ignoring protocol, Maddy stepped back to give them a moment before the clerk called the court to order.

The prosecutor read the charges against her, attorney Toby Bardo stood up and announced that he would be representing the defendant, and the judge asked if she was ready to enter a plea at that time.

"Your Honor, my client pleads not guilty."

"I'd like to hear it from her," the judge said.

"I can't believe you're trying to charge me with a crime when my child is the victim here," Lorraine said. "That maniac almost killed my son!" She pointed an accusing finger at John Lee.

"Ma'am, this hearing is about the charges against you, not about what happened at the school. Now, do you plead guilty or not guilty?"

"I'm not pleading anything! I didn't do anything. You all are just trying to protect this psycho cop of yours by shifting all the blame to me!"

"Mrs. Matthews, you can tell your story when it comes to trial. Now what's it going to be? If you want to plead guilty we can adjudicate things right now, or if you plead not guilty you can be released on bail and there will be a trial where you can tell your side of things."

"I'm not saying a word! This is nothing but a kangaroo court."

Judge Harrison Taylor had been on the bench for over 20 years and had earned a much deserved reputation for fairness and honesty. But he was not a man to challenge in open court.

"Mr. Bardo, please control your client."

"Nobody controls me!"

"You're wrong about that, Mrs. Matthews. You're in *my* courtroom and *I* control everything and everybody in here. Deputy Westfall, please take the prisoner back to her cell. We'll recess until 9 AM tomorrow morning. Maybe by then you'll be able to control yourself, Mrs. Matthews. But I warn you right now, if you come back into my courtroom with the same attitude tomorrow morning, I will hold you in contempt and you'll spend more time behind bars. Do we understand each other?"

"No! No, please don't lock my mom up anymore! It's all my fault, judge. Me and Stephen Atterbury, we did something really stupid and we know it. My mom was just mad and scared and stuff." Herbie was crying and his father had to restrain him from rushing to his mother's side.

Judge Taylor looked at the boy for a moment, then closed his eyes, listening to him sob. When he opened them again he said, "Mrs. Matthews, I'm giving you one more chance. Look at your son, there. You've both had a rough night and I think he needs his mother home with him. And that's where I'd like to see you go right now. But I need a plea from you to do that. Otherwise, my hands are tied. Deputy Quarrels has already told me he holds no animosity toward you and would like to see this put to rest without any more difficulty for any of the parties involved. If you plead guilty we can put this all behind us right now, or you choose to plead not guilty and I'll set a trial date. And for the sake of your son I'll release you on your own recognizance right now without any bail required. So what's it going to be?"

Lorraine shook her head stubbornly, refusing to reply.

"My client pleads not guilty, Your Honor."

"I want to hear it from her," the judge said evenly.

She held her head high and glared at him but refused to speak.

"Jesus Christ, Lorraine, quit being so god damn stubborn and answer, will you?"

She jerked her head towards her husband and hissed, "If you were more of a man, you'd have been the one kicking that prick's ass, not me, and I wouldn't be standing here. But no, I had to do your job. So don't you dare tell me what to do!"

"That's it," the judge said, rapping his gavel. "Deputy Westfall, take her back to her cell. And keep her there until this time tomorrow."

"No, please don't do that to my mom," Herbie begged.

As Maddy led the defiant woman out of the courtroom, the judge looked at the boy with sympathetic eyes and said, "I'm sorry, son, but I'm not the one doing it to your mom. She's doing it to herself."

***

"If I ever get that stupid and stubborn, promise me you'll shoot me," Maddy said an hour later as they sat across from each other in the bullpen. "I mean, it's not like Judge Taylor didn't give her plenty of opportunities to avoid going back to jail."

"Some people are just too dumb for their own good," John Lee replied.

"Your face looks terrible."

"Okay. Your ass looks too big in that uniform."

"I beg your pardon?"

"Oh, I thought we were trading insults."

Maddy gave him a haughty look and said, "I was showing concern for your injuries. And by the way, my ass looks just fine, in or out of uniform."

"Mea culpa. I think that's Latin for 'oops, my bad.'"

Andy Stringer came in and sat down at the table. "Did you hear the latest?"

"No, what's up?"

"Obie put in for sick leave. Said he's still having chest pains even though the ER over in Perry checked him out and said he's fine."

"Why am I not surprised? I wonder how long he'll ride that train?"

"Just as long as he can," Maddy said. "You know Obie, if there's a way to get out of work *and* get paid at the same time, he's going to milk it for all it's worth."

"I know what those boys done was stupid and all that," Andy said, "but I've got to tell you, it was funnier'n hell, too!"

They all laughed, picturing Obie huddling terrified in his car as the boys threw firecrackers onto the roof. Their fellow deputy had shirked his duty and made others carry the load for him too many times for anybody to have much sympathy for what he had gone through.

Andy studied John Lee's face and said, "That woman sure messed you up, son."

"It only hurts when I breathe."

"You making any progress on those skeletons yet?"

John Lee told them what he knew, and how he suspected the victims had come from one of the turpentine camps, but had no way to prove it at that point.

"Did you talk to anybody at Somerton? Maybe they have some old records or something."

"I talked to Troy yesterday. He said that big tornado that came through here back in the 60s destroyed a building where they had their old company records stored."

"How did that go?"

"What? Seeing Troy?"

"Yeah. Didn't you guys have some history back a long time ago?"

"We ran around together when we were kids," John Lee said.

"Okay. I was thinking there was a hassle about some girl or something. One of you stole the other one's girlfriend or something."

"Oh, those boys tried to pollinate anything within reach," Maddy said. "My brother was part of that rat pack."

"Yeah, we had us some fun back in the day," John Lee agreed. "What can I say? Life happens and sometimes people just drift apart. Troy did invite me to go fishing with him. Said he's been riding the desk pretty much all the time since his daddy semi-retired."

"So are you at a dead end in the investigation?"

"I don't know," John Lee said. "I was thinking about talking to some of the old timers around here to see if any of them can tell me anything about those days."

"Donald Perry."

"Who?"

"Donald Perry."

"Mister Donald? The janitor from when we were in high school?"

"Yep."

"Is he even still alive?"

"Yes, he is," Andy said. "He'll be a 95 years old on Thanksgiving. And he still gets around just as spry as if he was in his 60s."

"You're kidding me?"

"Nope. You know where Anderson Farms Road crosses Copperhead Creek?"

"Yeah."

"That's where you'll find him," Andy said. "He's down there most every evening, fishing off the bridge there. I just stopped and talked to him the other day. That old gentleman knows just about everything that went on around here back in the old days. And he's still sharp as a tack. You ought to look him up."

"Thanks for the tip, Andy. I'll sure do that."

"I always liked Mister Donald," Maddy said. "Tell him I said hello."

"I will," John Lee assured her.

He set off for Copperhead Creek, eager to talk to somebody who might help him take the investigation of the skeletons to the next level.

Chapter 39

A blue three wheeled bicycle with a wire basket attached to the handlebars and a larger wire basket mounted in back between the rear wheels was sitting beside the road, its paint faded and the fenders dented. An old black man wearing a wide brimmed straw hat was seated on a folding chair on the bridge. He turned when he heard John Lee's Charger pull up and smiled when he recognized his visitor.

"John Lee Quarrels! That you, boy?"

"Yes, sir, it is. How you doing, Mister Donald?"

"Not bad for an old nigga. How 'bout yourself?"

"I can't complain."

"Don't do no good anyway," Mister Donald said, extending a gnarled hand to shake. Even at his age, his grip was firm. "Nobody really cares, they just listenin' to be polite, and all the while you're talkin' they's ignorin' you and wonderin' what they goin' to say next."

"I expect that's true. You catching anything?"

"Got me a couple sunfish and a bullhead."

John Lee looked in the white five gallon plastic bucket next to the man's chair.

A pickup approached and slowed down as it came to the bridge, rattling across on the wooden planks. The driver, one of the Davidson brothers, John Lee wasn't sure which one, raised two fingers from the steering wheel in salute and John Lee waved back.

"You come out here for a fishin' report or you got somethin' else on your mind?"

"As a matter of fact, I do."

John Lee took the evidence bag from his pocket and removed the brass tag. "Have you ever seen one of these before, Mister Donald?"

The old man brought it close to his face and studied it for a moment, then handed it back. "Yep. Seen more than one of them in my time."

"They tell me it's from the old turpentine camps."

"That's a fact."

"Mister Donald, did you hear about those three skeletons we found out on Turpentine Highway a while back?"

"Heard somethin' 'bout it. Didn't pay much attention. Man gets to be my age, he don't much give a care about all that's goin' on in the world. If I can sit up and take nourishment in the mornin' and my bowels move sometime in the day, that's about all I kin ask for. Well, that and that those bowels let me know ahead of time what they're goin' to do."

John Lee chuckled. "I guess that is important, isn't it."

"Yes, suh, 'deed it is. Now why you askin' me about that there piece of metal, John Lee?"

"We found it with those three skeletons we dug up. Fellow over at the historical museum told me about the turpentine camps and said it was an ID tag for one of the workers there."

"He told you right."

"He also told me about how things were back then, Mister Donald. About how those workers weren't much more than slaves sometimes."

"That's true, son. Black or white, if you found yourself in one a those places you could kiss your ass goodbye, 'cause it belonged to the company from then on."

"I heard that sometimes people tried to escape. And I heard that when they did, sometimes they got beat. Or worse."

"Heard the same thing myself."

The old man's red and white plastic bobber dipped under the water and he pulled back sharply on the rod, setting the hook. He reeled in another palm sized sunfish and took it off the hook, dropping it into the bucket. Picking up an old tin can from the pavement next to his chair, he fished inside and brought out a night crawler, and re-baited his hook. Wiping his hand on his pants leg, he cast the line out again, never having gotten up from his chair during the whole process.

When he was done, he asked, "Why you messin' 'round in this stuff, John Lee? Whatever happened to those men whose bones you found, it was a long time ago."

"It's my job. I want to find out who killed them."

"Why? What good's it goin' do after all this time?"

John Lee shrugged. "It just don't seem right that whoever did it got away with it."

"Lots of things ain't right in the world, son. Never have been and never will be."

"I know that. But I just can't let this go and pretend nothing ever happened, can I?"

"I don't know. Can ya'?"

"No, sir, I can't."

"Probably whoever killed them has been dead forever."

"I expect so," John Lee said. "But I still want the world to know who did it."

"One thing a nigger learns pretty early in these parts is that sometimes it's best to mind your own business."

"I like to think those days are long gone," John Lee said.

The old man picked up his fishing pole and hooked a finger over the line and pulled backwards just a touch, feeling for any tug of resistance that might tell him something was near his bait on the other end. Satisfied, he leaned it back against the bridge's low railing.

"I'd like to think so, too. Don't get me wrong, it's a different world than what I grew up in. But even now they's people that liked it the way it was in the old days. Would like to see things go back that way."

"Yeah, that's true, Mister Donald. But they're wrong, and it's better now."

"Don't kid yourself," the old man said, turning his lined and leathery face his way. "There's people right now in this county who'd string a nigga up and not think a thing 'bout it, if they thought they could get away with it."

John Lee knew the man was right, and he nodded his acknowledgment.

"Did you ever hear of some of the things that happened out there at those camps, Mister Donald?"

"Heard a lot of things. Saw some things, too."

"What kind of things?"

"Didn't you hear what I was sayin' to you, boy? I didn't get to be this old by talkin' about things that weren't none a my concern."

"Mister Donald, I'm not looking to cause you any trouble, sir. I'm really not. But I don't know where else to go with this. I wasn't around back in the old days, when the freedom marchers were doing their thing and all that, but I learned all about it in history class. I learned about all those folks who come from up north to stage sit-ins and walk with the blacks to try to change things. That wasn't any of their concern, either. And some of them got beat up pretty bad. Some even died because they got involved. But they did it, because they wanted to make things right."

"When I was eight years old, me and my friend Joseph was playin' with matches and we wound up burnin' down his pappy's tool shed," Mister Donald told him. "When I was fifteen I was introduced to sex by my cousin Charlie's wife while he was workin' diggin' ditches up around Lake City somewhere. I think I was about that same age when I swiped a silver dollar from my grandmammy's purse. That was money she was saving up to buy a new dress and hat for Easter Sunday. I used that money to buy me a bottle of moonshine and I got so drunk I 'bout puked myself to death, yes I did. I done some other things I ain't proud of, too. Even cheated on my wife one time with a gal I met in a gin mill, back when I was a young buck, full of piss and vinegar. What I'm sayin' is, I've been carryin' around plenty of guilt for most a my life, just like most people. So you bringin' any more to me? It's goin' to be pretty low down on the list for me to worry about."

John Lee was frustrated and couldn't think of a way to get through to the old man, to unlock the secrets he had hidden in his memory.

"I'm sorry, Mister Donald. I never meant to try to put you on a guilt trip. I'm just so damn frustrated that somebody killed those three men. Tied theirI do hands behind them with barbed wire and made them get down on their knees and shot them in the back of the head like that when they were helpless. I was talking to a lady over there in Tallahassee at the crime lab, and she showed me the bones from one of them's wrist. She showed me gouges right into the bone from that barbed wire, where that poor man tried to get free. I just keep thinking about that, and I can't let it go. What could they have done so bad to deserve that?"

"Ain't nobody ever deserved that."

"No, sir, I don't think so either."

Another car went by, with a teenage couple inside. John Lee nodded at them but they ignored him. Three or four other vehicles passed by before Mister Donald reeled in his line to check his bait, then cast it out again.

"There was five of us families that lived close together in a group of little shacks. My friend Joseph that I told you about, my grandpappy and grandmammy, a family called the Wilsons, and my Uncle Wayne and his wife and kids. A few times a man on the run from the camps would come through our place. Sometimes they'd stop long enough to ask for a drink of water or directions or somethin' like that. They's always scared to death and desperate. Usually it weren't much longer before the woods riders with their dogs come through, right on their trail."

"What did your people do?"

"What could we do? We'd give those men a drink a water and point them in the right direction. That was about it. See, back in those days, if ya' tried to hide one of 'em, ya' was in for punishment. You might even find yourself carried off to one of the camps. Sheriff would say you was aid'in and abet'in whoever was tryin' to escape. So when the riders came to camp we jez' said 'yes sir' or 'no sir' and hope'd they go on about their business. Usually they did, but sometimes they'd decide to tear a little house apart, looking for whoever they was trailing. Don't think they really believed they was there, but they wanted to make their point about who was in charge. And if one of us tried to say anythin'? Best thing was going to happen to us was gettin' thumped upside the head with a club. I remember when Roland Wilson tried to keep 'em from paw'in through his wife's underwear drawer. They took him out in the front yard and tied him to a tree and whupped him with an old blacksnake whip. Whupped him half to death, a laughin' the whole time."

"Do you know of any men who disappeared from the camps during that time?"

"Lots a men disappeared, John Lee. Some escaped, a lot more just was gone. If a man died in one of the camps, all the camp boss had to say was he died from an accident or got sick or somethin' and they buried him out there. Weren't nobody gonna come around askin' questions."

John Lee pulled his cell phone from his pocket and found the picture he had taken of the photograph of the horse mounted man he had taken at the museum.

"Does this fellow look like anybody you would remember, Mister Donald?"

The old man looked at the picture and John Lee noticed his body stiffen. Not much, but there had been a reaction.

"No, suh," Mister Donald said, shaking his head.

"Are you sure?"

"Didn't I just say I didn't know who that was?"

"Yes, sir. I was just hoping..."

"Boy, I'm an old man. How you 'spect me to remember every cracker I ever seen in my life?"

John Lee was sure there was something there, but he didn't want to push the issue and have Mister Donald close up on him completely. He'd wait and try to ask him again another time, if necessary.

"I talked to Troy Somerton at the lumber products company, asking if he knew of any way to trace that tag number back to one of the workers. But he said all of their records got destroyed in a tornado a long time ago."

"I don't 'pect he'd tell you anythin' even if he did know," Mister Donald said. "Who do you think was runnin' those camps? It was Somerton Lumber Company. Do you suppose any of that crowd is goin' to admit anything about those days?"

"Do you think they knew what was going on in those camps?"

"Course they knew! How could they not know! You think back in the slave days the master didn't know that the overseer was out back whuppin' the slaves and screwin' their women if he took a mind to? Mr. Lincoln might'a have put an end to slavery way back in the old days, but people like the Somerton's? They never got that message. I don't know who pulled the trigger on the gun that killed those men you found out there, John Lee. But I can tell you one thing. It was Somerton money that paid for the bullets."

Chapter 40

John Lee tried to shave, but quickly gave that idea up when the razor touched his lacerated cheek. He had never worn a beard before, but thought that maybe he would grow one for the duration, while his face healed. He brushed his teeth, washed his mouth out with Scope, and walked naked into the bedroom, where Beth Ann was waiting for him. He sat on the side of the bed.

"You okay, John Lee?"

"Yeah, it's just been crazy lately."

She sat up and rubbed his back and shoulders. "You're all knotted up and tight. Here, you lay down on your stomach and let me give you a massage."

Beth Ann had gone to the Volusia School of Massage in Port Orange and was actually quite good at it, though she had never practiced the skill when she returned home to Somerton County. He stretched out on the bed and she began working on his legs, expertly kneading the muscles.

"Does that feel good?"

"It sure does. Damn good."

She worked her way up to his buttocks.

"How about that?"

"Uh huh."

Moving up to his lower back and then his shoulders, he could feel the tension releasing as she seemed to work every muscle, one by one. "Ya know, John Lee, there's a thing called a happy endin'."

"I think by the time you're done I'm going to be sound asleep."

She was straddling him digging deep into the muscles of his neck and shoulders.

"Oh, I think if I massage certain things enough you'll wake up to do what I need done."

"I'm just a piece of meat to you, aren't I, Beth Ann."

"Is that what you think?"

"Sometimes."

"And what's wrong with that. Ain't I just a piece of ass to you?"

"No."

She stopped for a moment, then asked, "Then what am I?"

"I don't know. Does it have to have a label?"

She resumed the massage. "I don't know. I never thought of it that way. I mean, I can't be your girlfriend. You're still married to my sister. And don't get me wrong, I don't want to be your girlfriend. And I don't think you want me to be, either."

He didn't answer because he didn't know what to say. No, he didn't want a formal relationship with Beth Ann. So what was it they had? They both filled a need for the other person on a purely physical level, but he didn't feel the emotional connection with her that one would expect for a lover.

"So we're just friends with benefits?"

"I guess."

"I don't have any problem with that, John Lee."

"Okay."

"We both know this ain't forever, right? I mean, sooner or later you'll find somebody and this'll end. I just want you to know that I'm okay with that when the time comes."

"Or you might find somebody."

Beth Ann laughed. "Not me. Least not for a long time. I'm just sowin' my wild oats, as Mama calls it. I'm not ready to be tied down to anybody yet."

"Okay."

He was totally relaxed and didn't want to talk. He just wanted to sleep. When Beth Ann told him to roll over on his back he did not hear her. There would be no happy ending to the massage. John Lee Quarrels was dead to the world.

Sometime, hours later, his full bladder woke him up and he got up to go to the bathroom. Back in bed he was drifting back to sleep when he heard a vehicle slow down out front. He was instantly awake, wondering if it was Maddy. But then it continued down the road and he recognized the rumble of Phil Robinson's Dodge diesel pickup as his neighbor returned home.

***

"Hi. It's John Lee."

"John Lee? Do I know a John Lee? Oh yes, I seem to remember a cracker deputy sheriff from someplace named John Lee. But you can't be him, because he's one of those guys who takes a girl to dinner and gets what he wants out of her and then never calls again."

"I'm sorry, Shania. It's been really crazy over here. I wasn't ignoring you."

"Sure you were. But that's okay, I understand. You've got good reason to."

"If you think it's the racial thing..."

"Oh, stop it, I was just pulling your leg. What's up?"

"I was wondering, is it possible to get any DNA from those bones we found after all these years?"

"How much do you know about DNA?"

He shrugged his shoulders, even though she couldn't see him, and said, "I don't know, I guess about as much as anybody else. Or at least as much as any average cop."

"Okay, DNA stands for deoxyribonucleic acid. Every organism has DNA. It's made up of four chemicals, which are called nucleotides. They are guanine, adenine, cytosine, and thymine."

"You lost me already. Remember, I'm just a boy from the piney woods."

"I'm sorry. Sometimes you sound almost civilized and I tend to forget that. Let me try to dumb it down for you."

He smiled at her sassy attitude as he poured milk into his morning coffee and spooned in sugar.

"From the moment somebody or something dies, DNA starts to degrade. But not nearly as quickly as soft tissue. A lot of it depends on the conditions where the body or bodies are located, just like I told you, with the condition of the bones themselves. Scientists have been able to extract DNA from mammoths and things like that that died 50,000 years ago."

"That's a long time."

"Did you ever see the movie *Jurassic Park*?"

"No. I'm not much for sci-fi and fantasy."

"Really? That surprises me, I pictured you as a man with a very active fantasy life."

"So are you still busting my balls because I haven't called before this?"

"Yes, I am."

"How long is this going to continue?"

"I don't know, John Lee. How long is it going to be before you call me again? Preferably a social call, not just to talk about bones."

He laughed and said, "I have a comeback for that, but I'm going to keep it to myself."

"Yeah, there you go, lying to me again. I don't think you keep a certain bone to yourself at all."

"If you were a real scientist, you'd know that's not a bone."

"If you were *real* good ol' boy, you'd be driving this way right now to prove it."

They both laughed, and she said, "Anyway, back to the movie. In *Jurassic Park* they found DNA from mosquitoes that had been preserved in amber. And while that was fiction, there's some basis in scientific fact. Amber is an excellent preservative. Some scientists have claimed they were able to extract DNA from organisms that died over fifteen million years ago."

"Okay, then that means you should be able to get DNA from the skeletons, right?"

"Possibly. But again, it depends on conditions. Just like it does with meat in a refrigerator, freezing can slow the rate of DNA decomposition. That's why when they find ancient people or prehistoric animals who were frozen in places like Alaska or Northern Russia they can extract DNA sometimes. Dry places help, too. They have recovered DNA from 20,000 year old dung found in caves in arid places like Nevada and Arizona. On the other hand, heat and wet conditions like we have here are just the opposite. They hasten the decomposition of DNA."

"So is it worth a try?"

"Anything is worth a try. I did an internship at the Armed Forces Institute of Pathology in Washington, D.C. when I was in college. Before they closed down they were able to use DNA to identify the remains of over 150 casualties dating all the way back to World War II."

"Why did they close?"

"Why does anything close with the government? Budget cuts."

"That sucks."

"There are other facilities that still work to identify MIA remains. The big one's in Hawaii and they focus on Vietnam War casualties. Anyway, yes, I can try to extract DNA and we can see if we can get a profile for you. But then what?"

"I don't know," John Lee admitted. "Is there any kind of a national database it can be entered into?"

"The FBI has the Combined DNA Index System, or CODIS for short. They obtain DNA profiles from federal, state, and local DNA collection programs and make it available to law enforcement agencies across the country for identification purposes."

"Wouldn't this fall into that category?"

"Yes, it would. But you have to understand, John Lee, this isn't something that happens overnight. First of all, we've got to be able to extract the DNA and create a profile, and there's no guarantee we'll be able to do that. If we can, then we enter it into the system. And then, if there is anything that matches, which is probably going to be somebody with a criminal conviction, or else a John or Jane Doe, you may have something to start with. But if you expect results this evening, you're going to be disappointed."

"I understand that," he said. "But I'd really appreciate it if you could try."

"I'm on it," she replied. "I'll let you know if I find out anything. But don't forget, you owe me. I'm thinking dinner the next time you're in town."

"Please tell me it's not gonna be sushi."

"I guess I could make you a mess of chitlins and black-eyed peas."

"You like screwing with me, don't you?"

"I don't know. At least not yet."

John Lee was taking a drink of coffee as she said that and spewed it all over the counter in his kitchen. He coughed and choked, then wiped tears from his eyes.

"Are you okay?"

"Yeah, I just choked."

"I don't know, John Lee, maybe I should take a rain check on dinner. Better yet, maybe you should just send me a gift card for Red Lobster or someplace like that. I'm not sure you could handle anything else."

"I'm gonna say goodbye now. I'll be in touch."

"Promises, promises. You have yourself a good day, John Lee."

Chapter 41

Dixie Landrum looked up when John Lee came into the newspaper's office. "I heard some woman tried to rip your face off the other night. Looks like she did a pretty good job of it."

"She did put some effort into it," John Lee said.

"What can I do for you?"

"Well, I really don't know. I'm trying to come up with something on the skeletons we found out there on Turpentine Highway, but I'm not making a lot of progress."

"How can I help?"

"I was wondering how far back the newspaper records go. I was thinking that maybe there might be something about those men coming up missing or something."

"Do you know when they might have gone missing?"

"Not really," he admitted. "The best the folks over at the crime lab in Tallahassee could say was at least 50 years, maybe more."

"Nothing like narrowing it down, is there?"

"I know it's a pretty tall order. I'm just grasping at straws here, Dixie."

She opened the wooden gate at the end of the counter and said, "Come with me."

Leading him back past a couple of desks with computer monitors on them, then past the office of Arnold Kelly, the newspaper's editor and publisher, she opened the door into a large bay of a room that was a warren of stacks of old newspapers piled chest high.

Waving her hand, Dixie said, "There you go, help yourself."

"You've got to be kidding me."

"Well I damn sure don't have the time to sort through all of them for you."

"How far back do these things go?"

"At least back to the 1940s, maybe even the 30s or 20s."

"How would I ever find anything back here?"

"Well the good news is, Arnold does have them semi-organized.

These stacks here? Those are from the last five years. The ones behind them go back another five years or so."

"It would take forever to find anything back here."

"What did you expect?"

"I don't know. I thought maybe you had things on file on a computer or something that you could look up."

"For the last five or six years we've done everything on a computer and we have searchable PDF files of those. But before that every issue was pasted up by hand, then they took it over to Lake City to get printed."

"Maybe this isn't such a good idea," John Lee said, disappointed.

"I wish I could help you more, but with Arnold in the hospital getting his hip replacement and then going to a rehab facility, it's all on me right now to get the next couple of issues out. But even if he was here, I just don't have the time John Lee. I'm sorry."

"Well, it was worth a try. Thanks anyway, Dixie."

He was back out on the sidewalk and opening the Charger's door when an idea hit him. He went back into the office and Dixie looked up from her computer.

"We're going to have to stop meeting this way. People are starting to talk."

"People have to have something to talk about," he said. "I just had an idea. What if I had somebody helping me? A couple of volunteers who would go through those old newspapers? Would that be okay?"

"I guess," Dixie said. "As long as they were careful and didn't rip the pages up or anything like that, and they put things back in order when they were done with them. But it's going to be dusty, boring work, so I don't know how many volunteers you are going to be able to find for something like that."

"Oh, I know where I can find a couple," John Lee assured her. "I'll be back in touch."

***

"John Lee. What's up?"

"How's your boy doing, Dave?"

"I think if his knee was hinged in the other direction he'd be kicking his own ass. I really am sorry about all this, John Lee. How's your face?"

"It only hurts when I eat, drink, or sweat."

"Lorraine is just... she's a bitch. I don't know how Gene puts up with her. Is she still in jail?"

"Yeah. The judge wanted to let her go yesterday but she had to be stubborn and she earned herself another 24 hours."

"Gene called and told me about that."

"Hopefully she'll be in a better mood when she goes back to court this afternoon."

"I hope so."

"Listen, the reason I'm here is I've got an idea. You know that D.W. said the boys have to do some kind of community service?"

"Yeah, they're not looking forward to that. Not doing the work, I think they both know they're getting off light. Just having all the other kids in town walking by and seeing them picking up trash or whatever."

"Then this might work out good," John Lee said. "Let me tell you what I've got in mind."

***

By the time she was led into court for the second time, Lorraine Matthews appeared to have learned her lesson. She kept her head bowed and only looked up when the judge asked her for her plea.

"Guilty, Your Honor."

"Before I pass sentencing, is there anything you'd like to say to the court or the victims. Victim, I guess, since Mr. Atterbury isn't here. But Deputy Quarrels is."

"I made a mistake. I got scared when I thought about my little boy being shot and I overreacted. I'm sorry."

The judge studied her for a moment before he passed sentence. "I have to tell you, Mrs. Matthews, yesterday I was inclined to give you some serious jail time after the way you acted out in this courtroom. However, Deputy Quarrels has asked me to be lenient with you. He thinks you deserve a break. I can't say as I agree with him, but if he's willing to turn the other cheek, literally in this case, I'll let it be. I'm fining you $1,500 and I'm putting you on one year's probation. I'm going to defer the payment of the fine and order you to get some anger management counseling. If you can bring me proof of completing a six week counseling program, I'll waive the fine, assuming you stay out of trouble for the duration of your probation."

"Thank you, Your Honor."

Judge Taylor studied her for a moment longer, as if he still wasn't sure he was doing the right thing, then he rapped his gavel and said, "Court is adjourned. See my clerk to handle the paperwork."

***

"If you asked me, those little bastards and that bitch all got off way too easy," Flag said.

"I don't recall askin' you," D.W. said.

"There was a time when we had chain gangs to deal with shit like this."

"There was a time when the Klan lynched anybody that got in their way. Those days are gone, too. What's your point?"

"My point is, you're too damn soft, D.W. You're soft on crime and you're soft on deputies, too. Lettin' those kids and that woman get off like that! And now you got Obie ridin' the gravy train claimin' he's got stress or whatever. You should'a canned his ass a long time ago."

"Did ya' just come in here to bitch and complain about what a terrible job I'm doin' Flag, or did ya' have somethin' else you wanted to talk about?"

"It ain't right D.W.! You need to let me start handlin' a lot of this stuff. That's my job."

"No, your job is to do what I tell ya' to do."

"Then what am I supposed to do? You keep take'n stuff away from me. I'm the friggin' Chief Deputy, but you override me on everythin'."

"That's because I don't trust you any further'n I can throw ya', Flag. You and I both know you're just bidin' your time and tryin' to work up the courage to run against me come election time."

"I haven't decided that, one way or the other."

"See, that's what I mean, right there. That's bullshit and you know it and I know it. You ain't man enough to look me in the eye and say it, because you're a chickenshit backstabbin' son of a bitch. I'd have a lot more respect for you if ya' had the balls to tell it like it is. But ya' don't. Only reason I don't fire you is I don't want to sleep on the couch. But I'll tell you right now, Flag, for you to run against me, you've got to resign your position first. It's written right in the county ordinances that way. And when you do, and when you lose that election and come back here tryin' to kiss ass and get your job back, it ain't gonna happen. Now get outta' my sight."

"You're a joke, D.W. You know that? You got one daughter who's supposed to be a married woman, but she's livin' with a dyke instead of her husband. And the other one ain't nothin' but a tramp who's sleepin' with her sister's husband. You ain't got the balls to put a stop to that, but ya' want to threaten me?"

"I said get out of here! That's an order, Deputy. And as long as I'm sittin' at this desk, you'll damn sure follow my orders. So either take that star off your shirt and drop it on my desk, or get on about your business. Either way, I'm done talkin to you."

They were almost nose to nose, both men leaning over the sheriff's desk, eyes locked on the other. Dispatcher Sheila Sharp was sure they were about to come to blows when she appeared at the sheriff's office door with a handful of reports she needed him to sign off on. But finally Flag backed down. For the moment at least. He brushed past her without a word as he went down the hall and back to his office

Chapter 42

"Most people have the courtesy to call for an appointment, not just show up unannounced," Charlotte said, looking at him with disapproval.

"I guess I'm not most people," John Lee told her.

"Mr. Somerton is a very busy man, I can't be interruptin' him every time you want to drop in and chat."

"Sure you can. You just push that little button on your phone and you tell him I'm here."

"Would you like to make an appointment, Deputy Quarrels?"

"No, ma'am, I'd like you to do what I said and push that little button and tell him I'm here. What's so hard about that?"

She folded her arms and glared at him. "My job is to see to it that Mr. Somerton is not bein' disturbed all the time by people *without* appointments!"

"I'll tell you what, I'll just do your job for you, since you don't seem to be up to it today."

He walked past her desk and knocked on Troy's door.

"You can't do that!"

"Sure I can! Didn't you just see me do it?"

"Stop that!"

He knocked again, then opened the door and said, "Troy, you got a minute. I wanted ask you about..."

He stopped abruptly when he saw his old friend hastily pulling up his pants while a very flustered and red faced Jolene Thompson held her blouse over her naked breasts.

"Excuse me," John Lee said, closing the door.

"What in the world is wrong with you? Don't you have a brain in your head? You're probably goin' to get me fired!"

"What do you want me to say, Charlotte? You could've said he was busy or that he had somebody in there, or something."

"And you could've called for an appointment!"

"Well I guess we both learned a lesson today, didn't we?"

Before she could reply, the office door opened and a very red faced

Jolene walked out, averting her eyes.

"John Lee, how you doin? Come on in."

John Lee followed Troy into his office. The other man closed the door behind them and came around his desk. " I'm afraid you caught me at a bad time."

"Yeah, sorry about that."

Troy laughed nervously and fiddled with some papers on his desk. "John Lee, it isn't what it looked like."

"None of my business, Troy."

"No really, we were just..."

"Troy, I don't give a shit," he said raising his hand in dismissal. "I'm not your preacher."

"Yeah, I guess not." Troy laughed again. "What can I say? It's not a serious thing, it's just..."

"What part of *its none of my business* didn't you get, Troy? If you want to boink one of your employees during lunch hour in your office, as long as she's willing and neither one of you is worried about your respective spouses finding out, have at it. I'm not exactly an altar boy myself."

Troy laughed, relief overcoming his embarrassment and worry about his illicit affair becoming local gossip. "Yeah, I guess that's true. You're livin' every man's fantasy."

"What you mean?"

"I hear tell you're doin' that wife of yours and that good looking kid sister of hers, too."

It was John Lee's turn to be uncomfortable, and he said, "People do like to gossip."

"Oh look at you, gettin' all red faced on me! This is Troy, John Lee. I know all your secrets and you know all mine from back in the day. Back then you'd diddle a rattlesnake if somebody held its head down. And so would I. Guess some things never change, huh?"

John Lee wasn't really interested in a trip down memory lane to relive all of their teenage conquests, of which there had been many. So he went to the subject of his visit.

"Anyway, I'm still looking into those skeletons we found."

"Man, you're like one of those pit bull dogs. When you get hold of something you just got to shake it to death, don't you?"

"I guess so."

"So what about those old bones? Have you learned something

new?"

"I was talking to Mister Donald yesterday..."

"The janitor from the school?"

"Yeah."

"He's still alive? I would've thought he died years ago."

"No, he's probably going to outlive all of us," John Lee said. "He still goes down there on Copperhead Creek and fishes off the bridge almost every evening."

"Well I'll be damned. I guess there's somethin' to be said for a life of hard work."

"I guess so."

"Hey, do you remember when he caught us smokin' in the bathroom when we were freshmen?"

"I've tried real hard to forget that," John Lee said.

Troy laughed and slapped his desk at the memory. "We had what, most of a pack of Camels I filched from my grandpa's desk? And Mister Donald told us we had two choices. We could smoke 'em up right then and there, or else he'd take us to the principal. Mr. Stanislaw, god, he was a prick, wasn't he? Neither one of us wanted to get our asses paddled with that big old paddle he used with the holes drilled in it. And we knew once he'd done that he'd still tell our parents and there'd be hell to pay when we got home, too. So Mister Donald stood right there and made us smoke those cigarettes one after another. Time we were done we were both puking our guts out!"

"You know, I haven't smoked a cigarette since then," John Lee said.

"Me, neither," Troy said, laughing out loud. "For the first year after that every time I saw Grandpa light up a cigarette I had to swallow hard to keep from losing my cookies right there!"

"Lessons learned."

"That old man was a better educator than some teachers we had. Do you remember Mr. Driscoll? Taught science. We called him Dry Driscoll 'cause his voice was a monotone and never changed, and he lectured on and on until most of us were fallin' asleep."

"Yeah. Those were the days."

"So what did Mister Donald have to say about those old bones you found?"

"He said back in the days of the turpentine camps, those workers weren't much more than slaves, Troy. I guess they were kinda' like coal miners working for the company store. All they did was work themselves to death and get deeper and deeper into debt."

"Well I don't know about all that, John Lee. That's one man's opinion, maybe."

"No, I've been doing some studying on it, and that's pretty much the way it was back then."

Troy frowned, obviously uncomfortable with the direction the conversation was going.

"What's your point, John Lee?"

"I read about these guys, they called them woods riders, they were sort of like the guards, and every camp had a captain who was in charge. I guess it could be pretty damn brutal, Troy."

"Don't believe everything you read. Who knows what kind of agenda whoever wrote that had?"

"No, it really happened. Mister Donald told me about how every once in a while somebody would escape from one of the camps and come by where he lived, and a posse would be right on their heels. I guess they weren't none too nice about trying to get the black folks around there to tell them what they knew if they were on somebody's trail. He said he saw some pretty terrible things back then."

"Whatever. That was a long time ago, we can't change the past."

"No, I guess we can't."

"Look, John Lee, I hate to cut this short, but I've got to get back to work. We had a whole load of plywood that was supposed to ship out this morning and something got screwed up in the production schedule. I need to get down there and make sure they get things back on track."

"Oh, sorry. I'll let you go, then."

Troy stood up and ushered him out of his office, saying, "Give me a call the next time you want to come by, I'll make sure to clear some time in my schedule for you, okay?"

"I'll do that," John Lee promised, but Troy was already ignoring him.

"Charlotte, come in my office We need to talk."

***

"I don't know why you're surprised by that," Maddy said. "The Somertons always did look down on the rest of us. You can't tell me this is the first time you got the cold shoulder from any of that bunch. I know better."

"It just strikes me as funny," John Lee said. "The last couple of times I was there Troy was talking about how we needed to get out and go fishing, and stop by anytime, and all that. Today he kept trying to steer the subject away from those turpentine camps, then blew me off and couldn't wait to get rid of me. He even made it a point to tell me to call the next time I came by so he could make time to see me."

"Maybe he didn't like talking about his family's dirty laundry. The Somertons are about the closest things we've got to robber barons in this county. They prefer to sit out there in that big fancy compound of theirs and forget about all the little people who blead sweat and tears to pay for all that."

He had not told her about walking in on Troy and Jolene, but did say he hoped Charlotte Thompson wouldn't be in trouble for him opening Troy's door unannounced.

"That woman," Bob Patterson said, with a look on his face like he had just stepped in something nasty. "I had to pull her out of Gator's Pub the other night when she got in an argument with Melinda Bridges. I don't know what started it, probably both of them wanting the same guy. At any rate, Charlotte threw her drink in Melinda's face and the two of them went at it. I got her outside and told her she needed to take a sobriety test before I'd let her in her car. She called me every filthy name in the book. I was sure she was at least twice over the legal limit, but she wasn't anywhere close to it. So it wasn't the booze making her be such a bitch, it's just who she is."

"At any rate, if you expect the Somertons to ever acknowledge anything bad about the family line, you're in for a big disappointment," Maddy told him. "Maybe money can't buy happiness, but in some cases it can make you oblivious to the rest of the world."

Chapter 43

John Lee spent the next morning on a computer at the sheriff's office, searching for any missing persons cases from Somerton County dating back fifty years, but there was nothing. Frustrated, he finally gave up and decided to walk across the street to the Subway sandwich shop for lunch.

The place was crowded with workers from the downtown stores and offices on their lunch breaks but he managed to find a small table in the rear corner. He was halfway through his Italian beef sandwich when a young man approached his table. John Lee couldn't think of his name but he remembered seeing him around the courthouse from time to time.

"Are you Deputy Quarrels? John Lee Quarrels?"

"That's me. I'm sorry, I know your face but I don't think I know your name."

"Perry McIntyre." He handed John Lee a stack of papers and said, "You've been served."

"Huh?"

"Have a good day, Deputy."

***

"Yeah, you're not the only one," D.W. told him in his office five minutes later. "She's suin' you, and me, and Patterson here, and the sheriff's office itself for emotional stress, assault and battery, false arrest, and unlawful imprisonment."

"See? That right there's what I was talkin' about! You let that woman off easy and she turned around and she's suing us for everythin' under the sun. There's your thanks, John Lee. You go to bat for her with the judge and she sticks it in your ass in return."

"I guess no good deed goes unpunished, Fig."

"Stop calling me that! My name is Flag."

"Yeah, and just like a flag, your lips flap all the time in the breeze. I did what I thought was right."

"Ain't nobody pay'in you to think, boy."

"Drop it. What are we going to do about this?"

"I've got a call in to the county supervisors," D.W. said., "This is gonna be a PR nightmare, I can tell you that right now."

"That's what you're worried about, D.W.? How it's goin' to look? Jesus Christ man, why don't you start bein' a real sheriff instead of kowtowing to whatever some damn reporter thinks? I'll tell you right now, if I was sittin' behind that desk..."

"Well you ain't, so shut the hell up! If you don't have anythin' useful to say, get outta' here."

The phone on D.W.'s desk buzzed and he picked up the receiver. "Yeah? Okay, put him on."

He punched the button for the speakerphone and the voice of Melvin Depew, the county attorney, came on the line.

"Sheriff, how are you this afternoon?"

"I was doin' fine until all this nonsense started, Mel."

"Don't sweat it," the attorney said. "This isn't anything more than a nuisance suit. People pull this crap all the time, you know that. At least once a month somebody one of your deputies arrested is threatening to sue us for something."

"Just ticks me off that we gave this woman a break," D.W. said. "She should'a done hard time."

"Well, hindsight is always 20/20. Here's what I want you to do. Have all your deputies file a full report on the incident with this Lorraine Matthews. Along with your dispatcher and anybody else who was there who witnessed it. I talked to Janet Opperman, the prosecutor who was in court with her, and she gave me a rundown on how the woman acted at her first arraignment hearing. I've got a call in to Judge Taylor, too, but he hasn't gotten back to me yet. But it's clear this woman's got some mental issues to go along with a piss poor attitude."

"What about where it says here that she wants Deputies Quarrels and Patterson relieved of duty until the outcome of the trial?"

"What she wants and what she gets are two very different things," Depew said. "You guys just continue on, business as usual. One thing I would say is, if you get any calls involving her, or her husband or her kid, you have somebody else handle them. I don't want those deputies interacting in any way with anybody from that family."

"Mel, John Lee Quarrels here."

"How you doing, John Lee Quarrels?"

"I'm like D.W., I was doing better before all this started, I'll tell you that. Listen, D.W. told those boys they could do some community service instead of us pressing charges against them for that stunt they pulled with the firecrackers. I've got them over at the newspaper office going through stacks of old papers, looking for anything that might relate to those skeletons we found out there on Turpentine Highway. Is that going to be a problem?"

"I think it's best if you have no contact with Herbie Matthews. I'll have somebody from this office call his parents and tell them to go pick him up."

"Okay."

"Again, John Lee, D.W., don't get yourself all worked up over this. These things happen. I've already talked to several of the county supervisors, we're all on the same page here."

"I guess we shouldn't worry too much," Bob Patterson said when the call ended. "But I gotta tell you, now I wish I'd given her a longer blast of that pepper spray!"

***

"Seriously, Mama Nell? Do we have to do this? The man's been dead for almost forty years."

"Don't you sass me John Lee! Jesus has been dead for almost 2,000 years, but I don't see anybody trying to do away with Easter."

His grandmother was wearing a black dress with a veil and had insisted that John Lee and Paw Paw wear suits to dinner. A large velvet portrait of Elvis sat on a side table with candles burning on both sides of it.

"If your Mama Nell wants to honor Elvis's death every year, that's what we're going to do," his grandfather said.

"I don't think it's too much to ask for the man who gave the world so much," Mama Nell said as she scooped salad out of a bowl with two wooden spoons and put them on his plate.

"Are we talking about Jesus or Elvis now?"

She rapped him across the knuckles with one of the spoons.

"Oww!"

"Show some respect, boy. This means a lot to your Mama Nell."

John Lee rubbed his knuckles but nodded. "Yes, sir. Sorry, Mama Nell."

"I can still remember it like it was yesterday," Mama Nell said. "I was at the Piggly Wiggly gettin' hot dogs 'cause we was goin' to have a cookout, and when I get up to the checkout counter Mary Lou Douglas was just cryin' her eyes out. Lord, I thought maybe she just got word that her daddy had passed on or somethin' like that. But it was worse. A whole lot worse! She told me that Mr. Elvis Presley had died. I'll tell you, I didn't believe her. I just stood there with my mouth hangin' open in shock. I don't remember driving home. I just remember bein' back here and sittin' down in front of the TV and watchin' the news bulletins about it. It wasn't like today when you got all those different news channels on all day and all night long, so I had to keep flippin' through the channels. I felt like a part of me had died with him."

John Lee had never understood his grandmother's obsession with the singer, but it had always been a part of his life, a force as strong as the tides or the hurricanes and tornadoes that sometimes battered their way through the county. In Mama Nell's eyes, Elvis Presley *was* a force of nature more than a mortal man. He guessed as obsessions went, it was relatively harmless. Sure, she had spent a fortune on her collection of Elvis memorabilia, everything from a life size Elvis mannequin that stood in the bedroom she shared with Paw Paw (he quickly pushed that image out of his mind, he didn't even like Magic watching him when he was in bed with a woman), to Elvis dolls, posters, and everything else. But his grandparents didn't seem to be lacking the money to live comfortably in their retirement, so what the hell? He darn sure didn't need or want to inherit anything from them. Especially all of the Elvis stuff!

So as they did every year on August 16th, they had their annual Elvis Presley Memorial Dinner. The menu never varied - fried chicken, cornbread, mashed potatoes, homemade country gravy, sauerkraut, and biscuits. Mama Nell had learned one time that those were some of the King's favorite foods, and it seemed to her only fitting and proper that that's what they dined on on the anniversary of his death.

Later, as *Blue Suede Shoes* played in the background, Paw Paw asked him about the investigation into the origin of the skeletons. John Lee told him more of what he had learned about the turpentine camps, and the Somerton family's involvement in that dark period in local history.

"What are you hoping to get out of this, John Lee? Whoever killed those men has probably been dead forever."

"I know, Paw Paw. You're not the first to tell me that. But I just want to know, and D.W. wants to say we closed the case."

His grandfather shook his head with a mirthless smile. "The only thing D.W. Swindle cares about is keeping the voters happy and getting reelected."

"I won't disagree with that," John Lee said. "But what's the alternative? Fig Newton?"

"Oh, hell no! That man is a walking example of everything ugly. Did I tell you he stopped me on my bicycle the other day?"

"On your bike? No. What happened?"

"I was riding down the road and he came up close behind me and gave me a blast on his siren. I never heard him and it just about scared the crap out of me! I stopped and he got out and come swaggering up to me wearing those mirrored sunglasses of his like one of the guards from that old movie *Cool Hand Luke* and chewed me out for obstructing traffic. Said he could confiscate my bike and lock me up."

"Was there any traffic?"

"No! Only vehicle I'd seen in twenty minutes was Gus Sanders in the mail truck."

"I've got a feeling this was more about me than it was about you, Paw Paw. Fig and I have been butting heads lately. I'm sorry if you're getting dragged into the middle of it."

"Don't worry about it, that blowhard doesn't worry me any. I was just mentioning it."

"I'll have a talk with him."

"No, don't do that," Paw Paw said shaking his head. "It'd probably only make matters worse."

John Lee didn't press the issue, but he made up his mind that he was going to let Flag know that he had stepped over the line when he took their personal issues outside of the courthouse and to his family.

Before he could say anymore, Mama Nell came in with a large cake adorned with 42 candles, representing Elvis Presley's age when he died. He resisted the urge to ask her if it was a death cake instead of a birthday cake, because his knuckles were still smarting from getting smacked earlier. So he just closed his eyes while Mama Nell offered a prayer up to Elvis, and ate his cake without comment.

Chapter 44

Stephen Atterbury was drenched in sweat, his hands and face were streaked with black from the ink on the old newspaper pages, when John Lee checked up on him late the next afternoon.

"You look like you could use something cold," John Lee said, handing him a milkshake from Dairy Queen.

"Thank you, that sounds good."

"Any luck so far?"

The boy shook his head. "No, but I'm only back to 1962. Miss Dixie said to just look through the front sections where the news was. We were wasting a lot of time going through every page, where there was a lot of stuff about weddings and funerals and advertising and stuff like that. And with Herbie gone, it's not real fast."

"Yeah, I'm sorry about that," John Lee said.

Stephen shook his head. "Sometimes I wish I never met Herbie, to be honest with you, John Lee. I mean, I'm not trying to blame him for me being involved with that stuff the other night. He didn't have to try too hard to talk me into it. But he always wants to do something like that. His dad's a nice enough guy, but he's kind of pussy... uh, I mean..."

"Were you gonna say pussy whipped?"

Stephen's face was red, but he nodded. "Yeah. Mrs. Matthews orders him and Herbie around all the time and they both just do whatever she says. I think sometimes that's why Herbie gets into some of the stuff he does. Like it's his way of fighting back or something."

"You know something, Stephen? Everybody's got to follow their own path in life. Why does someone like Mr. Matthews let his wife walk on him like that? I don't know. But the fact that you're willing to stand up on your hind legs and take responsibility for what you did, and not try to say it was all Herbie's idea, that tells me a lot about the kind of man you're going to be. Makes me proud of you."

"I know what we did was wrong, John Lee. But I have to tell you, it was kind of funny, too. Up there on the roof of the school we could hear Obie yelling, "Don't shoot! I surrender. I give up!""

John Lee laughed so hard tears came to his eyes. "That *is* funny, but if you ever tell anybody I was laughing about it, I'm gonna have to kick your ass."

"I promise, I won't tell," Stephen said, holding up his fist to bump with John Lee's.

"I tell you what, it'd take forever to go through all these, and you probably wouldn't find anything anyway. When you finish your milkshake, go ahead and clean up and go home."

"But I've still got like eleven hours to go to work off what Sheriff Swindle said I needed to do."

"How about we call it early release, credit for good behavior and all that?"

"No sir," Stephen said shaking his head. "I made a deal with the sheriff and I aim to keep my end of it."

John Lee looked at the boy and then slapped him on the shoulder as he stood up. "You know what, Stephen? Once you get a few more years behind you, if you ever decide to become a deputy, I'd be damn proud to ride patrol with you."

"Really?"

"Yeah, really."

"Thanks, John Lee!"

He left the boy there amid the piles of newsprint, chatted with Dixie for a few minutes on his way out, and then went back to the courthouse for a staff meeting and briefing on the investigation into Ray Ray Watkins' murder.

All of the deputies were disheartened that no progress had been made on the case. The State Crime Lab and the FBI had exhausted every avenue available. The best pieces of evidence they had were the bullets and empty cartridge cases found at the earlier shooting scenes, and the tire tracks that had been recovered when Greg Carson had come under the sniper's fire. But they all led to nothing. The FBI said the tire tracks were from a very common Goodyear model of tire that could be found on hundreds of pickup trucks and sport utility vehicles in the region. Ballistic tests had determined that the bullets had been fired from the same rifle and the cartridge cases were all from the same lot and had been sold at least a decade earlier.

"We don't want this case goin' cold," Flag said. "Ray Ray deserves more than that. I know you've talked to everybody you can think of, but go talk to 'em again. Somebody out there knows somethin' and it's our job to pry it out of 'em."

"Flag's right," D.W. said. In spite of their personal animosity, the Sheriff and the Chief Deputy tried to put on a good front for the troops. Not that any of them were unaware of things happening behind the scenes. "I heard a sayin' one time that nobody lives in a vacuum. What that means is we all know and talk to other people some way or other. Whoever did this ain't braggin' 'bout it, but maybe somebody recalls somethin' and they don't know how important it might be. Could be somethin' as simple as somebody askin' about it, askin' if anybody heard anything new. Now, I know people been talking about it all over the place, but that's startin' to die down. So if somebody's still askin' if anybody's heard anything, that might be one of them indicators that he's takin' more interest in it than others. Makes you wonder why. Or maybe somebody recalls seeing somebody out target shootin' with a rifle with a scope on it. Anything at all."

Maddy raised her hand. "Has anybody thought to check the tire shops?"

"Pretty common tread. Three places in the county sell those kind of tires. And accordin' to the FBI they weren't new."

"But could it be possible that whoever did it changed tires? Like, they wanted to get them off their vehicle, even if they weren't worn out?"

"Don't know if we ever thought about that," D.W. said. He looked at Flag, who shrugged his shoulders.

"You and Bob make a list of every tire shop around and start contactin' them. Not just in Somerton County, but every place within a hundred miles of here. That's good police work, Maddy."

"Has that reward that Somerton Forest Products put out done us any good at all, or just brought in a lot of dead ends and nuts?"

"Not yet, but you never know. We keep followin' up on everything we get. Okay, anything else? No? Well keep at it, people. We're not goin' to give up on this. Sooner or later we're goin' to find this guy, and when we do, we're goin' to come down on him with both feet.

As the meeting was breaking up, John Lee approached Flag. "Got a minute?"

"What do you need?"

"We need to talk in your office."

Flag didn't say anything, just turned and led the way upstairs and then down the hall to his office. He sat behind his desk and asked, "What do you want?"

"Stay away from my family."

"Say what?"

"I didn't stutter, Fig."

"You talkin' about me chewin' out your grandfather the other day?"

"Don't do it again."

"You need to watch yourself, Deputy. You're steppin' over the line."

"No, *you* stepped over the line. Don't do it again."

"You think just because that old hippie is kinfolk to you means he don't have to obey the law? I'm supposed to turn my head the other way and ignore it when he's creating a traffic hazard? Hell boy, I was lookin' out for his own good! Somebody could'a come down that road and run him over. You ought'a be thankin' me for lookin' out for him 'cause he damn sure needs someone to keep an eye on him. Probably fried his brain with psychedelic mushrooms or some shit like that fifty years ago."

"First and last warning, Fig. You got a problem with me, let's you and me handle it, whenever you're ready. In the meantime, don't be going after Paw Paw because you don't have the balls to take me on directly."

The Chief Deputy shot out of his chair and started around his desk. John Lee braced himself, fists balled and ready to fight. Flag had a couple of inches and at least 75 pounds on him, but John Lee wasn't worried. In fact, he was looking forward to settling things between the two of them, once and for all.

"Both of you, stand down right now!"

They had not been aware of D.W. coming to the door of Flag's office, drawn by their shouting.

"I'm done takin' shit from this mongrel," Flag said. "I'm goin' to mop the floor with him, and I'm goin' to do it right now!"

"If you two want to fight it out, I got no problem with that at all," the sheriff said. "But you ain't doing it here. We can all go out in the garage where there ain't no citizens watchin' and you can beat each other to death for all I care. But not here."

"Let's do it. I'm ready," John Lee said.

Flag looked at the younger man like he wanted to tear him limb from limb, but after a moment he backed down.

"You'd like that, wouldn't you D.W.? Then when I whip his ass you'll use that as an excuse to fire me."

"Ain't gonna do no such thing. You're both grown men, go settle it like men."

"That's what you say now. But as soon as it's over with you'll forget all about that."

Flag was backpedaling and all three of them knew it.

"If it makes you feel any better, I'll let you throw the first punch," John Lee said. "Because you're gonna need it."

"Fuck you, you little maggot. Fuck both of you. I ain't got time for this shit."

"Yeah, just what I thought," D.W. said. "You ain't got time. You got your chance, Flag. It's put up or shut up time. What's it goin' to be?"

"Why don't you go kiss ass with some reporter somewhere, D.W.? And you, why don't you find one of his daughters to stick your dick into? That's all you're both good at." Flag shouldered his way past the sheriff and walked down the hall.

Looking after him, D.W. said, "You're goin' to have to kick his ass or kill him one of these days. You know that, don't you, John Lee?"

"Yeah, I do. And I'll tell you something D.W., at this point I really don't care which one it is."

Chapter 45

Stephen Atterbury had long since put in his twenty hours of community service, but he continued to go to the newspaper office every day to spend time searching through the old stacks. John Lee wasn't sure if it was dedication, a desire to help find something that would be useful in solving the mystery of the three dead men, or the obvious crush he had developed on Dixie Landrum.

The deputy couldn't blame him. Dixie was in her mid-20s, and though she carried a couple of extra pounds, she was a good looking woman, confident, intelligent, and with a great sense of humor.

"He's a good kid," she said. "Says he's fascinated by all those old newspaper stories. Maybe we've got a new journalist in the making. What do you think?"

"I think maybe he's more fascinated by what he sees up here in the front office than all of that dusty stuff in the back," John Lee said.

Dixie smiled and looked toward the back room. "You noticed that, too? I was thinking it was just my imagination."

"Fifteen year old boys are not exactly subtle," John Lee said.

"And the sad thing is, he's one of the nicest guys in town, present company excepted," Dixie told him. "I wish he had an older brother."

"Are you saying the pickings are slim?"

"Oh, there's some nice guys. Problem is, most of them are married. And I just haven't clicked with any of the ones who aren't."

"Give the kid two or three years and he'll be legal," John Lee said "Meanwhile, you can train him right."

"Don't think I haven't thought about it," Dixie said with a laugh. "Unless you've got any brothers."

"Not that I know of. I guess I could do one of those Ancestry search things and see if I can find one for you that I don't know about."

"Well if you do, send him my way."

"I'll do it," John Lee promised.

"Hey, John Lee, come look at this."

He went into the back room, where Stephen had an old newspaper laid out on top of a stack.

"This don't say nothing about those skeletons you found, I just thought it was interesting because it's about one of the Somerton's."

The yellowed newspaper, dated March, 15, 1962, had a black and white photograph on the front page of two dump trucks parked alongside the road, along with a police car. The bold headline in 72 point type stretched across the top of the page and read "Standoff on Turpentine Road".

John Lee read the story with fascination:

Yesterday Sheriff William Allen and his deputies were involved in a three hour standoff on Turpentine Road when Richard E. Somerton accosted workers involved in the widening project of the road. According to Sheriff Allen, Mr. Somerton claimed that the construction crew was trespassing on property owned by the Somerton Lumber Company and threatened to shoot them if they continued. The Somerton Lumber Company has extensive landholdings in the county and had resisted the road widening project in court until the county prevailed under eminent domain laws. The newly improved road, when finished, will be blacktopped and run all the way to Live Oak. County Supervisors have said the thoroughfare will greatly improve traffic and be a boost to commerce throughout the county. The standoff ended when Mr. Somerton was taken into custody and later released after paying a $50 fine for disturbing the peace. Mr. Somerton, age 35, is a World War II veteran and the assistant manager of the Somerton Lumber Yard. When questioned about the incident, he said that he felt it was important for citizens to stand up for their rights and that the Somerton family does not believe the county's confiscation of a right-of-way through their property is legal.

"That's pretty cool, isn't it? I mean like, not cool that he was out there with a gun, but still pretty neat, don't you think?"

"What I think, Stephen, is that you may have found something that's going to help us figure out where those skeletons came from after all!"

John Lee slapped the young man on the back, then took the paper out front to show it to Dixie.

***

It had been fourteen years since John Lee had been to the Somerton family compound seven miles from town, and a lot had changed in that time period. The big house was still there in all its glory, a true antebellum mansion complete with four white columns in front. But off to the side there was now a sprawling ranch house, which he assumed was where Troy lived with his wife Melinda, who had been a year behind them in high school.

John Lee stopped the Charger in front of the main house and got out, memories flooding through him as he walked up the three steps to the porch and crossed to the huge door. He pushed the doorbell and heard chimes sounding inside. A moment later a tired looking black woman in a formal maid's uniform opened the door.

"Can I help you?"

"Yes ma'am, is Mr. Somerton in?"

"Which one?"

"Grandpa... I mean Mr. Somerton, senior."

"He's resting. He takes a nap about this time every afternoon."

"Okay, how about Mr...."

"John Lee? Is that you?"

The woman was nothing short of striking; tall, with thick, long chestnut hair, brown eyes, high cheekbones, and perfect skin. The years had been very kind to her.

"Hello Ashleigh."

"Well come in! Mary, would you get us some tea? Or would you prefer lemonade, John Lee?"

"Neither," he said, stepping through the door.

The maid left them there in the wide foyer and Ashleigh said, "Look at you, all handsome in your uniform and everything. How long's it been?"

"Not long enough," he told her.

She feigned a pout on her face. "Don't be mean."

"I came to talk to your grandfather. Or your father, either one."

"Come and sit with me, John Lee. We need to catch up after all these years."

"I've got nothing to say to you, Ashleigh. Like I said, I'm here to talk to your father or your grandfather."

"You used to have lots of things to say to me back in the old days."

"Yeah, I did. And you never listened."

"Come on, John Lee. That's ancient history. Don't dredge up the past."

"It may be ancient history to you, but I don't forget."

She frowned at him. "Be nice. You're going to hurt my feelings."

"I don't give a damn about your feelings."

"There was a time when you cared a lot about my feelings."

"You're right, there was," John Lee told her. "That was before you killed our baby."

Chapter 46

It had seemed so romantic back then. The most beautiful girl in the county, daughter of the richest family around, and the boy from the wrong side of the tracks, if Somerton would have had any railroad tracks. Over her parents' strong objections, or maybe because of them, John Lee and Ashleigh were inseparable during their senior year in high school. He was head over heels in love, as only a young man can be with a beautiful, passionate young woman like her. It didn't matter that he had no future, all they cared about was the moment. And many of those moments were spent in the back seat of his old Chevrolet.

A month before graduation he learned that she was pregnant. He didn't hear it from Ashleigh herself, who had suddenly become withdrawn and was avoiding him. He didn't know what he had done wrong and was frantic to try to make up for whatever it had been. The news had come to him from her best friend, Darcy Jackson. When confronted, standing in front of her locker one afternoon after the last class of the day, Ashleigh had admitted the truth and told him her parents had ordered her to stay away from him.

John Lee had immediately gone to her father and told him he planned to do the right thing. Yes, he knew they were young, but that didn't matter. They loved each other and they would make it work. They'd get married and he'd worked two jobs or whatever it took to support his wife and child.

Richard Somerton, known by everyone as Junior, a name he despised, had laughed in his face and called him white trash. "Get outta' my sight boy, before I shoot you. You think my daughter's going to spend her life with a mongrel like you?"

"I know this isn't the best way for things to start out, sir, but I love her. And I know she loves me!"

Ashleigh's father had walked across the polished hardwood floor of his den to one of the pair of matching big oak gun cabinets, opened one of the glass fronted double doors, and taken out one of the beautifully engraved Purdey side-by-side shotguns that he had custom-made by a company in England. "I'm not going to tell you again, you little bastard.

Get out of my house and off my property. If you ever come near my daughter again I'm gonna blow you in half and nobody will do a damn thing about it. You hear me boy? Now git!"

John Lee wasn't going to give up that easy. He caught up with Ashleigh the next day at in the school cafeteria and begged her to run away with him to Georgia that weekend. "We can get married and be back here in time for class Monday morning. Nobody will know anything about it. You turn eighteen two weeks after graduation and then there's nothing your father can do to keep us apart."

She had laughed and said that was very noble of him, but he was putting way too much into the relationship. " Get real. It was fun, John Lee. But I don't plan to spend my life in a house trailer married to a good old boy, with half a dozen kids hanging onto my ankles."

"But I love you!"

"Well I don't love you. It was just good times, okay? That's all. Get over yourself."

He had begged, actually dropped down on his knees and begged, but she just looked at him without pity and turned and walked away, dismissing him like one would some insignificant life form far down on the evolution timeline.

Soon after, Ashleigh's mother had taken her to a private hospital in Miami, where she had gotten an abortion. A week after graduation she and her mother had taken off on a tour of Europe. Heartbroken, he had joined the Army, vowing never to return. But when his enlistment was up three years later, that's just what he had done. He had never known why, except that it was home.

By then John Lee's friendship with Troy had cooled, understandably, but he heard Ashleigh had gone off to some fancy college up in New England somewhere. There had been news once in a while, a piece in the newspaper when she married a lawyer from Savannah, another story a few years later about her coming back to Somerton County that did not mention the husband. By then John Lee didn't care, but he was never able to forget what might have been, or to forgive her.

***

"John Lee Quarrels. What the hell you doing here? Didn't I run you off years ago and tell you never to come back?"

Ashley's father was a big man with a shock of white hair and thick, bushy eyebrows that reminded John Lee of two albino caterpillars making their way across the top of his forehead.

"Now Daddy, that's no way to talk to our company."

"He ain't company, he's a mutt, just like he's always been."

The man was standing in the door of his den, the same den where they had had their last conversation, so many years ago.

"I need to talk to you, Mr. Somerton."

"I've got nothing to say to you. Get the hell out of here."

"This is official business."

"Whatever it is, you go back and tell D.W. Swindle to come talk to me himself, or else to send somebody else."

"I'm not leaving here until I talk to you. Now, we can do it here in front of your daughter and the help, or we can do it in your den. Makes no difference to me."

He stared at the deputy for a moment with a look on his face that showed exactly how little he thought of him or his badge.

"You always was a hell raiser, John Lee."

"Where's it going to be?"

He didn't like it, but he could tell by the look on John Lee's face that he wasn't going anywhere.

"Get the hell in here."

Nothing much had changed in the den. The same huge desk, the cigar store Indian standing in the corner, the trophy bucks hanging on the wall, the Frederic Remington prints, the same gun cabinets with their expensive rifles and shotguns.

Somerton sat down behind his desk, leaving John Lee standing there.

"Say what you came to say and get out of here."

"Do you know anything about those skeletons we found out on Turpentine Highway?"

"Just what I read in the newspaper. Why?"

John Lee took out the brass disc and showed it to him. "Have you ever seen one of these before?"

"Yeah, I know what it is. Troy told me about it. Why are you nosing around in our business, anyway?"

"Because three men got killed out there. Because someone's been shooting at deputies and because one of those deputies is dead."

"First of all, whoever killed those niggers a long time ago is probably dead by now. And whoever it was, there's no way to prove they had anything to do with Somerton Lumber. That little piece of junk could've come from anywhere. Even if one of them had it on them, that don't mean nothing except they were on the run, which was against the law back then. As for someone shooting at deputies, that don't have a damn thing to do with those bones. Probably some kind of crazy person. Now, I'm sorry that your friend got killed, but it has nothing to do with me or my family. But I will say, as far as I'm concerned, the wrong one took that bullet in the head."

"What about this?"

John Lee opened up a copy of the newspaper story about the standoff on Turpentine Road so long ago. Somerton looked at it and flipped it back across his desk dismissively.

"What about it?"

"That's your father, right?"

"So what? What's that got to do with anything?"

"Why was he out there waving a gun around trying to stop those guys working on the road way back then?"

"How the hell do I know? It says here he was mad because they were taking part of our property. My Daddy never was one to bend over and take it in the ass. None of us Somertons are. We stand up for ourselves. When someone pushes us, it don't matter who, we push right back. And we don't stop pushin' 'til we win. You need to think about that when you come here throwin' your weight around."

"I want to talk to him."

"Daddy? Forget it, he's 88 years old and probably don't remember nothing about those days."

"Don't let age fool you," John Lee said. "I was just talking to a man who's older than him the other day, and he remembers a lot."

"What are you getting at? What are you trying to prove, coming out here like this?"

"I think some of your thugs are the ones who killed those people way back then. And I plan to prove it."

"My thugs? Christ, man, that happened years before I was born."

"Maybe not your thugs, but they worked for Somerton Lumber."

"I don't have any idea what happened to those men, and neither do you. Now, you haul your ass back to town and don't you dare come out here again! You remember when I pointed a shotgun at you last time you were here? Well, I've still got it, and I meant what I said that day. I see you around here again I'm gonna blow you in half!"

"Are you threatening a deputy?"

"No, I'm threatening a piece of shit who don't know his place in the world and never did. If you think I'm impressed by that god damned tin badge of yours, you're only fooling yourself. Now get on outta here! I mean it!"

John Lee was almost hoping the man would try to point a shotgun at him again. But he knew that those feelings were based more on the past than the present.

"I want to talk to your father," he repeated.

"Then you go get yourself a warrant and you show up back here with a whole bunch of backup. Because I promise you right now, you're going to need it."

Chapter 47

"Do ya' sit up at night thinkin' of ways to make my life more difficult? Do you know that Junior Somerton was on the phone to me two minutes after you pulled out of his driveway yesterday?"

"That doesn't surprise me, D.W. But I'm telling you, he knows something about those skeletons we found."

"Everybody knows something about them! Hell, it was on the news for three or four days in a row!"

John Lee noted that his father-in-law's language was drifting back towards the norm. He wasn't sure if it was because of the stress from the things that had taken place in recent weeks, or if his short lived religious experience was wearing off now that it seemed like he wasn't going to keel over from another heart attack anytime soon.

"I really need to talk to the old man."

"Richard Senior? You stay away from there, John Lee! I mean it."

"Are you telling me to drop an investigation into a triple murder because you don't want to offend the Somerton family? Because if that's what you're saying, D.W., I'll turn in my resignation right now."

"When did you get so damn dedicated? There was a time when all you wanted to do was put in your time, drive fast with lights and sirens on, and go home at the end of the day."

"There was a time when I had something to go home to."

The sheriff averted his eyes and shook his head, and his tone of voice became subdued. "I wish it was different between you and Emily. I really do. Me and her mama, we've talked to her 'til we're blue in the face but it don't do no good at all."

"I know the feeling."

"For what it's worth, it ain't you, John Lee. I know that."

"It is what it is," he said.

D.W. spat a brown stream of juice into the spittoon, then sighed.

"When did life get so darned complicated?"

"Well, those that go to church might say it was back when Eve took a bite of that apple. I don't know, D.W. Emily keeps telling me to give her more time, and I keep asking her how long she needs."

"I love my daughter," the sheriff said, "love both of 'em, even though I don't approve of a lot of what they do. But I'm goin' to tell you this, John Lee. Not as your father-in-law, but man to man. Both those girls are jerkin' you around like a puppet on a string. Sooner or later you're gonna have to cut the strings from both of them and get on with your life."

"I'm not ready to give up on Emily yet. Sometimes when I wake up in the morning I think I am, but by the next day I'm right back where I started."

"And what about Beth Ann? How long do ya' think that's goin' to go on?"

"I don't know. Look, D.W., I appreciate you trying to help, but with all due respect..."

Before he could continue, Sheila Sharp barged into the sheriff's office without knocking. Both men looked at her, startled. "Somebody just found a dead body out by Copperhead Creek. Looks like it was a hit-and-run!"

***

John Lee's stomach sank when he pulled up behind Danny Ray's patrol car a quarter-mile past the bridge and saw the mangled remains of the old three wheeled bicycle. He walked up to where the other deputy stood on the shoulder. Down in the ditch was the broken body of Mister Donald. The old man was halfway on his side, eyes opened as if staring at him. John Lee knew that he was dead, but it felt like the accusing eyes were blaming him for getting the old gentleman involved in something that had kept him from dying in his sleep like a man his age deserved to do.

"A couple of kids on dirt bikes found him and went home and told their dad," Danny Ray said. "He come down here to see for himself, then called it in. No skid marks on the pavement, it's like whoever hit him did it on purpose."

"Son of a bitch!"

John Lee crawled down the steep embankment and squatted beside the body. Mister Donald had laid there a long time. He was sure he had been run down the night before when he finished fishing and started for his old mobile home not far away. Blood had trickled from the old man's mouth and nose and crusted on the side of his face. John Lee brushed away the flies that were hovering over him. He heard sirens coming from off in the distance, the noise growing louder. He felt like telling the ambulance crew to slow down, that there was nobody here left to save. Instead he took the old man's stiff hand and said, "I'm sorry, Mister Donald. I'm am so damn sorry!"

***

Mister Donald had been more than a janitor, he had been an institution at Somerton High School. Generations of students had known and admired the crusty old man who greeted them all by name every day and never hesitated to offer a friendly word of advice, whether it was to a lovestruck boy (don't let the little head do the thinkin' for the big one, son) or a girl who might be tempted to trade her virtue for a class ring (ain't nobody goin' to buy a cow when the milk is free, missy).

Over three hundred of those students came to his funeral, filling the bleachers on one side of the small high school gymnasium. James Nelson, the superintendent of schools, gave the eulogy, reminding those in attendance that while Mister Donald was gone, his legacy would live on inside all of them who had been touched by the humble, hard-working man who had bridged racial barriers and social status to become a friend to all.

"Whether you were a student, a member of the faculty, a school administrator like myself, or a parent, we were all equal in Mister Donald's eyes. He never cared who you were or what your name was, he cared about *what* you were. He cared about the kind of human being you were. And I believe all of us are better human beings for having known him."

The overhead lights dimmed while teachers and former students went to the podium and shared their memories of Mister Donald. As they spoke, a projector showed yearbook pictures from over the years on a large screen. One was of the janitor posing jauntily with his mop and bucket, a big smile on his face. Another showed the captain of the football team presenting him with the game ball from a homecoming victory long ago. There were other pictures, candid shots of Mister

Donald and students taken by members of the school photography club and yearbook staff who were now grown up and had children of their own, and in some cases grandchildren, attending Somerton's schools.

Watching the slideshow and thinking about the old times and Mister Donald, an image flashed on the screen and suddenly John Lee felt his skin began to prickle. He had heard the term about one's "blood running cold" but had never experienced it until that moment.

Feeling his body stiffen in the seat beside her, Maddy turned to him. "Are you okay?"

He couldn't reply, barely managed to nod his head.

She looked at him with concern. "What is it?"

Again, he didn't reply. The last of the speakers was finishing, the lights were turned back up, and the pallbearers came forward to carry the casket outside to where a hearse was waiting to take Mister Donald for his last ride.

By the time they made their way through the crowd the doors of the hearse had closed and it was pulling out of the parking lot, followed by a long line of cars, all headed toward the cemetery.

"What is it, John Lee? You look like you saw a ghost or something?"

"No," he said, shaking his head. "Not a ghost. I saw a killer."

Chapter 48

Three days later he followed the silver gray Mercedes G-Class SUV at a distance until they were two miles outside of town, then turned on his overhead lights. It took the driver a moment to notice him, but when he did the SUV pulled to the side of the road. He checked to make sure his dashboard camera and body cam were working before he got out of the Charger and walked up to the Mercedes.

The driver was waiting with license and registration in hand.

"What did I do, officer?" Then recognizing who had pulled him over added. "John Lee. What are you doing?"

"Step out of the car, please."

"Really?"

"If you would, please."

"Okay. Why so formal?"

"I want to show you something."

The driver got out and asked, "What is it?"

"This."

"The *Guardian*? You pulled me over to show me a high school yearbook?"

John Lee opened the book to a marked page and pointed to a photograph of four young men.

"Look familiar?"

"Why, sure it does. Me and you and Patrick McKibbon, and Dan Westfall. What about it?

"What were we then? Sixteen, seventeen years old?"

"I guess. If you want to reminisce about the old days, can we do it someplace besides standing alongside the road at the end of the day?"

"You were a good looking kid back then."

"I like to think I'm still halfway decent looking."

John Lee turned to the back of the book and pulled out a photograph.

"What's this?"

"It's your grandfather, Troy. It's a print of a picture I took on my phone at the historical museum a while back. Something about it looked familiar and I couldn't place it. I didn't until we were at Mister Donald's funeral and they were showing all those old pictures from back in the school days. They had that picture of the four of us up on the screen. Do you remember seeing it? Oh, that's right, you didn't make it to the funeral, did you?"

"I wanted to. I really did. But I was stuck down in Gainesville in a meeting. I'll tell you, John Lee, there are times I think the worst thing my Daddy ever did was turnin' the business over to me to run. It's like I never have any time to do anything I want to any more. Hey, we still need to get out on a boat someplace and catch us some fish."

"You weren't at Ray Ray Watkins' funeral either."

"Ray Ray? I didn't really know him all that well. He wasn't in our class. I think he was a couple of years after us."

"Did you know the FBI and the State Crime Lab had people up there taking pictures at his funeral?"

"Why would they do that?"

"They said sometimes murderers go to someone's funeral. I don't know if they do that to make sure the person's really dead, or to gloat, or what."

"I guess you can never know what goes through somebody's head that would do something crazy like that."

"You know what I think, Troy? I think there might be some people who stay away from the funeral of somebody they killed, too. Maybe because of guilt."

"Maybe so. Like I said, crazy people do all sort of things."

"Is that going to be your defense, Troy?"

"What the hell you talking about, John Lee?"

"Is that going to be your defense? Are you going to plead insanity? I imagine with your family's money you could find a high dollar lawyer that might get you off that way. Sure, you'd spend some time in one of those fancy treatment facilities, where you could play tennis all day long or something, but that's better than getting the death penalty."

"This conversation is over."

"Like I said, that picture was familiar to me. But I figured whoever that guy was on the horse, he was probably dead a long time ago. Then when I saw that picture of the four of us up on the screen at Mister Donald's funeral, those eyes and that nose and forehead. Your grandpa would've been nineteen or so back then. The family resemblance is amazing, isn't it? You were the spitting image of him when he was a young man."

"Okay, I'm out of here. If you've got anything else to say to me, you can talk to my attorney."

"I remember that .308 rifle," John Lee said. "What was it, between our sophomore and junior year, when your dad bought it for you when he took you to Montana to go deer hunting? You came back with that big old ten point buck. Your old man's still got it hanging in his den. What did you say it went field dressed? Three hundred pounds or something like that?"

Troy didn't respond.

"You always were a hell of a shot. I remember when we were kids plinking with .22s, you were the best shot of any of us, even with open sights. I imagine with the scope it wasn't hard at all, was it?"

"John Lee, you're crazy."

"No, we've already had that conversation. You're the one who's going to plead insanity. Otherwise they're going to take you to Raiford and stick a needle in your arm."

"Are we done here? I already told you, if you want to say anything else to me..."

"I don't think you meant to kill Ray Ray. You're too good a shot for that. The way he was twisted in the seat, those folks from the state think he turned to look in the back for something just as you pulled the trigger. There was no way you could have prevented that. Well, except for not shooting in the first place. No, I think the first time, out there at the construction site, you were just reacting without thinking. You heard about those bones and you remembered how your grandpa used to talk about the war and how much he loved killing the Japs. When we were kids, that was exciting. I also remember him talking about riding hard on the niggers. Back then I thought he meant making the black folks at the company work hard. But I was wrong, wasn't I, Troy? No, he was one of the camp captains. And he liked it. He liked having that kind of power. Maybe he couldn't kill Japs anymore, but who was going to miss a stray nigger now and then?"

"Don't talk about my grandfather that way, John Lee. You don't know what the hell you're talkin' about. That man was a hero! He fought his way halfway across the Pacific."

"No, he didn't," John Lee said. "He went in right at the tail end of the war, and when I was able to pull his records from back then from the Department of the Army, they said he never saw any combat. He spent his time guarding prisoners in the Philippines long after the shooting was done there. But I think he got a taste of it then. Who knows? Maybe one of them tried to escape and he shot him? Or maybe he just shot a couple of them because he wanted to. I figure Japs were just another kind of nigger to him. Who cared if he killed one now and then? But apparently somebody did care. He got a General Discharge. That's what they give you when you're unfit for service, but they can't prove you did something bad enough to court-martial you for."

"You shut up! You shut up right now!"

"Or what, Troy? Are you going to kill me like you did Ray Ray? Oh, that's right, that was an accident, wasn't it? But running down Mister Donald, that wasn't any accident. I showed that old man the picture on my phone, the picture of your grandfather. He said he didn't know who it was, but he knew. I blame myself for that as much as you. When your dad said your grandpa was too old to bother, I told him about the old man I talked to. A man who was a lot older than him, and still sharp as a tack. When we do talk to your grandfather, I wonder what he's going to have to say."

"Grandpa is batshit crazy. He could say anything, that doesn't make it real!"

"So anyway, here's the way I see it. You heard about those skeletons we found, and either your grandpa told you about killing them men or you'd figured it out before, I don't know. But the way that old man used to talk, I think you knew. That's why he was out there when they were widening the road so long ago. He thought the road crew back then was going to dig them up, but they didn't. But over time the road expanded. Hell, they even started calling it a highway. Then they went and widened it again and uncovered your family's dirty little secret. Did you think firing a couple shots our way was going to make us forget the whole thing? Then when you realized how stupid you'd been, that's when you shot at Greg Carson's car, and then at Ray Ray. You were thinking that would throw us off the trail and we wouldn't connect the two things, right? Who cares about some guys that got themselves killed a lifetime ago when somebody's shooting at deputies today? And as terrible as Ray Ray getting killed was, it totally took the focus off those skeletons, didn't it?"

"I'll say this for you, John Lee, you're wasting your time being a cop. You ought to get yourself a typewriter and start writing detective stories, because you've got one hell of an imagination!" Troy walked back to the driver's door of his Mercedes and opened it. "Now like I said, and I'm telling you for the last time, anything else you want to say, you say to my attorney."

"I hope you hire yourself a good one," John Lee said. "And I wouldn't wait too long to call him. Because I've got everything I need to convict you and I'm taking it back to D.W. right now. I guess maybe that grandfather of yours is too old to prosecute, but I really hope the stress gives the old bastard a heart attack so he can burn in hell."

"Don't do this, John Lee."

"I'm just doing my job."

"I can make it worth your while. How much? Name your price."

"You might be able to afford to buy fancy cars and boats and even women like Jolene Thompson. But you'll never have enough money to buy me, Troy."

"We're friends."

"I don't have friends who are murderers."

"Please, John Lee, I'm begging you. I never meant to kill Ray Ray. It was just like you said. He moved at the last minute just as I was squeezing the trigger. And Mister Donald? Come on, he was like a hundred years old. It's not like he had long left in this world anyhow, and who's going to miss an old nigger anyway?"

"Come on back here so I can put handcuffs on you, Troy."

"That's not going to happen. Not today, and not ever."

"You're under arrest for the murder of..."

The gun had been in the door pocket of the Mercedes, a .40 Smith & Wesson semi-automatic. John Lee saw it in Troy's hand as he turned back to him and was already diving sideways when the first shot rang out, the bullet passing so close by that he felt the hot buzz from it on his face.

John Lee rolled behind the back of the Mercedes and pulled his Browning from its holster.

"Drop the gun, Troy."

"I'll see you in hell before I do that!"

John Lee rose up and scooted to the passenger side of the car as Troy came around the back end, pistol at the ready.

"Drop it!"

But Troy didn't drop it. Instead he pointed his gun at John Lee. The deputy felt the Browning's recoil as he fired three quick rounds. The first one hit Troy in the chest and staggered his old friend backward, but he managed to raise his pistol again. The second and third shots hit within three inches of the first, the jacketed hollow point bullets shredding muscle and tissue on their deadly path. Troy's gun dropped from his limp fingers and he fell backward onto the hood of John Lee's Charger, then slid to the ground.

The distance between them had only been ten feet at the most, but it felt like a mile as John Lee cautiously approached, ready to shoot again if necessary. One look told him he didn't need to do that. He slid the safety up on the Browning to engage it and holstered his weapon. He stepped over Troy's body to get to his radio and called the dispatcher.

"This is County 16, officer involved shooting on Washington Road two miles east of town. Suspect down."

"10-4, County 16, units responding. Are you okay, John Lee?"

He wanted to tell Sheila that he wasn't okay, that he didn't know if he would ever be okay again. But all he said was, "Suspect is down. I'm not hurt."

Epilogue

John Lee was put on two weeks paid administrative leave while the Florida Department of Law Enforcement conducted the investigation into the fatal shooting of Richard Troy Somerton. There was some question about why he had chosen to confront Troy Somerton alongside a road instead bringing him to the Sheriff's Department or at his office, but nobody questioned his explanation that he wanted to save his old friend from embarrassment in the event that John Lee was wrong in his accusations. After all, everyone in the county was accustomed to handling the rich and powerful Somertons with kid gloves. But the video and audio from John Lee's dash camera and body cam made it obvious that the deputy had no choice, and had only resorted to deadly force when the murder suspect refused to surrender and had attacked him with a handgun. When investigators executed a search warrant at the dead man's home and found the scoped Remington Mohawk .308 bolt action rifle used in the shootings, there was no question about Troy's guilt. John Lee was cleared of any wrongdoing in the case and allowed to go back to work.

He delayed his return to uniform by one day so he could attend the joint funeral of the three men whose remains had been discovered on Turpentine Highway. Shania Jones, wearing a conservative black dress and heels, attended the funeral. John Lee liked the way she looked in it. Not many women in Somerton County wore dresses any more, except to church and funerals. She told him she was sorry that they had not been able to recover enough DNA to identify the murder victims. "It's just been too long. Time and weather and the elements destroyed anything we might have been able to find."

"That's okay, I know you tried," he told her. "That's all any of us can do."

There were only a half dozen or so people at the funeral and they had all left except for the two of them, lingering to watch the common grave being filled back in.

"If it's any consolation to you, I hear the old man is bragging about how he and his posse chased them down and taught them a lesson. That should be enough to get a conviction, shouldn't it?"

"I wish it was," John Lee told her. "But he's also telling people about how he was riding on the same tank with General Patton when he rolled into the concentration camp at Auschwitz, and how he helped raise the flag on Iwo Jima. Swears he's one of those guys in that picture of the flag raising. Also swears he shot Lee Harvey Oswald in Dallas after he assassinated John F. Kennedy."

"So he's not competent to stand trial?"

"At his age, what good would it do?"

"What about the lady that's suing you and the county for you almost shooting her kid?"

"It's not going to go anywhere," John Lee said. "That's the least of my worries."

"Hey, you were exonerated for the shooting right?"

"Yeah."

"So except for your messed up love-life, and the fact that the Chief Deputy still wants to kick your ass, and that you've got that pretty blonde deputy friend of yours standing on the sidelines, what else do you have to worry about?"

The cemetery workers had finished filling in the grave and were patting the dirt down with the backs of their shovels.

"I'm worried that when I take you to dinner tonight, you're going to find some place that serves sushi."

Turn The Page For A Sneak Peek At
The Gecko In The Corner, **The Second Book In
The John Lee Quarrels Series, Coming Soon!**

Pain. A depth of pain he had never experienced before. A depth of pain he had never known existed. The beating had been terrible, but it was only the start. At some point he had passed out and his tormentors had stopped hitting and kicking him and had waved an ammonia capsule under his nose to bring him back to consciousness. Then they brought out the pruning shears.

They didn't take off his left pinkie finger all at once. That would have been too quick. And too kind. Instead they had removed the tip, then used the same ammonia capsule to revive him while they took off another section. He had passed out a third time and once more they had brought him around, the acrid smell of the ammonia ampule doing its job, awakening him so he could experience the agony as they finished the job.

***

How long had he been driving? Hours only, but it seemed like days. He wanted to stop and sleep, but he knew if he did they would find him. Not those two, they were dead. But Torres had more where they came from and he knew whoever he sent for him this time would be even more brutal.

How much further? Could he make it before fatigue and pain and loss of blood took their toll and his abused body finally gave out like an old jalopy that had been pushed to its last mile before finally disintegrating into a heap of rusted metal and rubber and glass with it's oil and gasoline and grease spilling out onto the blacktop, just like his blood was leaking out of him? He looked at the GPS, finding it hard to focus his eyes. Three more miles. Three more miles was nothing. He could do that. He had come so far already, what was three more miles? Three more miles might as well have been the distance from the Earth to the Moon. If he could just pull over and rest for a few moments. Just close his eyes and rest.

No! He knew if he stopped he would never move again. It was only three more miles. He could make it.

Chapter 1

When he first saw the gecko on the wall in the corner of his bedroom a week earlier he was going to catch it and put it outside. But it had been too fast for him. Three times he had tried to snatch it and three times it had scurried out of his reach. Frustrated, had gone into the kitchen and found a plastic flyswatter.

"Don't kill it," Beth Ann had pleaded.

"I'm not gonna kill it, I'm just gonna knock it out so I can throw it out."

"Don't do that, John Lee. They're good luck."

"No, rabbits feet are good luck. I've never heard of lizards being good luck before."

"I bet rabbits don't think their feet are so lucky, if people are always killin' 'em so they can hang them on those little chains."

"I never thought about that," he admitted. "Hold still, you little bastard."

John Lee slapped at it with the flyswatter and missed. The gecko ducked behind the corner of his dresser.

"And even if they ain't lucky, they eat bugs. Long as he's here you won't have no bugs in your house."

"This is Florida, Beth Ann, there are always going to be bugs in the house. And so what if he eats them all? I've got a lizard in my house instead of a bug. Is that any better?"

"Just leave him and come back to bed. I promise I'll take your mind off of it."

"I don't like Magic watching us in bed. I damn sure don't want a lizard watching us."

"Come on, John Lee, come back to bed."

So he had, and Beth Ann had had been right. It only took a few minutes for him to completely forget about the gecko.

Since then he had come to grudgingly accept the freeloading lizard. Mostly because he couldn't catch the damn thing anyway. So they seemed to have come to an agreement of sorts. As long as the gecko kept the insect population in control and minded its manners, John Lee would think of it as a living bug zapper. But the first time he found it in his bed there was going to be hell to pay.

Magic, his 100 pound protection trained German Shepherd, had not been as quick to welcome their new roommate. But over time the dog stopped growling at the gecko, though he followed it with his eyes whenever it moved.

John Lee was asleep when the dog growled, waking him up. But it wasn't the noise he used to signal his displeasure with the gecko. This was a lower, deeper growl. One of warning. One that there was trouble nearby.

The red numbers on the digital clock on his nightstand said 3:28. He swung out of bed and walked into the darkened living room. Beside him, Magic growled again.

"What is it, boy? Somebody out there?"

He peered through the wood Levolor blinds. It had rained earlier and the moon and stars were hidden behind the thick clouds cover. Even so, he managed to see the dark shape of a strange vehicle in his driveway.

Going back into his bedroom, John Lee pulled on a pair of jeans and a dark blue T-shirt and slipped his feet into tennis shoes. He went to his spare bedroom and retrieved his Bushnell Lynx night vision binoculars and returned to the front window. The car was still there, a silent trespasser.

Kneeling down at the bottom of the window, he pushed the blinds up enough to be able to see out and trained them on the car. The green tinted image showed somebody inside, sitting behind the wheel unmoving.

John Lee called the Somerton County Sheriff's Office and when the dispatcher answered, he said, "This is John Lee. Who's on duty tonight?"

"Maddy and Barry."

"Are they busy?"

"Maddy's working a one car accident out by the EZ Rest. A couple of kids ran off the road and into a ditch. No injuries. Barry's at the Harris place. Tom caught a couple of kids siphoning gas from his pickup and was holding them at gunpoint. Did you need something John Lee?"

"I don't know. There's a car parked in my driveway."

"Do you want me to see how soon I can get somebody out there?"

"No, not yet I'm going to go out and check on it, see what's up."

The dispatcher's name was Tony Ramsey and there was concern in his voice when he said, "Don't do that, John Lee. Let me see if I can call somebody at home to give you some backup."

"It'll be okay," John Lee assured him. "I've got my dog and he's pretty good backup. I'm taking my radio with me. If you don't hear from me in ten minutes, called out the cavalry."

"You think it's somebody from... well, you know?"

"I don't know, probably not. Probably just kids necking or something."

Months earlier John Lee had killed a man in an on-duty shooting. Though the Florida Department of Law Enforcement had ruled the shooting justifiable, the man's father had sworn to get revenge. Since he was the richest man in the county, he certainly had the resources to send hired guns to get even with the deputy.

"I really wish you'd wait and let me call somebody."

"We'd both feel pretty dumb if all it is is a couple of teenagers making out. Hang tight, Tony, I'll be back with you in just a couple of minutes."

John Lee tucked his 9mm Browning Hi Power pistol into his pants behind his right hip and picked up his 12 gauge Remington tactical shotgun and a high-intensity LED flashlight and went to the back door of his house. "Come on, Magic, let's go see who's visiting us at this time of night."

He scanned the back yard with the night vision binoculars, looking for anybody who might be waiting in ambush. Seeing nothing, he eased out the door, giving Magic the command to stay close at his side. He went to both back corners of the house and looked through the binoculars again. Nothing. Moving at a crouch, he crossed the open side yard, every sense alert to danger.

Keeping to a line of trees at the far edge of his property, John Lee and the dog made their way toward the front. He hoped there were no snakes around. John Lee hated snakes and feared them more than he did any bad guy with a gun or knife.

He moved stealthily until he could cross behind and approach the strange vehicle from the rear. The person inside had not moved. Holding the flashlight away from his body with one hand and resting the shotgun on the trunk lid, John Lee pushed the button to turn on the light.

"Show me your hands!"

Nothing.

"I said, show me your hands. Get them up in the air where I can see them!"

He thought he saw the head make a slight movement, but not much.

"Show me your damn hands or I'm gonna shoot!"

When there was no response John Lee left the shotgun and drew his pistol. He eased his way up to the side of the car. The man inside still hadn't moved. John Lee looked at the man through the window. Brown hair, maybe early to mid-50s. It was hard to say because his face was covered in blood. The driver's window was down. He knocked on the door with his flashlight and the man managed to turn his head enough to look at him.

"Are you John Lee Quarrels?" The voice was weak, not much more than a tortured whisper.

"That's me. Who the hell are you?"

"I'm your father."

Made in the USA
Coppell, TX
02 December 2019